GW00888867

Also available from Headline MAN2MAN

Danny Boy
Big Business
Rude Boys

NEIL

Dylan Delaney

Publisher's message

This novel creates an imaginary sexual world. In the real world, readers are advised to practise safe sex.

First published in 1998
by HEADLINE BOOK PUBLISHING

A HEADLINE MAN2MAN paperback

10 9 8 7 6 5 4 3 2 1

All characters in this publication are fictitious and any resemblance to real persons, living or dead, is purely coincidental.

ISBN 0 7472 6066 4

Typeset by CBS, Felixstowe, Suffolk
Printed and bound in Great Britain by
Mackays of Chatham plc, Chatham, Kent

HEADLINE BOOK PUBLISHING
A division of Hodder Headline PLC
338 Euston Road, London NW1 3BH

NEIL

Chapter One

'The brain is a wonderful organ, Armstrong. It starts working the moment you get up in the morning and, in your case, doesn't stop until you get to the office.'

'Yes, Mr Gee.'

'Now take this, sort it out and bring it back to me when you're sure it works.'

Arnold Gee slid the thick manila file of drawings and plans over his desk. It knocked a biro onto the carpet. The biro landed silently in the thick beige pile.

'I'm sorry, Mr Gee. It was an oversight. It won't happen again.'

'Too bloody right it won't. Get your act together, Armstrong.'

I stooped and picked up the biro and dropped it on his desk. By the time I had stood up, Arnold Gee was already looking back at the papers on his desk, furiously scribbling notes in the margin of a letter with his legendary red pen. His balding head shone at me in the afternoon sun. I picked up the file and left.

Marilyn, Arnold Gee's secretary, was typing at her desk outside his office. She paused and looked up. Although she was barely forty, her eyes looked tired. She had been Arnold Gee's secretary for fifteen years.

'How'd it go?'

'As predicted.' I tried to smile.

'Oh never mind, you know what he's like. Such a stickler with his red pen. Still, it's not real life is it?' Her eyes crinkled as she gave me a smile. 'Liquorice Allsort?' She offered me a box of brightly coloured sweets. 'The aniseed ones have gone

I'm afraid, if you were looking. I've had stress this morning with you-know-who.' She nodded towards the door of Arnold Gee's office.

'No thanks, Marilyn. I'll pass.' I patted my stomach.

Marilyn looked up at my six foot one frame and curled her lip. 'The trouble is you ruin it for the rest of us. I bet there's not an ounce of fat on you. All the girls in the office are potty about you.'

'But you know I only have eyes for you, Marilyn!' I leant on her desk and smiled. My brown hair flopped into my eyes.

'Don't you start that, Wade Armstrong! I may be a single girl of a certain age, but I do have my reputation to think of!'

Marilyn grinned and dropped a large yellow Liquorice Allsort into her mouth.

'If it's your reputation you're concerned about, I'd check your spelling again. When I left old Gee, he was busy with his red pen on some of your letters.'

Marilyn curled her lip and let out a silent wail.

'Still, it's not real life, is it Marilyn?' I kissed a finger, touched her forehead and made my way back to my desk.

There were days when I wondered just what I was doing with my life. Here I was stuck on the fifteenth floor of an anonymous glass tower block with the afternoon ozone haze of London spread out before me. All my dreams of being a world-leading architect, a free spirit designing innovative buildings, had been lost; vacuumed into the dust bag of Allsop and Gee Ltd. The last eighteen months of my life had been wasted designing the plumbing system of another anonymous glass box. And now Gee, who hadn't designed anything for ten years and who leached his drawings from underpaid and overqualified staff like me, had just had the supreme satisfaction of patronising and belittling my work by pointing out that I had sewage disposal pipes running in at the same place as the fifth and sixth floor electrical ring main. And whose fault was that? Not mine. The plans I had spent a month working from were out of date, since my colleague, Neil Rogers, had 'amended' them to suit his electrical plan. It was

Neil who I was heading to see now.

Neil's desk was empty, but I spotted him standing by the photocopier talking to one of the secretaries. He had his jacket off and the sleeves of his shirt rolled up. I could see the V-shape of his torso underneath and already I felt my anger subside. The curve of his firm arse further soothed my anger. Neil was tall, with a mop of dark blond hair, the most piercing blue eyes and a year-round tan. He had befriended me on my first day at Allsop and Gee and that evening had taken me to the gym next door for a work-out. I had always thought I was in pretty good shape until I saw Neil standing in a white Gold's Gym vest and navy rugby shorts. His pecs were broad and firm, the dark areolae of his nipples just visible at the edge of his vest. His abdominal muscles were clearly defined, three smooth-cut valleys that would fill with sweat as he bench-pressed beneath me. Rippling over these were the smoothest blond curls imaginable. I remember on that first evening at the gym preparing to bench-press with Neil standing over me. As he leaned forward to support the barbell, I caught a glimpse up the inside of his vest, the downy mat of hair moist with sweat and clinging to his mass of muscle. I was lost.

'How'd it go?'

I was shaken from my memory by Neil's voice. He had turned to me and was leaning on the photocopier. His eyes were bluer than sapphires. He smiled and focused on me in his intent way that was always disconcerting. Did he know how I felt about him?

'Not good, actually.'

'Bummer!'

'It would seem that I have been working from out-of-date plans for floors five and six. Does this ring any bells?'

Neil's brow furrowed. 'I don't think I'm gonna like the next bit, am I, Sport?'

'Sport.' That was what he called me. I loved the intimacy it suggested, but not at this moment.

'No, you're not going to like it, because you stuck a load of wires where I've got pipes and as you're Baldie Gee's golden boy, I get the shit and you get to keep your wires where they are.'

'Fuck. I'm sorry.' Neil planted his big hands on my shoulders. I shook them off. His physical intimacy was more than I could stand.

'Don't be sorry, just let me know what's going on. I looked a right pillock in there and had a happy half-hour eating humble pie, rather than drop you in it.'

'You should've told him!'

'What? Criticise you to old Gee? You know how he loves you. You never put a foot wrong as far as he's concerned.'

'Yeah, but I can handle him. I give him a smile, a pat on the back, ask about his wife, Maureen.'

'It's Margaret.'

'Margaret then, and it's all alright.'

Neil was using the same technique on me. It worked. He was impossible to dislike, even for a moment. The secretary giggled by the photocopier.

'And how is your wife, Neil?' I shot the secretary a stare. If I couldn't be familiar I didn't see why anyone else should get to flirt with him.

'So so, you know.'

'Yes, I think I do.' I flicked my eyes towards the photocopier.

I thought I saw Neil blush. The secretary scooped up the papers and left.

Neil called after her. 'Just leave them on my desk, Cheryl. Thanks.' He turned back to me. 'Not necessary, Sport. She's only a girl.'

'And your wife is only your wife, so maybe you should think about her a bit more. If things aren't going too well at home then maybe you should pay her a bit more attention and avoid those little distractions in short skirts.'

'Hey, hey, calm down. You're right, Sport.' He draped his strong arm around my shoulder. Even at six foot one, Neil's six foot three, broad frame dwarfed me. He was wearing his cologne again. Not strong, but just a faint odour. I breathed it in deeply. He ruffled my hair. His powerful hand squeezed my shoulder. 'How about we go through those plans and sort it out?'

'Not now.' I knew that after Gee's dressing down I wouldn't be fit to concentrate. The added presence of Neil next to me, breathing on me, brushing up against me, would be too much. Already I could feel warm blood pumping into my cock and straining against my white Calvins. I dropped the manila file to hide the swelling. Nine inches of fat, hard man-meat straining in a business suit is easy to spot and I didn't want to get a reputation. 'I think I'll call it a day and get in early tomorrow. Just leave the revised plans on my desk, will you?'

'Will do. You sure there's nothing else I can do?'

For a moment the picture of his firm arse in the shower came to mind. The warm soapy water flowing down through the small of his back and then spreading out over his muscular white cheeks. The mark of his Speedo swimming trunks scorched by the sun, leaving the dark tan of his upper body to give way to the milky skin of his arse. And down the middle of this glorious butt, the crest of light brown hair in his crack darkened by the water and with the promise of so much more . . .

'How about I fix you up with Cheryl?' Neil continued.

The image disappeared.

'Thanks, mate, but no thanks. I just need to get home, have a beer and crash out.'

'OK, OK.' Neil patted my chest. 'Don't say I don't try to help. A good fuck's what you need on a day like today. And a woman like Cheryl . . .'

'Is nothing like a good fuck. Yeah, I get the message.' Neil grinned at me like a naughty school boy. 'But still, no thanks.'

I grabbed a few papers and left the office. Outside the afternoon sun was shining and the city was sweltering. The air conditioning and tinted double glazing of the office had severed me from the reality of life outside. I was hot. I loosened my tie and took off my jacket. The afternoon's events had left me feeling uncertain. Gee's reprimand was uncalled for. Neil's apology combined with his physical closeness and the offer to fix me up with Cheryl had left me feeling horny and lonely. I hated being away from Neil. Not only was he a physical god but he was also clever and charming. Everyone fell in love with him. He was impossible to resist; and I was no exception. But he was as straight as they came. He'd been married to Karen for three years and, although they had their ups and downs, on the one occasion I had been to their small house I was struck by how close and how much in love they were. Karen had been very welcoming, but after that one visit I swore I would never go again. It was too painful to see him hug and touch and love her in a way that I knew he would never feel for me. I was jealous and knew if our friendship was to survive I would have to keep my distance. When Neil told me he was having trouble at home, I tried not to get involved. It would be impossible for me to be a neutral bystander.

I normally took the tube home, but the weather was so hot I opted for a bus. The thought of being trapped two hundred feet underground, pressed up against a bunch of sweaty, irritable people was not good.

The number nine came into view just as I was wondering what to do. I climbed aboard. Upstairs was full, so I was forced to stand downstairs, pressed against the row of sweaty, irritable people I had been trying to avoid. It wasn't my day. Still, there was a nice breeze blowing in through the back of the bus and I was finally on my way home.

We had been going for ten minutes when the bus stopped to pick up more people. The conductor called out that there was only room for one. I doubted there was even space for one of the Seven Dwarfs the bus was so full, but when a young guy climbed aboard holding three large brown boxes, my opinion changed and I gently pushed the standing line of people further down the bus.

'Hold tight.' The conductor rang the bell and we trundled slowly away.

Next to me the young guy steadied himself. He couldn't have been more than twenty with a shock of medium-length, jet-black hair. He had deep brown eyes, like chocolate buttons, surrounded by thick lashes. His olive complexion was clear, covering a strong nose and square chin. He looked boyish, but the curve of his thick biceps clearly labelled him a man. I tried not to stare, but kept finding myself turning on the spot, pretending to look out of the back of the bus, in order to catch sight of him. Beads of sweat rolled down his nose and his fringe hung in wet ribbons on his forehead.

'Hello.'

His voice startled me. Rather than the light tone I had expected, it was rich and deep, as dark and as chocolate brown as his eyes.

'Hi,' I answered, unsure whether he was really talking to me or if he was just pissed off because I had been staring at him.

'How you doing?'

He was definitely talking to me.

'Fine. You've been shopping.' I nodded towards the boxes he held.

'Yeah, new stereo. I don't want to drop it after paying cash.'

It was too good an opportunity to miss. 'You want me to take one?'

'Would you? It's not far to my stop and I don't want to put it in the luggage bit 'cause someone'll smash it up.'

'No problem.' I dropped my file on the top box and lifted it off the pile. It was surprisingly heavy. The kid was stronger than he looked.

'Cheers, mate. What you doing out of the office at four o'clock then? I thought you guys in the city worked till midnight.'

'Not if I can help it.' I smiled. 'Bad day, you know.'

'Yeah, I know; arrive late, take a long lunch break and leave early. All my jobs are like that.'

'What do you do?'

'At the moment I deliver pizzas. Great eh!'

'It's a job'

'I need the money. I'm studying art at St Martin's. Another year to go and then maybe I'll be able to earn some proper money.'

A bead of sweat rolled off his nose and splashed onto the box in front of him. He shifted his weight and turned at an angle to me. He was wearing long khaki shorts and a green T-shirt with the sleeves cut off. On his feet were white Nike trainers. His legs were long and brown covered with the same jet-black hair as his head. The muscle definition on his legs was clear, his calves firm and his thighs thick. Beneath his shorts I could make out the curve of his arse. His T-shirt had rucked up beneath the stereo box so I could see a thin line of black hair leading over his flat stomach and into his shorts.

'Not too heavy for you?'

'No, it's fine.'

'You look as if you work out. I expect you're used to lifting heavier weights than an amplifier.'

'I try to keep in shape. How about you? You look pretty fit yourself.'

'Swimming. Can't stand the gym, too boring. But I love swimming. Nearly made the British team once, but I'm too short. Believe it or not five foot eleven is not tall enough. Guys of six four always touch the side before me, no matter how fast I go. I could've done with being your height.'

He smiled at me. I felt acutely self-conscious. 'Well, I try and keep in shape . . .'

'Looks as if you're doing a lot more than that!' The guy laughed. I laughed too. My cock brushed against the side of my leg, the head tickling my thigh as it grew into life.

'This is my stop. Here, drop that box back on top. You can have the rest of your journey in peace.'

The conductor pressed the bell and the bus pulled into the side of the road. The guy turned to let me place the amp back on the top of the pile. For the first time I looked at his face straight on. He was so beautiful. From underneath the top band of his T-shirt a thin wave of smooth black hair curled out. This was no boy.

'Hey, what the hell. I'm off at the next stop. I'll get off here and give you a hand,' I lied. There was miles to go, but this guy was worth the delay.

'You sure?'

'Yeah, sure I'm sure!'

We stepped off the bus and began walking along a parade of small shops. 'I really appreciate this you know.' He turned to me. 'I was sure I was going to break something before I got home; either the stereo or me. By the way, my name's Kyle.'

'Wade,' I nodded, 'nice to meet you. I won't shake your hand.'

'Better not. That amp alone cost over two hundred pounds. It takes a lot of bloody pizzas to get that sort of money!'

Kyle stopped by a door sandwiched between a dry cleaners and a stationery shop. 'Home.'

We climbed a steep set of stairs and came to a yellow door.

'It's gonna be a mess. It's always a mess. I'm happy in my mess. I hope you don't mind mess.'

'Suits me.'

Kyle swung the door open and took me though a narrow hall into the large living room at the front. Apart from a few old newspapers on the floor it was remarkably tidy. The room was lit by the afternoon sun pouring through two long sash windows. Propped up all around the walls were paintings. Bright colours, unusual shapes an designs, intriguing.

'Dump the box anywhere and I'll get us a beer. I think we've earned it.'

I placed the amp on top of the boxes Kyle had placed by an empty shelf obviously readied for the arrival of the stereo. I studied his paintings. They were really good.

'What do you do for a living then?' Kyle asked, handing me a cool Rolling Rock.

'Architect, supposedly.'

'Wow. Then you can help me put this stereo together.' He clinked his bottle against mine and we began ripping the stereo boxes open. Within minutes we were surrounded by cardboard, bubble wrap and small glaciers of white polystyrene chipping. Kyle stood back and studied the wires in his hands. With one wrist he brushed his fringe from his face and I caught sight of an armpit of soft dark hair. He lifted one of the units and tried to balance it on his knee while attaching the wires to the back.

'You need a hand?'

'If you could hang on to this CD player it would be great.'

I leaned around him and took hold of the unit, my chest pressing against his warm back, my cock pushing into the crack of his arse. His hair smelt clean, freshly washed. Kyle fiddled with the wires while I bear-hugged him from behind. My cock, still swollen from the bus journey, grew with a vengeance, pushing upright against my fly, held in from the top by my belt and growing out into Kyle's firm arse.

'Feels like something pressing against my arse back there.'

I was uncertain of Kyle's tone. Was this some guy who was gonna try and thump me one and throw me out of his flat? He dropped the wires and half turned to me, a wicked grin on his face.

'Feels like you had a stressful day. This any better?'

He pressed his arse against my blood-gorged cock and wiggled it a little. The movement rubbed against my mushroom cock-head and I let out an involuntary groan. Kyle reached his arms behind him and pulled me into his back. 'You're fucking gorgeous, man!'

'You're pretty hot yourself,' I answered, placing the stereo unit on the shelf and hugging Kyle to me.

I slipped my hands up underneath his T-shirt. His stomach was smooth, apart from the line of hair I had noticed earlier which let up over his washboard stomach to his chest. Here I could feel the mat of fur spread out over his chest. Not a lot, just a fine dusting that spread towards his nipples which were pert and hard. I twisted them slowly and Kyle groaned.

'I fucking love that!'

I twisted them again, harder and sharper, and Kyle groaned once more, pressing his arse against my cock, spreading his legs to the outside of mine so that he could get nearer to me. He dropped one arm beneath his legs and under my crutch. He gently stroked between my legs, massaging my balls and caressing my inner thigh. My hand slipped down his chest, which was moist with perspiration, and beneath the waistband of his shorts.

'No underwear? You dirty fucker!'

'You have no idea how dirty!'

We both laughed. My fingers brushed against his damp pubes and onto his cock. It was already semi-erect. I squeezed the base of it and felt the blood surge in. This was no kid cock. It was already thick and fat and, as my fingers traced along its shaft, I could feel the head damp with pre-come. I cupped his balls in my hand. They were heavy and coated with the same down as his chest. I pulled out my hand and licked my fingers. His juice tasted sweet.

I pulled off his T-shirt as Kyle lifted his arms into the air. Now he stood in only shorts and trainers, his cock standing out like a tent pole. I pulled off my tie and Kyle slowly undid the buttons of my shirt while gazing silently into my eyes. He pulled open the shirt and slipped it from my back. He pressed his face into my chest, nuzzling between my smooth pecs, kissing the skin and licking out towards my dark nipples. The hours in the gym were worth it for moments like this, looking down to see that glorious black-haired man with his lips under my pecs, his chin pressed against my abs, moving up to suck on my nipple, his teeth teasing the teat, pulling on it, stretching it, chewing it.

I put my arms around him and slid my hands into the back of his shorts. His cheeks were clenching in time to his chewing. I eased his shorts down and felt his hard cock spring out and brush against my leg. His arse was smooth, tickled with dark hair, firm and solid. My fingers probed his crack. It was hot and moist, his hole damp and sweet. Kyle stopped biting my nipple and looked up at me. Slowly he undid my belt and unzipped my fly. My trousers slid to the floor. I stood out of them, kicking off my shoes and tugging off my socks. My white Calvins stood out, showing just how aroused I was. My cock curled upwards to the right, like the path of a bonfire-night rocket, the tip already damp with an explosion of pre-come.

Kyle pulled my underwear slowly down, freeing my

manhood, which slapped upright against my stomach. Free at last, my balls swung beneath. I've always been proud of my cock. Nine inches of thick circumcised shaft with the best bollocks hanging beneath them like ostrich eggs. As my underwear dropped, so did Kyle. He gazed at my strong cock and flicked his eyes up at me before running his tongue along the length of the shaft, tracing the outline of a thick, dark vein before coming to rest with a kiss on the slit at the top. My cock-head was already sticky and Kyle used this and his spit to work his way down the shaft. I closed my eyes as Kyle's mouth took in my tool. I held his head in my hands, his soft hair running between my fingers. He worked his way down my cock, eventually taking in all nine inches, his nose buried in my pubes. I thrust my hips slowly forward so my balls would momentarily bump into his chin. He slurped on my cock and I forgot about the tensions of the day; about Baldie Gee and his fucking drawings, about Neil and his blue eyes, sensuous mouth and broad chest.

Kyle slipped my cock from his mouth and stood up, his chin wet from work. For the first time I got a clear view of his body. He was certainly a swimmer; clear olive skin with a dusting of hair, broad defined pecs, smallish hard nipples. Powerful legs and a hard butt took second place to his cock, which at eight inches was already pretty impressive, but it was also thicker than any I had ever seen before. His pubes were thick and black. I stroked them and they were smooth and soft. Not like the wiry pubes I had, more like silky hair. I squeezed the base of his cock. My hand couldn't fit round it.

'That is some thick piece of cock.'

'You're not bad yourself,' Kyle grunted, before pressing his lips against mine.

We kissed deeply, our tongues flicking over each other, fighting for supremacy as our mouths ground together. We held each other tightly. My smooth, hard body pressing against his. Our cocks entwined. Kyle slipped his hand down to my arse and pulled my cheeks apart. This had always been my favourite. I groaned as Kyle toyed with my puckered arsehole. His fingers probed, two fingers stretching and playing, then three, while the other hand held my cheeks apart.

In turn, I cupped his balls in my hand and pulled. His nuts were strong, fighting to draw up to his stomach in joy whilst I held them at bay below. Still we kissed. He pushed his knob between my legs so that the head rode against my sac. I pulled my head back and sucked on my fingers. I traced my hand down his back to his arse. Still he played with my hole, roughly finger-fucking me. I plunged two fingers into his arse. Kyle gasped and pushed his arse outwards to take them in.

'Oh, yeah. Fuck me, Wade, fuck me.'

I plunged my fingers in again. Kyle's arms went limp behind me. I turned him round and crouched by his arse. My cock was purple with blood. The tip was smooth, pre-come seeping from the head. I licked at this delicious arse and slowly nosed the cheeks apart. The smell was heavenly, a man-smell that can't be found anywhere, other than here in the cleft of a man's arse. The hairs in his crack tickled my nose. I pressed in, Kyle bending over to allow me free entry into his hole. As he curved over, his cheeks parted like Aladdin's cave.

'Open Sesame!' I muttered to myself as my tongue darted in to taste the treasure within. His sphincter was smooth like the surface of an ice cube that melts on your tongue. The taste was strong, his musk overpowering. Unable to control myself I began to suck deeply on his hole; licking and savouring every sweet taste that filled my mouth. I pulled Kyle's arse to my face and Kyle nuzzled his hole into me.

'Oh yeah,' he groaned.

With my eyes closed my senses were overpowered. In front I could feel Kyle pounding his cock, his foreskin stretched back over his gigantic cock-head, just the spit on his hands lubricating his fingers. I touched my cock and a bolt of ecstasy jolted through me. I shoved two fingers up my own arse. My insides began to unravel with delight.

'Oh fuck me, fuck me!' Kyle called.

I pulled my head away from his arse and Kyle pulled a condom from his shorts. 'Just in case,' he grinned.

Kyle knelt by my cock. He sucked the head of it between his lips, drawing out more juice and running the taste around his lips.

'This cock's gonna take some work. Promise me you'll be kind?' Kyle grinned again as he rolled the condom down my shaft.

'I promise,' I replied, holding his head as he rose to his feet and planting a big kiss on his lips.

Kyle led me over to the sofa. He lay on his back and I lay gently between his legs. Our cocks touched. I lifted his legs up and apart and dropped my head back to his hole. I licked his crack upwards. Kyle moaned. I licked his manhole and spat into it. From the work I had given it already, I could tell he was lubed and ready. I stretched his legs apart. Kyle's fat cock slapped against his stomach. He reached down and pulled his arse cheeks apart. His pink hole twitched for some action. His hips bucked slightly towards me. I placed the head of my cock against his hole and pushed. I could see his sphincter relaxing as it began to take my head. Kyle tugged at his cheeks. It was as if he wanted me to cleave him in two with my cock. I pushed harder. I could feel the resistance of his arse to this invasion.

'Yes, yes, push. Fuck me, Wade. Get your cock in me. I want you in me, Wade.'

I pushed harder. Kyle gave a small yelp and then my cock slipped in. I eased the shaft inwards. Kyle groaned in ecstasy. His eyes closed with sheer joy at having another man inside him. I pushed my cock in hard. My balls slapped against his arse and I held my cock there, feeling the sensation of him tight around me, his sphincter pulling in my man-meat, eager for more. I shifted the base of my cock around his hole. I tried to hold it there, but nature took over and I began to withdraw. I felt the head of my cock come almost out before shoving my load as firmly as I could back into him.

Kyle grunted. 'Oh yeah. Fuck my man-cunt. Fuck me hard.'

I began pounding his arse, stretching his legs up and out while Kyle thrust his arse towards my oncoming piston. I fucked him rigid. Sometimes I bent over him and kissed him, or pulled his nipples in my teeth, but always I fucked him with all my strength. Kyle would reach his hands up and stroke my chest, run his fingers over my abs, but still I fucked him. Soon I was covered in sweat; the sweat gathered from a hard fuck. Outside the world continued to turn, but I had no cares apart from the tight arse that was hugging my thrusting cock. This was when I really came alive. This was when I was a man; when I had another man with me and we were as one.

The orgasm began to unwind in the pit of my stomach. Kyle lifted his arms and held his legs open. He pulled them back and as he did I saw an arc of come shoot from his cock and on to his chest. Then another, his juice pumping from him in time to the thrusts of my cock.

'Yeah!' Kyle cheered. He opened his chocolate eyes and smiled at me, come still squirting from his fat cock.

I dipped my finger in the pool of jizz on his chest and put it to my lips. The salty tang hung on my tongue. It was too much. I swept up four fingers of come from his chest and sucked on them hungrily. My cock pounded into his arse and I came. Thrust after thrust, the come shot out of me. I clenched my arse to squeeze every last drop of juice from my sac. His come was sweet now. I pounded his arse for a few strokes after I had come, eager for it to continue.

As my cock softened I dropped onto him. My face in his chest, his come on my cheek. I licked at his salty stomach as my cock slipped from his arse.

'You are gorgeous,' Kyle said, stroking my hair. 'Just gorgeous.'

'Thanks.'

'Feel better? Tension gone?'

'You bet. Your arse has just melted it all away.'

Kyle slipped the condom from my cock. 'Looks like you got a month of jizz in here!' My wet cock slapped from the condom and onto my nuts. Kyle kissed the tip of my dick.

'Tasty come. You should've let me know. This juice I could swallow.'

I smiled at him and held him close. Our hot bodies pressed

against each other. I cradled him in my arms.

We lay there in silence for some time as the dusk settled outside.

Finally Kyle broke the silence. 'You gonna help me get this stereo to work then or not?' He laughed.

'Sure,' I laughed back. 'Where'd we get to?'

Chapter Two

I slept well after the evening with Kyle. I was in the office the following morning at eight. Neil had left the plans on my desk as promised. I had not been reworking them for long when Karl Parker sidled up to my desk. Karl was short and plump. His voice grated and he always had a scheme to put me down. He had worked for Allsop and Gee for five years, three more than me, and yet I knew I was already paid more than him. It was, however, his delight to see me fail.

'You're in early,' Karl sneered. His face was red. He was perspiring.

'Yup.' I kept studying the plans in front of me.

'Where's the sewage going this time? Down the lift shaft?' He sat on my desk, partly covering my work.

'Ha. Ha.' I pulled the plans from under him.

'Oh come on, it's an easy mistake. When you've been designing for as long as me you'll know where the sewage goes.'

'When I've been designing for as long as you,' I stared at him, 'I hope someone else will be dealing with the sewage.'

'Touchy!' Karl stood. 'Not my fault you got it wrong.'

He strode off. I sat at my desk and felt bad. I had been rude unnecessarily and it would come back on me. Karl knew everything about Allsop and Gee; in particular, how to cause trouble. I tried to study the drawings but found it difficult to concentrate. What was I doing here? I never intended that at twenty-eight years of age I should still be processing other people's inadequate work. I had studied architecture in order to create something new, something individual. And yet even a company as big as Allsop and Gee were struggling. The market had suffered a glut in the late 1980s and we were all still reeling from the recession and property crash. The chances of me going anywhere in the next five years were slim. It was a depressing thought. Great talent; no capital and no contacts. The only sniff of a job I'd had in the last twelve months had been to design up-market kitchens. I couldn't stand the thought of some wealthy housewife dithering where the fridge could go. I wonder if Leonardo da Vinci had this trouble? 'Mr da Vinci, when you've finished with the Sistine Chapel, could you put my waste disposal unit next to the sink, please?'

'You look glum, Sport.'

Neil sat on my desk.

'You look smart,' I noted, changing the subject. 'Something up?'

'Armani suit. Gee's got some wealthy clients coming in and wants me to schmooze them. They've got a site in Hammersmith to develop.'

I smarted at this exclusion.

'Good luck.'

'How's the waterworks?'

'OK.'

'Did I just see poxy Parker with you?'

'Yeah. Gleeful at my fall and ready to stir it with Gee at the drop of a hat.'

'Fuck him. You're better than that.'

There was an uneasy pause. I wanted Neil to stay. He sat in his navy suit looking wonderful; strong, clever, charming. His broad thigh lay firm along the edge of my desk. His buttock teasingly close. His tanned hand spread out on the desk close to mine. I eased my forearm forward and let it touch him. His finger was warm. I felt comforted and calm.

We remained in silence for almost a minute, Neil examining the plans and me just soaking up his presence. Then he lifted his hand and put it on my arm. I looked up.

'You know, if you need a hand, I'm more than willing to spend some time with you tonight.'

'No, I'll be fine. I can see a few possibilities already. Besides, you've got Gee to contend with.'

'That's lunch. How about the gym this evening. You got your stuff?'

'Sure.'

'Seven o'clock?'

How could I refuse?

He sprang off the desk and wandered through the open-plan office to his desk. He whistled as he went, stopping occasionally to flirt with the office women who were arriving. It was no wonder he got so much attention. He was beautiful, and it was this beauty that Gee was selling to his clients. 'Never mind the building, just feel the staff.'

The morning drifted by in a haze of plans. It should've been simple to reroute the sewage, but my mind couldn't concentrate. The work was boring. Neil was visible on the other side of the office, usually laughing with a woman or on the phone. I had to snap out of this crush. Why did I always fall in love with straight guys? At college I had become smitten with Gary Hammersley. We played rugby together and in the final year he became team captain. Tall and blond, powerful, with an infectious laugh. I spent the last year as his roommate on campus. I lied to keep his various girlfriends away from each other, comforted him when a woman he loved dumped him. We even stood by the lake on the campus and wanked together after winning the University's Cup. He had a fabulous cock. It hung like white salami between his legs. The size of it was well known on campus; a good eight inches flaccid rising to eleven inches of thick man-meat when erect. I longed to be ploughed by that tool. The nearest I came was on that moonlit night, watching him milk the come from his cock, the thick milky liquid being squeezed from the tip onto the thankless soil. The image of that dick kept me sane through my finals. And here I was five years later, still lusting after straight boys. For someone with supposedly above average intelligence, I was behaving like a fucking dunce.

At twelve thirty a party of men arrived. Their leader was a thoroughly groomed man of about forty, his hair greying at the temples. Gee welcomed them. Neil smiled, told jokes and introduced them to the office. They approached my desk.

'And this is Wade Armstrong.' Neil held out an arm and I stood to greet the men. 'Wade is one of our high-fliers. He's only been with the company for two years but already he's in hot demand; particularly amongst the women.'

I blushed and threw Neil a look.

'And modest too. Believe me, Allsop and Gee are very lucky to have the talents of Mr Armstrong.'

'I look forward to working with you, Mr Armstrong.' The man in charge offered me his hand. 'Miles Stone.'

I shook Mr Stone's hand. He had a short, firm grip and an air of quiet authority.

Neil winked at me. 'I just hope we can keep him.'

'You're not going anywhere are you, Armstrong?' It was the voice of Arnold Gee bellowing out of a severe dark suit. His piggy eyes glared at me. His cheeks puffed out like a frog.

'Not as far as I know, Mr Gee. You can't beat this company, one of the best in the City.' It caught in my throat to fall into this public relations chatter.

'Not one of the best, but *the* best in the City, Mr Armstrong.'

I smiled and sat down as the parade passed me by. Miles Stone gave me a nod as he left.

'And this is Karl Parker. A great technician.' I heard Neil introduce a bloated and pasty-looking Karl, who had already sprung to his feet to tell them all about his work. The easy charm of Neil shone next to this performing warthog.

Something Karl had said about the lift shaft had stuck with me. Maybe it wasn't such a stupid suggestion. So much of the space at the back of the shafts were wasted. Here was an area to hook up the water system, allow easy access and separate the electrical from the sewage.

I skipped lunch and worked all afternoon revising the plans. It was brilliant. The new drawings worked like a dream. Neil was out all afternoon with the clients looking at the site in Hammersmith, so I had no distractions. Cheryl spent a few minutes lolling by my desk droning on about Neil, about how much she was in love with him and did I think he'd leave his wife.

'Neil is not someone you want to get involved with,' was my terse advice.

'But he's gorgeous and he's got a lovely bum.'

'If Neil left his wife for you, what makes you think he wouldn't leave you for someone else?'

''Cause I'm different. She don't understand him.'

'And you do?'

'Yeah. I would listen to him and take care of him. With me he'd change.'

'That is the oldest story in the world.'

'I thought that was prostitutes?'

'No, that's the oldest profession in the world.'

'Oh. What about you then? Who you seeing?'

'No one at the moment.'

'You like Janice?'

'In accounts?'

'Yeah. She loves you. Says you've got the best skin of any man in London.'

Cheryl giggled at her forwardness.

'She's very nice, but I'm not interested.'

'Pity.' Cheryl sucked on a finger and examined the nail.

'Cheryl, I'm sorry, but I have to work.'

'Oh yeah. Gee gave you a bollocking for cocking up the pipes or summat.'

'How did you know?'

'Karl said.'

Cheryl grinned at me and slipped away. Trust Karl. The entire office knew about my mistake. Great.

I was still working as the light faded behind the windows. Inside, the strip light held the encroaching night at bay.

'You done?' Neil pulled up a chair and flopped beside me.

'Just about. I need to draw these up to scale. What do you think?'

Neil studied the papers. His face concentrated, showing no sign of emotion. Then he looked puzzled and turned the papers around. I loved to see his mind at work. With his public charm turned off and alone, he was at his most loveable. Then a smile broke out. He understood what I had done and was impressed. He looked at me and I fell into the blue pools of his eyes.

'You are one clever son-of-a-bitch. This is genius!'

'Thanks.'

'Fuck! You really are something special. What are you doing in this dump?'

'I ask myself the same question everyday!'

'Listen, let's get out of here.' Neil stood, picked up his jacket and slung it over his shoulder. 'I've had a fuck of a day being nice and I'm shagged. How about a steam and a beer on me?'

'Sounds good.' I would miss my work-out, but time spent with Neil was never wasted.

The steam room was hot. Neil lay next to me, his arm over his eyes. I sat upright, my cock and balls laying between my legs, large and sluggish from the heat. Neil looked beautiful. It was unfair that genetics should give him such a perfect body. His dark blond hair was swept back, thick and shiny with water. On his face stood little pools of perspiration, running in trickles onto the plastic bench beneath. His chest rose gently as he breathed deeply. His pecs were firm, nipples enticing and all nestling within a mat of smooth blond curls. His V-shaped torso ran to a tight waist, held in place by six powerful abdominal muscles. His white butt cheeks caved sensuously just behind the front of his hips. His cock was beautiful. I loved these opportunities to study it. It lay upwards and onto his stomach. Circumcised, the head was broad and smooth. The outline of the helmet rose above the shaft. The piss slit urged me to kiss it, lick it, take it in my mouth. But I had never taken a cock as big as that in my mouth before. I doubted I would be able to swallow something so large and succulent.

I felt my cock begin to swell. Fuck! I held my dick between my legs and thought of Margaret Thatcher's minge. A drop of salty sweat dropped in my eye. I rubbed it away.

'What you thinking about?' Neil stirred into life.

'Pussy.'

'Whose?'

'Margaret Thatcher's.'

Neil let out a howl of laughter. He bucked upright and I watched his cock plop heavily to one side. 'You crack me up, Sport.'

'Well what are you thinking about?' I retorted.

'Not some moth-eaten old bit of fanny, that's for sure!'

We both laughed and the sound echoed and re-echoed around the steam room.

'You ever thought about making it with another guy?' Neil turned his eyes to me. He was serious. Did he know about me? Guiltily, I turned away and pretended nonchalance.

'Not really,' was my half-hearted reply, the vision of his cock still in my mind.

'Just wondered. There are a lot of fags here and I've seen them staring at you and just wondered if you'd ever thought of giving it a go.'

'Stare at me?' I gasped. 'Every man, woman and child ogles you the minute you enter a room, how can you say they're looking at me?'

Neil chuckled. 'I think you're looking in the wrong direction, Sport. You're a horny-looking lad. Rich, dark-brown hair, those hazel eyes that Janice in accounts is always going on about. You're built like a brick shithouse, are phenomenally bright and from what I've seen are hung like a donkey. Of course people fancy you! Wise up.'

I was taken aback by this praise. It made me love Neil even more.

'Wanna run my fan club?' I patted Neil on the shoulder. He was hot and damp. Neil put his hand on mine. He squeezed it and held it there. The closeness was almost unbearable.

'I think there are others in the queue ahead of me for that job,' he said cryptically.

Our hands remained together. I thought I felt him clench it

again. Then he suddenly stood up.

'I'm off for a shower, need to cool down. I'll see you in Reception.'

He left the steam room. I was alone.

What was all that about? I rubbed the sweat from his shoulder on my face and tongue. The saltiness was mouth-watering. I felt my cock growing and opened my legs to give it room. I pulled on my balls and squeezed my shaft. Blood rushed in and the head swelled. I pulled back my foreskin and gazed at the now purple head. What was it about cock that I loved so much? Why did I want to suck it, drink its juice, feel it in my mouth and up my arse?

The door swung open and on old guy with a beer gut covering his groin tottered in clutching an *Evening Standard.* I pushed my cock back down and closed my legs, the erection slowly subsiding.

By the time I had showered and got into the changing room, Neil was already gone. He was waiting for me in Reception.

'The usual?'

'Yep.'

We wandered around the corner and into the Cork and Casket. Neil bought a couple of beers and I found a table by the window overlooking the street. Outside, workers were hurrying home. Buses were full. Taxis honked impatiently at some nearby lights. I remembered the fun with Kyle.

'Sorry about that, Sport.' Neil placed two beers on the table.

'About what?'

'In the steam room. I'm having trouble with Karen.'

'What is it this time?'

'The usual. We row, she says I don't care, don't take enough notice of her; that we're strangers living under the same roof.'

'Do you care?'

'Of course I do. I love her, I'm just not sure that I love her enough. It was a mistake getting married.'

'But surely you can make it work. Turn on some of that

legendary charm of yours. How could she resist?' I slurped at my beer. It was cool.

'My charm has run out as far as she's concerned.'

We drank in silence.

'I've got a big favour to ask.' Neil looked at me. I wasn't sure I liked the way this conversation was going.

'Sure, whatever.'

'If I needed to kip with you for a few days, a week max, would it be OK?'

'Yeah. But things aren't that bad, are they?'

'I just need some space. To think.'

'Whatever.'

We finished our drinks with small talk. My mind was racing at the thought of having Neil live with me. On the one hand I knew it was a recipe for disaster, but on the other; to have him with me in the morning and last thing at night; to have him use my shower, piss in my lavatory, drink the milk from my fridge was too wonderful to conceive.

I wanked that night long and slow, pumping my shaft, lubing the head with KY and letting my fingers tickle the surface while my balls twitched with delight. I pictured Neil in the steam room, ploughing my arse with that long, fat, clean-cut cock. When I came, it was in long spurts, bolts of white cream forking onto my chest and melting there as I lay and dreamed of Neil.

The next day was not, however, what I thought we had agreed.

I was in early to draw up the plans. Neil arrived shortly after and dropped a duffel bag at my feet.

'I've cleared it with Karen. We're going to spend a week apart to think about where we're going.'

'Is she OK?'

'Tears and the usual wailing – that was from me – but she was fine.'

'Did you tell her where you were going?'

'Yup. She thought it was a good idea. She likes you. Thinks you're sensible and a good influence.'

Little did she know.

I drew all morning. The only odd thing that happened was when Cheryl brought me a cup of coffee mid-morning.

'You've changed your tune pretty quickly, haven't you?' She cooed.

'Meaning what?' I replied. It was difficult to be angry with someone as bubbly as Cheryl.

'It's women's intuition. I knew, so did Janice. You men give off vibes. You're so easy to read.' She shook her curly hair coquettishly.

'What are you talking about?' I was confused.

'Ta, ta! Big boy!' She winked.

I carried on working, the success of my drawings easily pushing Cheryl's mundane conversation aside.

In the afternoon, however, things became a little clearer. Taking a break from work I wandered over to Marilyn. Baldie Gee was out with clients so the coast was clear.

'How are you?' I asked. I liked Marilyn. She worked hard and deserved better than Gee as a boss.

'I'm fine. How are you?' She sounded terse.

'Good, yeah, very good.'

'I should think so too.' She didn't sound as if she meant it.

'My drawings have come together really well. Looks as if that little bit of trouble earlier in the week could've been a lucky break.'

'And so you're off to celebrate with a couple of floozies?' Marilyn began typing harder, the keys clacking away beneath her fingers.

'No,' I replied, now thoroughly confused.

'Don't lie to me, Wade Armstrong. I may sit here out of the way, but I'm the eyes and ears of this office and when you and Neil Rogers decide to whip a couple of members of staff out on a drunken evening, and then do God knows what with them afterwards because they know no better, don't think I don't get to hear about it!'

'What are you talking about?'

Marilyn stopped typing.

'I've had all the details from Cheryl about how you and Neil are taking her and Janice for a night on the town. And don't tell me it's out of the goodness of your heart. They're young girls and they're easy targets for men of the world like you. Besides which, unless the situation has changed in the very recent past, I understood that Mr Rogers was married.'

Marilyn's outburst winded me. I stared at her flabbergasted.

'That's very interesting Marilyn. I think I need to talk to Neil about this. Would you excuse me?'

Without a word Marilyn returned to her work.

Neil was out. I worked all afternoon with one eye on the door. At six he entered, the usual cocky grin on his face. He came up to me.

'Too much work makes Jack a dull boy!'

'I think I'm happy being dull.' I waited for him to tell me of the evening's plans.

'Good day?'

'Illuminating, yes.'

'Got anything planned for this evening?'

Neil was nothing if not predictable.

'Not as far as I know.'

'Good.'

'Unless, of course, the foursome you've got arranged just happens to include me. In which case, yes, I am busy. I've got to wash my hair.'

This Neil took in his stride.

'Look, I don't know what you've heard. All it is, is that Cheryl's been nagging me to take her out to the cinema. I didn't want to go alone because of the Karen situation. So I rather hoped you would help me out and come too, so it doesn't look as if I'm playing away.'

'Why didn't you tell me in advance? Why does the whole office know about it before me?' Neil's charm was great, but it bugged me that he used it to get his own way so much. First the electrical plans fiasco, and now this. 'I had Marilyn giving me the third degree this afternoon.'

'Sorry about that, Sport. I wanted to tell you, but I had to go out. Client meeting. If you don't want to come though . . .'

'No, no, I'll come. You need someone to watch over you. Just as long as there's no funny business, alright?'

'Gimme a break, Wade! You're beginning to sound like Karen.'

And I was beginning to know how she felt.

The evening started well. We saw a film which, although I wasn't keen, turned out to be good. Cheryl and Janice laughed a lot at Neil's jokes and I found myself swept along by the tide of happiness he created. We had pizza and plenty of wine. Still everything was going well. We were just four colleagues having a good time. We had good food and too much to drink.

When we left the restaurant the warm night air was intoxicating. I felt at last that I was just like all the other people I had seen out at night; drunk, laughing, enjoying myself. My isolation and depression with work was momentarily lost. I soaked in the atmosphere.

'How about we go back to Wade's for a nightcap, ladies?' It was Neil.

The three of them looked at me. What the hell? We were having fun. I didn't want it to end any more than the others did. We caught a cab back to my flat.

I have a small one-bedroom ground-floor flat in West London. Luckily I had tidied it due to the possibility of Neil coming to stay. More importantly I had stuffed my sizeable collection of porn into a bag in the wardrobe. It was just as well because, as we entered, Cheryl and Janice went into yelps of delight about how fabulous it was and ran in to every room to check it out. My collection of *Hung Studs* and a fat dildo would certainly have given them plenty to talk about in the office. I opened the French windows onto the night-time lawn. Behind me the girls were buzzing. Neil was drunk and leaning against the kitchen door.

'Nice place.' He said through half-shut eyes. 'Big.'

'That couch is a sofa bed.' I pointed to a green sofa. 'Coffee?'

'Brandy.'

'I don't know if I've got any.' More alcohol was not a good idea.

'Yes you have, here it is!' Cheryl opened the cupboard where I kept the drinks. I hadn't realised she was there. I had to be drunk.

The brandy came out and soon we all had a glass. Neil collapsed on the sofa bed with Cheryl snuggling up to him. Janice came and sat on the opposite sofa with me. She kept running her fingers through her red hair. I could feel her eyes on me. Conversation died. I dozed for a moment – and awoke as Janice curled her legs on the sofa and laid her head on my shoulder. Opposite, Cheryl and Neil were making out. I watched him kiss her hard on the mouth and pull her head back to kiss her neck. He caressed her breast and held her in his arms as if she were a paper toy for him to crumple. Janice began to stoke my chest. I stiffened.

'You OK?' Janice asked sitting up, her green eyes looking dopily at me.

'Just pissed. Sorry, I'm not up to this.'

I had made a resolution when I left college that I wouldn't make out with girls again, unless I really wanted to. Too often I had slept with women to hide my sexuality, to fit in, to be one of the lads. Now things had changed. I knew what I wanted and I didn't have to apologise for it. I didn't have to proclaim my love of cock to the world, but I could still be true to myself.

'I'm going to bed. Sorry.'

'That's OK. Another time.' Janice stroked my hair. I felt bad. I wanted to explain to her that it wasn't her fault, but now wasn't the time. I got her coat.

'You going?' It was Neil.

'Yes,' Janice replied. 'I've got a busy day tomorrow.'

'You'd better go too, Shell.' He pushed Cheryl upright. She was not pleased.

'Alright, alright, you don't have to shove me. I get the message.' She grabbed her coat.

The two women left hurriedly. I had broken the atmosphere

and yet I wasn't sorry. After they had left, Neil looked sheepish.

'I'll sleep here then.'

'Yeah. Bathroom's there.' I pointed down the corridor. 'I'm at the end.'

'Thanks.' Neil rubbed his blue, blue eyes. 'Look, I'm sorry, Sport. I didn't mean for this to happen.'

'Sure you didn't.' I was angry.

'Don't get cross . . .'

'Look, you leave your wife and invite yourself over here. Then I find out on the first night away that you've fixed up to go out with the office bike. Then you rope me in on it too, with some half-hearted excuse about us all being friends. And I believe you and go along with it. Then: wham, bang, at the end of the evening I look up to see you practically eating her on the sofa opposite me and, what's more, I have to explain to the date you have arranged for me, that sorry, I'm afraid she's just not my type. How the fuck do you think I feel? Fucked over, that's what!'

Neil was silent. 'I'm sorry. I didn't plan it.'

'And don't start with the lost puppy look. I've seen you give it to so many people and watch them ooh and ahh and let you off the hook. It ain't gonna work with me.'

'Look I'm a shit alright? Is that what you want to hear?'

Neil's outburst took me by surprise.

'I'm a second-rate cunt who can't hold a marriage together and who's fucking average at his work. I haven't got your talent or your strength of personality, OK. Feel better?'

I didn't know what to say. Neil was beginning to cry.

'What the fuck is it? What do people want from me?' He went on. '"Bring in charming Neil, he'll seal the deal". And what do I do, I bow and scrape and keep everybody laughing and cheerful. And yet I am bored shitless by my whole life.'

He was becoming very loud. I tried to calm him but he shook off my arm.

'What the fuck am I supposed to do? Why have I made a mess of everything? I love Karen, I love her, love her, but we can't be together.'

He was sobbing now, uncontrollably. I took him in my arms and calmed him. He hung onto me. His strong frame leaning over me, drained of energy from his outburst. My shoulder became damp from his tears.

'It's OK. Calm down, calm down.'

I hugged him close and closed my eyes. His warm musk infiltrated my body. I never wanted to let him go. I stroked his back, feeling the muscles ripple beneath my fingers.

There was a knock on the ceiling from the floor above. Neil giggled through his tears.

'Think I did a bit too much, Sport.'

'Don't worry about them. God knows they've kept me awake many times with their parties.'

Neil stood back and looked at me. His cobalt eyes were bloodshot. His cheeks damp with tears. He sniffed. I gave him my handkerchief.

'I'll send them some flowers tomorrow. Say sorry.' Neil blew his nose.

'Don't worry about it,' I reassured him, 'They'll get over it. Save your money.'

'Not going to be my money. I'll use the company florist. Gee can pay.' Neil laughed. His eyes twinkled momentarily.

'In that case, who am I to stop you?'

We laughed.

'You sure you're OK?' I asked seriously.

'I'm fine. Drunk. Need some sleep. I'm sorry about all that. I shouldn't have let it happen and I shouldn't have yelled like I did. I was out of order.'

'Don't worry about the yelling. If you're not happy you need to talk about it. I had no idea you were so unhappy. You always seem fine.'

'Ignore it. It's the drink talking.'

'We'll chat tomorrow. How about I cook for you?'

'No, tell you what. I'll cook for you. It's the least I could do.' Neil smiled and held my shoulders.

'OK. See you tomorrow. Sleep well.'

'Wish you'd told me earlier,' Neil added as I left the room.

'Told you what?'

'That you'd caught onto the "puppy dog" act. I'll have to think of something new to handle you now.'

We smiled at each other, some invisible bond holding us before I left the room.

After cleaning my teeth I remembered Neil would need a duvet. I took one from the airing cupboard, placed it in a cover and took it to the living room. Neil was already asleep. He lay across the opened sofa bed in just a pair of boxer shorts, his body lit by the moon outside. His broad feet hung over the edge of the bed. I wondered that even his feet were golden brown with a crest of hairs on the top of each foot and little crops of a few blond curls on the top of his big toes. Already he slept deeply; that power at rest. I looked at his body for a moment longer before placing the duvet carefully over him. He grunted and curled over, wrapping himself in the covering like a baby.

'Goodnight,' I whispered before going finally to bed.

Chapter Three

The next morning I lay in bed waiting to hear some movement from Neil. All was quiet in the living room. I switched my alarm off before it had the chance to ring. I pulled on some old sweat pants and tiptoed along the hallway. Neil was asleep. Next to the sofa bed were his boxer shorts. He lay on his front, his face crinkled into a pillow. The morning sun shone, decorating the room with pyramids of bright light. I sneaked into the kitchen and switched on the kettle. The tiled floor was cold beneath my feet. My head ached. I heard Neil groan and turn over. I looked into the living room. He was laying on his back now, the duvet swept aside with the sun's warmth, his face lightly creased by his night's sleep. His muscular chest rose and fell gently with deep breaths. His legs straddled apart slowly, kicking the duvet further away to reveal his firm, erect cock. I couldn't take my eyes off it. It had to be twelve inches long, thick and strong, his balls laying between his legs, jostling for position. The head was broad and pink, the piss-slit just visible. I was rooted to the spot, looking at this object of beauty. I rubbed my cock as it hardened in my sweat pants, my arsehole ached and twitched for the attention of this rigid pole. Neil stirred again. His moan made me step defensively back into the kitchen. I paused a moment. Behind me the kettle burbled. I peeped again. Neil now had one arm over his eyes and one hand stroking the back of his cock, slowly tugging at his balls, causing his cock to lift gently from his stomach, the curve and thickness of it now clear to see. By now my dick was firmly erect, the head twitching for action. I stroked it gently and my balls shivered in delight. The kettle clicked off.

Neil moaned again and I returned to the kitchen.

'That you, Sport?' Neil grunted, his voice deep and gravelled.

'Yeah. Coffee?' I replied, unable to return to the living room without my stiff dick being all too apparent.

'Yeah. And aspirin, something like that,' Neil moaned. 'I feel like shit!'

I made the coffee with one hand whilst trying to push my cock down with the other. But this was one erection that wouldn't go away. My mind continued to lust after that humungous dick.

By the time I took in the coffee and aspirin my dick had subsided a little, but it was still begging for attention. Neil sat upright in bed, the duvet pulled around his waist. His pecs overhung his muscular stomach, the tight skin on his abs crinkling into little rows as he rested forward. I looked down on his broad shoulders, the muscles packed tightly beneath his brown skin. He looked up. His eyes were still cobalt blue and his smile, even now was devastating.

'I've got a mouth like a badger's arse. Where's the aspirin?'

I laughed and sat on the edge of the bed. Neil swallowed the pills and slurped at his coffee.

'I think I owe you an apology for last night.'

'Forget it,' I began.

'No, I was an arsehole. I was out of order and I'm sorry.'

'Yeah you were.' I smiled. 'But you're forgiven.'

Neil slapped his arm on my shoulder. 'Thanks, mate. I appreciate it.'

We sat for a few moments in silence. I wanted it to go on for ever.

'I'm going to jump in the shower.' I stood up. 'I need to get into work.'

'You need to have a bloody good wank, mate.'

Neil startled me. I looked down and saw my cock standing rigid beneath my sweat pants. I felt my face go crimson. I tried to fiddle my reluctant dick into a less prominent position.

'Yeah, always happens in the morning,' I muttered halfheartedly, turning away to wrestle with it some more.

'Must be sweet dreams of that Janice,' Neil taunted.

I half turned to him. 'Something like that, yeah.'

As I jogged to the shower I heard Neil call behind me, 'Don't be too long, I've got to get ready too you know.'

I stood in the shower my cock aching for attention. I began to wash my hair and yet was continually drawn back to the overwhelming need in me to fantasise about what I had just seen. As I soaped my arse, a finger slid into my hole. I groaned with delight and my cock twitched as I pulled the foreskin back. I forced a second finger in. I dreamed of Neil thrusting into me, my arse cheeks forced apart by his strong thighs, his thick cock mixing agony and ecstasy as it filled me. I imagined being bent double, my ankles by my ears, the full weight of Neil resting on me as he pumped into me, my sphincter tight around his cock, holding onto his tool as it slid into me. I could see his powerful pecs above me and the down of his chest hair between my fingers as I reached for his hard nipples. The thought of his tongue darting over my face and his look of pleasure as he pumped my hole filled my mind. I imagined smelling of him after he had come, after having had his juice inside me, his sweat on me, his tongue over me. It was this awareness of his scent that sent me over the edge. I came in long ribbons of come, groaning as I did, seeing the white jizz shoot onto the shower wall and slink away amongst the shampoo. My cock, now drained, hung between my legs, long, thick and exhausted by the wank.

Even though I had come, I was still not sated, not satisfied. If anything, this had awakened a deeper hunger within me, a stronger yearning to have a man of my own.

We journeyed into work silently and at the office separated with little said. I was frustrated and hungover. I looked at the work on my desk and felt as if I was viewing it through double glazing; it was all there but somehow removed from human contact.

'Well?'

It was Marilyn, leaning over my desk. She was always in early.

'I expect a full report of last night's activities. As you know, I am the eyes and ears of this place and if you don't get your version of events in first, I'll only have what Janice and Cheryl have to say about things to go on – and you don't want that, believe me.'

I smiled groggily.

'Alcohol was consumed I take it by that somewhat distant look in your eyes.'

I nodded.

'Then it'll have to be twenty questions.'

I nodded again, this time with a smile.

'You went to see a film. Something rated eighteen with more violence than sex and with a lot of men saying "fuck" and "shit" before shooting each other in the name of good versus evil. And all this to save a woman with overly curly hair, a lot of make-up and liberal amounts of lip-gloss.'

I nodded.

'And our hero had a funny accent?'

I nodded again, enjoying the game.

'Arnold Schwarzenegger?'

'Jean Claude Van Damme,' I corrected her.

'Right, so less plot, but more karate kicks and a liberal sprinkling of people being called "mother-fucker".'

'That's the one.'

'Then off for something to eat. Neil was in charge, so it will be tasty, but basic – I know our Mr Rogers. I would lay money on a pizza.'

'Correct.'

'In that case you would have something vegetarianish, Neil would have pepperoni with lots of chilli and Janice and Cheryl would have something they couldn't pronounce and think they were being very sophisticated.'

I laughed.

'Too much to drink; wine and beer by the looks of you this morning and then what . . . ?'

I looked at my desk.

'Thought so. You left the restaurant, Neil suggested a nightcap, the girls giggled whilst ferreting in their little boxy handbags to see if they had a fistful of condoms, and then you all went back to your place. You agreed because you're a wimp at heart and didn't want to upset anyone.'

'Were you following us?' I enquired.

'And then what?' Marilyn looked at me. She was serious.

'We went back to mine, drank a little and then the girls left,' I ventured.

'Nothing happened?'

'No. Janice was keen, but I said no. Cheryl and Neil were . . .'

'All over each other liked crazed ferrets.'

'Something like that, but nothing happened. I bollocked Neil later. He took advantage, but I can't blame him, I was happy to let him.' I looked sheepishly at Marilyn. She pursed her lips and thought for a moment.

'You and Neil need to get things sorted out between yourselves . . .'

'Yeah, I'll talk to him tonight.'

'No, you need to sort things out between yourselves!' Marilyn emphasised what she was saying whilst drawing a circle with her finger on the desk top. The silence was excruciating. What did she mean? Had she guessed at my feelings for Neil? Were they that obvious? Should I ask him to leave my flat?

The silence was broken by Marilyn.

'But first things first. You'll need a lunch appointment for today.

'Why?'

'Because if I can guess the way your minds work as easily as I have, you bet your firm little arse that I know what Janice and Cheryl are thinking. Now Neil is out with Mr Stone this lunchtime to discuss the Hammersmith project, and you, Mr Armstrong, are going to take me for something to eat. It's about time we caught up on the news.'

'Yeah, OK,' I stammered.

'Unless you would like to meet with Janice for a quiet little tête-à-tête?'

'No, no, you're right, Marilyn. Thank you. I'll see you at one.'

It was mid-morning when I looked up to see Cheryl lingering by my desk.

'Hi,' I said with a faint smile, still feeling hungover.

'Hi,' Wade. How you feeling?'

'A little rough,' I confessed. 'How about you?'

'Oh I'm fine. Takes more than that to get me pissed!'

Cheryl leaned on the desk. She feigned interest in the plans I was working on. I knew she had something else on her agenda.

'Janice had a nice time too,' she cooed.

'Good. It was a lot of fun.'

I returned to the plans but Cheryl continued, 'Think it must be over for Neil and his wife. I said so. I think he loves me. I've got a sore tit 'cause of him.'

'It's good to see that romance isn't dead.'

'I was gonna see him for lunch but he's got some meeting or other. And then he says he's out tonight, something personal he said.'

My mind raced. Who could he be seeing? Was there someone else? Was he going to see Karen and make up? I felt jealousy coil around my stomach. Why hadn't he told me about his plans? It was pointless. I resolved to push Neil to the back of my mind and find someone else.

'What you doing for lunch then?'

My mind snapped back. 'What?'

'What you doing for lunch? Janice isn't doing anything and she wanted to know if you wanted to go out with her and have something to eat?'

'I can't. I'm seeing Marilyn.' I thanked Marilyn for her foresight.

'Can't you cancel it? Janice really fancies you. She says you're a great kisser!'

'What?' I thought back over last night. I knew I hadn't touched her.

'You've gone all shy. Cat got your tongue?'

'No . . .'

'Between you and me, Janice wants you to park your car in her garage, if you know what I mean . . .'

I looked at Cheryl. She really was just a girl. 'I'm flattered, but I'm afraid I'm only taking the bus at the moment.'

Cheryl looked confused. I pictured the curve of Kyle's biceps, the trail of hair from his navel down to his luscious creamy cock, his low hanging balls and his tasty puckered hole. Public transport did have its advantages.

'Sorry, Cheryl, but I really have to get on with my work.'

Cheryl hopped off the desk and scuttled over to the other side of the office. I could just make her out deep in conversation with Janice. Neither seemed to know what to make of my response. I kept my head down and concentrated on my work.

Lunch with Marilyn had been fine up until coffee. We had chatted about life, work, the pain of having Baldie Gee as a boss and the fact that although the company were always pleading poverty, there was always masses to do. There was always another project looming on the horizon and Baldie Gee was always preparing to change in his company car for yet an even bigger BMW as soon as the ashtrays on his previous model were full. Talk of pay rises were forbidden and the belief purveyed that we should all be grateful that we had a job at all, let alone one as prestigious and as rewarding as working for Allsop and Gee. I started to moan about Karl but Marilyn warned me off.

'Take it easy with him. He has connections that could make your life very difficult.'

'With Gee you mean?'

'Something like that. They are very close. And I mean very close. If one clicks his fingers it is likely that the other will spring to his defence. So keep away.'

'What do you mean?' I marvelled that Gee would actually

spring to the defence of what was so obviously a second-rate architect and office gossip.

'Never you mind. I'm not going to sink to Karl's level and gossip – my job's not worth it – but just take my advice, keep out of Karl's way.'

'That's easier said than done,' I replied. 'You don't have to take his snide comments and taunts.'

'Oh really, Wade! Take a look at yourself! You're six foot two and gorgeous. You have a body that would make a male model blush, more sex appeal than that Brad Pitt – whose nude pictures I happened to stumble across on the internet this morning . . .'

I smiled and made a mental note to check them out.

'And if what Janice says is true, you have a baseball bat swinging between your legs.'

'What!'

'Calm down, I know she made it up, but I told you, office politics are a carefully crafted thing and Miss Janice has just scored a major advantage in convincing the office that she and you are biblically involved. You have been voted Mr Number One Hot Totty in the secretaries' monthly sweepstakes for the last three months.'

'Me?'

'Yes, you. And if your ego needs boosting any more, I can tell you that to win that dubious award you unseated Mr Neil Rogers who had held the title for over a year.'

'So what had changed for me to win?' I knew that Neil was seriously cuter than I was.

'A change in the scoring. If you're married you lose three points – and that was all it took for Master Neil to slip to the number two position.'

'Well, I'm flattered. I don't know what to say.' I took a sip of my coffee. It was hot and bitter.

'Don't count your chickens, Wade. He's living with you now and a separated man is counted as a single man.' Marilyn smirked. She always did end up on top of the conversation.

'Well maybe not for long,' I countered.

'Why's that?'

'He told Cheryl that he's got some romantic dinner arranged for tonight. So something is on the cards.'

'We'll see. I can't imagine a man as attractive as Neil being alone for long.'

'No, neither can I,' I replied with more longing in my voice than I had intended.

That afternoon I delivered the final proof plans to Gee for approval and left early. After getting off the tube I wandered aimlessly towards my flat. Businessmen were hurrying homeward. Women in smart suits clutching brief cases were out-walking them, their sharp heels clicking on the pavement. On a street corner a young guy stood laughing into a mobile phone. Traffic thundered by, the petrol fumes swirling about my head. I crossed into a quiet street and dawdled along. A row of terraced houses were being renovated. The first three were completed, clean white woodwork surrounding navy doors, with newly manicured handkerchief lawns in front of dark windows. Towards the end of the row the lights in the house shells were on. As I ambled past I saw that the front door was open and through the window I could see two workmen were finishing up in the living room. One was older than the other, wearing a tatty torn jumper spattered with paint, his vast stomach pushing through the knitted weave. He was puffing on a cigarette. The younger guy was no more than eighteen or nineteen. He had straight white-blond shoulder-length hair that hung in his eyes. I watched as he flicked the fringe clear and hooked some hair behind his ears. His soft teenage stubble was the colour of amber, the patches of bristles surrounding a perfect set of white teeth. He was wearing a torn T-shirt that revealed a severely toned body beneath. He had tight hips, a perfect pair of hard buns jutting out of an almost shredded pair of shorts that clung to his arse and thick thighs. I stopped, rooted to the spot at this sight of masculinity. I could sense the testosterone in the evening air. I envied those who worked in such a male atmosphere, surrounded by fit guys, able to soak up their company. The young guy's hand went down and pulled at the heavy packet in his shorts. He shook his right leg slightly as if he was freeing something. I couldn't help but stare. The picture of this horny guy playing with himself through a lighted window was like watching a porn film come to life.

'Can I help you, mate?'

It was the older guy. He stood in the doorway looking accusingly at me.

'Er, no, it's OK,' I fumbled. The blond guy noticed me through the window and smiled. He looked down and his fringe fell back into his eyes. The old guy continued to stare at me while I held onto the low wrought iron gate that stood at the entrance. I didn't want to leave.

'Well, yes, about these houses, when will they be finished?' I bluffed to gain a few more minutes to glance at this young god.

'Not sure. Nice bit of work though. All gutted. New fittings throughout. You should talk to the estate agent.' He pointed to the 'For Sale' sign outside the completed properties.

'Yes, of course,' I continued, fighting for something to say. I looked towards the window. The blond guy had gone. I was about to start walking again, the vision still strong in my mind when I heard another voice.

'I can show you round if you like, mate.' It was him. He was Australian and he stood almost silhouetted in the doorway with a cheeky grin on his face. The older guy, who was obviously in charge, was less keen.

'Yeah, Scott, but I'm just locking up.'

There was little I could say, but the Australian continued, 'Oh leave it to me, George, I've got the keys and I know the alarm. It'll only take a few minutes. You get off.'

The foreman paused. 'Alright then. Remember the windows and I'll see you at eight tomorrow.'

I swung open the low gate at the front of the garden and George came through.

'You have a look round, sir, and if you're interested then

have a word with me. I may be able to do you a little deal if we don't go through the estate agent.' He tapped his nose conspiratorially.

'Thanks very much.'

George took a last drag on his cigarette and screwed it into the ground with the ball of his foot. He called out goodbye and whistled as he climbed into an old white transit van.

'Don't mind him, mate,' the Australian said as he ushered me inside. 'All talk and no action, you get me?'

I nodded and smiled as he swung the front door closed behind him.

'This place is about halfway done. The hallway goes along here and this is the main living area.'

He led me into the living room where I had first spied him. Now I had entered the picture that had captured me and I was inside looking at the dark street outside. The room was warm, a gas stove roaring in the corner. The wooden floorboards creaked beneath my feet. The sound echoed around me.

'Fresh plaster on all the walls,' the Australian continued, 'and the floorboards will be sanded and sealed. You can have carpet or rugs then, depending on what you want.'

'It looks good.' I feigned an interest, all the time trying to see as much of my fit young guide as I could.

'This plaster will take a while to fully dry out, you may get some hairline cracks, but it's a good job.'

He stood with his palms on the wall, his back towards me. I took in his full frame. His blond hair hung in a shaggy mane almost on his shoulders, which although not overly broad, were clearly defined beneath his thin white T-shirt. His lats gave his torso a bold V-shape. With his arms outstretched I could see the clear definition of biceps and triceps in his smooth arms. His hands were big, decorated with paint and plaster, fingernails white with the day's work. His back tapered to a tight waist, the T-shirt hanging off his shoulders and flapping around. And then I saw his arse; the cheeks were firm, rock solid. They jutted out as two hard mounds before tapering back into his thick thighs. His shorts clung to them, as I wanted to, the back seam slipping lightly into his crack to emphasise their definition. His legs were hairless, long sinewy hamstrings held in place by strong knees, before his legs flared out again with his solid calf muscles. His feet stood in a pair of battered trainers.

'Not bad, eh?' he guy said, turning to look at me.

'Not from where I'm standing,' I replied, the smirk hard to wipe from my face. 'How about upstairs?' I enquired, eager for our interview to continue.

'Come and have a look.'

We began to climb the stairs, but the Australian guy was slow.

'Sorry about this, but it's my leg. I've pulled something, giving me a fuck load of pain whenever I go up or down.'

My mind filled with witty replies, but I fought them back. No use scaring him off while his cute arse was just inches in front of my face as we slowly climbed the stairs.

'What did you do to it?'

'Not sure. It's back here someplace.' His right hand felt down his butt and onto his hamstring. His fingers massaged deeply into the muscle. 'Here, just here.'He stopped on the stairs, my face next to his hand and leg. I breathed in deeply. The smell of plaster and paint gave way to a warm masculine odour that filled my nostrils. It was too good an opportunity to miss.

'About here?' I asked, my hand slipping beneath his and feeling the muscle. It was taut and sinewy, surprisingly warm, and his skin was smooth as sheet metal.

'Yeah, that's the place.' He eased his leg back, pushing against my hand. I massaged slowly. 'I got some Deep Heat stuff from the chemist. I'll have a bath tonight and give it a bit of a work over.'

'Good idea.' I continued to massage, the two of us frozen on the stairs, me breathing in his scent, him moaning slightly and pushing his arse closer and closer to my face. For a moment time stood still. I felt my cock flex into life, the pent-up frustration of the day unwinding within me.

'You should do this for a living,' the Australian said, moving away awkwardly and continuing his climb of the stairs.

'I'd like to,' I admitted in all honesty.

We reached the master bedroom.

'Plenty of space, I know it's a bit of a mess, but here's the en-suite bathroom which we fitted at the end of last week. Sorry its untidy, but some of the guys have been using the bath and stuff after work. Save stinking on the way home.'

The bath was bright white, with a pile of newspapers on the floor which had been used as a bath mat. The overhead lighting was harsh.

'It's bright,' I commented.

'On a dimmer though.' The light faded as the Australian turned a switch. I could hear it buzz.

'Good idea.' I stood looking at him. 'How's the leg?'

'Sore.'

'Well, you've done a good job here. I'll have a think about it.'

'Yeah, do.'

He looked at me. His eyes twinkled. Neither of us moved. Through the bathroom window over his shoulder, I could see that it was now dark outside.

'When will they be ready?'

'Oh, six weeks or so.'

'You still be here then?'

'Yeah, probably.'

'Well, my name's Wade.'

'Scott.'

'Nice to meet you Scott.'

'You too, Wade.'

I stood looking at Scott. He smiled at me. Was I reading these signals correctly? My aching dick was telling me that Scott was one hundred per cent horny, but was he just a young kid ready for a night out in the pub followed by a quick shag after a hard day's work? He limped slowly towards me. I held my breath.

'Better be going then . . .'

'Yeah.' I stood still. 'Thanks for your time, Scott.'

'No problem. He flicked the bedroom light off and I took a

step out onto the landing. The bathroom light was still on, the faint buzz from the dimmer switch just audible.

'Better get that,' Scott said returning to the bedroom.

He disappeared from view and I made my way to the top of the stairs. I could see the front door at the end of the hallway ahead of me, the exit from this fantasy world with Scott. I was about to walk down when I heard a yelp from the bedroom.

'Scott? You OK?' I called out. In the bedroom, Scott was on his knees. I flicked on the light. 'What is it?'

'The leg, mate. Don't worry, just a twinge.'

'No, you come here.' I pushed my hands beneath his armpits and lifted him gently to his feet. I could feel his pecs flex beneath my fingers.

'It's always worse at the end of the day. I reckon that bit of massage must have loosened something.'

I lifted his arm over my shoulder and carried him to a pile of dust sheets in the corner. 'These clean?'

'Yeah, they came today. They're for the second bedroom.'

I dropped him lightly on to the sheets. He sat there rubbing the back of his leg and flinching.

'You couldn't give it another rub could you, mate?'

'Sure.'

I held his leg and felt the hamstring behind. It felt tight. Scott groaned and leaned away. He lay on his back with one leg in my hand, crooked slightly upwards.

'I'll get the Deep Heat. Where is it?'

'In my bag. In the kitchen.'

I raced downstairs and found a small black ruck sack which contained the tube of liniment and dashed back up to Scott. He was still laying on his back, one arm now bent over his eyes. I tried to push the leg of his shorts up, but the thick muscle on his thigh prevented it.

'You're gonna have to slip your shorts down so I can get to this,' I ventured. Without a sound Scott undid the buttons and slid the shorts down. He moaned slightly as he raised his stiff leg. I pulled the shorts off. Underneath he wore an old pair of faded red briefs. The elastic was going, but they were still tight enough to reveal a mound of Australian cock-meat the size of a large fist. Scott groaned again. I eased his legs slowly apart and spread the Deep Heat on my fingers. Scott's arm remained over his eyes. Between his legs I saw the side of his scrotum hanging slightly out of his underpants – a white flap of skin with wisps of pubic hair covering it. It was the first hair I had seen on his body. As I rubbed the ointment in I gazed at his cock. I could make it out clearly now, curving sidewards around his body, his luscious bollocks filling up the bottom of his pants. Beneath my fingers the muscle spasm rippled. I slid my fingers further up towards his buttocks, the smooth skin sliding beneath my fingers, while Scott moaned almost silently from beneath the arm covering his face.

'Better?' I ventured.

'You bet,' Scott whispered.

I looked again at his cock, which now was unravelling from his waist and was punching slowly upwards. My cock stirred too. With one hand I massaged his leg whilst with the other I silently undid my belt to give my cock space to breath. In the half-light I watched Scott's member come to life, first straightening out and then pushing up against the tatty white waistband of his underpants. The old elastic was no barrier for a man-rammer as strong as this one and the mushroom head slid out, pushing back the elastic. It flexed with the pulse of his young heart, lifting up from his smooth stomach beneath. I continued to massage his leg. Now my hand was up to his arse, I lifted his underpants and slipped my hand onto his buttocks. His butt was firm, solid, the skin stretched tightly over the muscle with no fat between.

Scott groaned. He pulled up his T-shirt with his free hand and tugged it effortlessly over his head. I gazed at his torso, the white smooth skin vacuum-packed onto his youthful muscles. With a free hand he tweaked at his nipples. Delicately, so as not to hurt his leg, I lifted his buttocks upwards and pulled his underpants down. His dick sprang free, with a slap onto his stomach. His legs slid apart and two weighty balls glided down between his legs, left hanging in their white fuzzy sac. Still I massaged with one hand whilst kicking off my shoes and pulling my trousers down. Only for a moment did I let go of this Adonis, to undo my tie and slip off my jacket and shirt.

Soon I was naked too and we were both laying on the dust sheets as the night settled outside. I looked at Scott, who turned his head towards me, that cheeky grin that I had first noticed through the window back on his face.

'Sure am glad you stopped by.'

I wiped my hands clean and slowly massaged his balls. They were the size of my palm.

'This good?'

'You bet. If this is what it's like to sell a house, I reckon I'm going to become an estate agent.' Scott's hands lifted to my head and his fingers ran through my hair. 'Must be my lucky night.'

He kissed me deeply, his tongue flicking over my teeth. I could feel the soft stubble tickling my face, the hair too young to scratch. We kissed passionately. Our lips pressing against each other, while our hands felt and discovered each other's body. Scott's fingers dug deeply into the muscles on my back. I stretched my arms down to that hard arse of his and lifted him onto my lap. My cock was sticky with pre-come and slipped beneath his legs, sliding over his balls, creating a wet trail of juice up between his crack, leaving the shaft of my dick pressing against his hole. His cock in turn pressed into my stomach, his chest rested against mine. Still we kissed. I pulled his head to mine, wanting as much of this young man inside me as I could. Scott wanted it too and leaned against me, hugging me, pulling at me, his hands running over my body, tugging at my nipples, clenching me between his muscular thighs.

We kissed, the passion raging within us. I toppled backwards, with Scott's face nestled against mine. My legs flipped up and Scott adjusted his dick to rest between my arse cheeks. My buttocks clenched that long Aussie cock and he began to dry hump me. And still we kissed. My eyes still closed, I gave way to the sense of ecstasy and pleasure that filled my body. I could feel Scott's cock, the sticky head pressing against my sphincter as his dick rode my arse crack, his hands punching down on my chest, pinching my nipples, my dick solid, pumping, purple and hard.

My eyes remained closed as I felt Scott move on top of me. The vision of this beautiful youth in my mind was so perfect that I wanted nothing to destroy it. I loved the smell of him, his smooth warm skin sliding against mine. I lifted my arms above my head and groaned in pleasure.

And then it got better. I felt those soft downy lips that had been pressed against mine slip onto the tip of my cock. My shaft shivered in delight as he took my head in his mouth and began to flick his tongue across the piss-slit, slurping at my seed. His mouth began to slide my foreskin back as more of my dick went into his warm, wet mouth. I breathed in with excitement and as I did I smelled his sweet arse, now pressed towards my face. My hands moved forward, my eyes still closed. I could feel his butt edging along my chest towards me. I gently prised his cheeks apart and buried my head at the source of this man-scent. There were just a few hairs in his crack to tickle my face as my tongue darted in and out to savour this dish. I found his puckered hole and probed deeper. Scott moaned, my dick slipping further down his throat as my tongue pushed into his tangy tight hole.

My hips bucked upwards as my cock was worked over. I concentrated on his arse, pulling his cheeks apart, fingering the creamy hole and slurping in the taste of this Australian juice. I could feel Scott take the whole of my dick down his throat, but still he seemed to want more, pulling at my bollocks in an attempt to get more in his mouth, my pubes brushing his soft chin. I stretched his puckered hole open and roughly licked along his crack. I could feel Scott punching his arse back onto my face in return, the savoury hole gliding over my tongue, my taste buds alive with his nectar. His dick had been gently dripping pre-come onto my chest and I could feel the stickiness lubeing his dick-end as it rubbed against my chest hair. Taking a last mouthful of his fabulous arse, I lifted his firm butt into the air and positioned his creamy dick-head on my lips. Slowly

Scott lowered his dick into my mouth, the darkness from his body covering my face. His cock-head was wide, salty and hot. My lips savoured this new taste of man-milk as much as that of his arse which was still sparkling inside my mouth. I dropped my jaw as his shaft came into my mouth. Christ! He was big. My eyes had now been closed for so long that I'd had no idea that Scott was so well hung. I was going to need all my technique to service this joystick. He gently let his dick pass over my tongue, letting it pause as the steamy heat of his tool filled my mouth, before it continued its journey to the back of my mouth and then down my throat. I took a deep breath as his dick filled me. Still I could feel my cock warm and safe within Scott's mouth as slurping noises filled the room. I was almost tipped over the edge as I felt his sac fall onto my face, his heavy man-sized bollocks resting on my nose, his soft blond Aussie pubes tickling my chin. I pulled his arse apart and shoved two fingers into his already moist hole. Scott groaned and I moaned in reply as we lay there, our mouths impaled on each other's dicks.

I felt Scott's hand part my butt cheeks and begin to finger my man-cunt. Then he slowly lifted his dick up. I could breath again, but not for long. He slid his shaft back down, filling my throat as he began to fuck my face. I spread my legs in ecstasy and I felt Scott finger fuck me in time with fucking my face. My arsehole was already moist from Scott's own pre-come and the juice spilling from his mouth. He fucked my face and sucked my dick down to the root. His bollocks slapped against my face. I opened my eyes briefly to see his great balls suspended above me, his legs tight around my head, his smell encasing me in delight, while all the while he teased the juice from my cock with his tongue. My arse was stretched some more. I could feel that he had three fingers in me now and his cock was pumping a rhythm down my throat, his haunches bumping against my face. More; I wanted more. I wanted all of Scott in me; his come, his arse juice, the sweet saliva from his kiss. Still he fucked me, riding my face like a tight arse, thrusting down my throat while the salt of his pre-come oiled my mouth and lips. I bucked my hips to his face as he worked over my tool. I could bear this no longer. I could feel my balls unwind, the man cream about to burst free. His taste filled my every sense, the sound of him fucking my face, his mouth sliding over my cock, the slurp of my arse begging for more fingers.

And then pure ecstasy. He came. It seemed like a gallon of his jizz sauce cascaded down my throat, bubbling up into my mouth, spilling out over my lips and on to my chin. The sweetness was overwhelming as he filled me with his juice. My hips flew upwards and I came too. Scott let out a guttural groan and thrust his face down on my cock, eager to take all of my boy-gravy, unwilling to waste a drop, his throat sucking the ribbons of jizz that flew from my tool. And still he pumped into my mouth. More and more man-shake filling me. My tongue lapped against his cock-head, relieving him of every drop of jism.

The pumping of his dick eased slowly, but he was still pulling at my cock-head, demanding more pecker juice. I squeezed my sphincter around his fingers, urging the last drop from my balls, keen that he should drink everything from within me.

I felt his cock soften slightly. I didn't want it to end. I wanted more. I let his cock slip from my mouth and relaxed backwards onto the dust sheet. I looked at his beautiful schlong and kissed the tip of it. Scott turned and curled up next to me.

'Fuck, man! You have one beautiful cock,' he said, gazing at me, 'and the sweetest jizz ever.'

I lay there filled with his flavour, filled with his juice, feeling both exhausted and more alive than I had been for ages. He was beautiful and his juice was royal nectar. My skin was coated with a thin layer of sweat from both our bodies. I pulled Scott on top of me and held him close. Our smells continued to blend even after the sex had finished.

'Fancy a quick bath before home?' Scott asked.

'Only if you share it with me.'

'I think that can be arranged . . .'

Scott stood and his great tool fell between his legs. I kneeled next to it and sniffed in its aroma.

'You sure there's not a drop more juice left in these balls?'

I watched as his cock began to grow.
'I reckon there just might be, Wade . . .'

Chapter Four

It was almost nine before I got home. I was surprised to see lights on in my flat. I opened the door tentatively. The television was on and sounds of singing were coming from the kitchen. It was Neil. He was a little drunk.

'You alright?' I enquired.

'Just in time, Sport,' came Neil's response through billowing steam. A pan lid clattered. 'Surprise! Thought I'd make up for last night's fiasco. Spaghetti Carbonara, my speciality, well sort of.' He offered me a steaming plate of pasta. 'Table's set, go on through.'

I sat at the table and began to eat. It was good food and after the hour with Scott I was hungry. Neil dropped into the chair opposite. He poured the dregs of a bottle of red wine into his glass and uncorked another.

'Drink?'

I nodded, my mouth full.

'You've got a bit of catching up to do.' He slurped from his glass and began to eat. I continued, filling my mouth with the creamy pasta and sauce.

'Take it easy, Sport, there's plenty more if you want it!'

We ate in silence. I paused only to sprinkle on more parmesan or to gulp down the wine. Finally, I pushed the plate forward and sat back in my chair.

'Good?' asked Neil, flushed and grinning.

'Excellent. Just what I needed.' I smiled, feeling similarly merry. I had never been so comfortable with a person as I was with Neil. His blue eyes smiled at me from under his dark lashes. Neither of us said anything. I could feel his leg, warm, leaning next to mine under the table, his foot tapping gently. I pictured his cock that morning, long, thick and hard with the head rising above his stomach. And I thought of Scott filling my throat with his lovely Aussie dick and I longed to do the same for Neil, to be filled with his love and to see his face turn to ecstasy.

'You handed your plans into Gee?'

'Yup. Pretty good job too, if I say so myself.'

Neil picked up his glass, the red wine swilling inside. 'To Wade Armstrong. The most brilliant man at Allsop and Gee. And also, I hear on the grapevine, the sexiest.' He winked and his smile temporarily dazzled me.

'To Neil Rogers. Great in the kitchen, great at work and according to the same grapevine, the greatest in bed.' I was drunk, I knew it and couldn't help but flirt. I knocked back the wine while Neil roared approval.

'Great in bed? You better believe it.' He drained his glass and stood. 'They don't call me *Donkey Dick* for nothing!' He howled with laughter and grabbed his crutch. Through his jeans I could see him cup his balls, his cock laying out of the palm of his hand while he thrust the tantalising package towards me. 'I've had Cheryl begging for it!' He bellowed. I laughed and poured us more wine. Neil wrestled me from my chair before I had a chance to drink and pushed me to the floor. He was stronger than I had imagined. I was laughing too much to fight back, even if I had wanted too.

'Oooh, Cheryl, you are a tease,' he said sitting on my chest and pinning my arms under his knees. 'Now what do you say?'

I continued to laugh. The last time I had been pinned down like this was by my brother when I was eight. 'Sorry, Mr Rogers,' I replied in my best Cheryl voice.

'I didn't hear that,' Neil cooed back, sliding his arse further up my chest so that his large packet was now directly in front of my face.

I could smell him again. That sweet musky fragrance that I always associated with Neil. His arse was hot against my chest. I found it difficult to breathe because of the pressure on my chest and because I was laughing so much. My dick stirred into life, still moist from the encounter with Scott. My balls were suddenly bursting for similar action from Neil.

'I said I didn't hear that, Missy Cheryl!' Neil dropped his head to within inches of my face. His breath, still sweet from the pasta, blew across the bridge of my nose and into my eyes. I could see a slight five o'clock shadow on his chin. His hair flopped over his eyes, shadowing them from the glare of the overhead light. I was powerless. All I could do was laugh. My cock continued to swell.

'Something funny, Cheryl?' he asked, leaning closer to my face. I breathed in his wonderful scent as he spoke to me, his air filling my lungs. I closed my eyes and savoured it. Feebly, I tried to wrestle him off, but he was bigger and stronger.

'Nothing, nothing's funny,' was the only reply I could giggle from my burning lungs.

'Then why are you laughing, girlie Cheryl?' With this he thrust his hips downwards, causing me to exhale. My cock was like a truncheon. I prayed that he didn't turn around and see it. I tried to wrestle it to one side, but Neil saw this as an attempt to escape and pinned me down even harder.

'Are you a girlie gossip, Cheryl?' He shook his head and his auburn fringe tickled my face. Then he did it again. It was excruciatingly erotic and yet he had no idea, laughing all the while at my apparent discomfort.

'Yes, I'm a girlie gossip, I'm a girlie gossip,' I bellowed, my ribcage collapsing with heaves of laughter.

'Then take this you, girlie gossip.' One damp palm was planted on my forehead to keep my head still. I closed my eyes waiting for some new torture. Neil made a sound like Tarzan. I howled too and then I felt him press his lips roughly against mine. I gasped. My eyes flashed open. I could see his closed eyelids, the row of sooty eyelashes. I felt his tongue roughly probe into my mouth, the sweetest taste of his saliva mixing with mine, his soft lips fringed with the light bristle of his beard. His tongue darted around my mouth for an infinitesimal moment which left me paralysed beneath him. And then it was gone and Neil was upright again grinning down at me, licking his lips and wiping the saliva away from his mouth with the back of his hand.

'Take that, girlie Cheryl!' He jumped off and grabbed his wine. I lay temporarily winded on the carpet. Quickly I rolled over to hide my thumping erection and began to laugh. 'More wine?' he asked.

'Yeah, go on.' I staggered to my feet, my hands in front of my crotch and sat down. There was a banging from the ceiling. We both looked up.

'Looks like I made too much noise again, Sport.'

'Fuck 'em,' I replied, grabbing my glass and downing it in one. Neil cheered. The banging repeated above us.

That night I lay in bed and repeated the evening's happenings. Neil had kissed me and even though it was only in jest, it seemed that one of my prayers had been answered. I felt loved, and although Neil couldn't really love me as I wanted him too, I knew that we had a special bond between us. I fell asleep, still tasting his beautiful breath, my cock warm and engorged between my legs.

'Something's up.'

'What?' I stood at Marilyn's desk the next morning at work. I was in an effusive mood and was ready to tell Marilyn all about the great evening I had had with Neil (minus one or two of the details, like Neil's kiss and my stomping erection).

'I don't know,' Marilyn continued, 'Gee was in early today and that's not like him and then he asked me to get you as soon as you came in. Be careful, Wade. I don't know what it is, but I've worked here long enough to recognise when that blood-sucking freak of nature in there is about to pounce.'

'It can't be,' I reasoned. 'I left the revised plans on his desk last night and they're genius, if I say so myself. Even Neil thinks they're perfect and he knows that project better than anyone.'

'Well, where you're concerned I think our Mr Rogers thinks everything's perfect, so that doesn't mean a lot.'

I was about to challenge this when the door to Gee's office opened. Karl Parker came out. He nodded to me and strode past Marilyn, his greasy, thin lips pursed.

'Ah, Mr Armstrong, do come in.'

Marilyn mouthed a 'good luck' at me as I hesitantly entered the lair of Arnold Gee. My plans were spread open on his desk, together with my notes about the plumbing system in the lift shafts.

'Very impressive work, Wade.'

'Thank you.'

'Please, sit down.'

With the plans spread between us I took Gee though the modifications I had made, together with their associated cost savings. I confirmed that Neil had seen the plans and that if further designs were modified it could save the project a considerable amount of time and money. Gee seemed pleased. He smiled and nodded as I explained my workings.

'And this is all your idea, is it?'

'Yes.'

'And you drew these up all by yourself?'

'Yes.' I was getting confused. What was he leading to? This line of questioning had a bite at the end and too late I realised I had walked straight into its open jaws.

'Then how do you explain this?'

Gee dropped a sheaf of papers on my desk. They were all prototype sketches of my designs. Dumbfounded I flicked through them. Clipped at the back were printouts of e-mails from Karl Parker. The first was some half-hearted sympathy message for the last bollocking I had received from Gee after Neil hadn't given me the proper plans and my initial plumbing system was made redundant. Added to this was a promise to let me know of any ideas Karl may have to resolve the problem. The second, more interestingly, was a suggestion that I should use the spare space in the lift shafts together with a rough outline of where the pipes could be fitted. The third e-mail, dated at the beginning of the week, was a full outline of the plans, proposed cost savings, the offer of help with drawing the plans up, as well as an offer to go and see Gee to give him the good news. Graciously the e-mail ended with a suggestion that we could both share the responsibility and honour for this brilliant idea, with Karl taking credit for 'just helping out and giving the initial nudge that led to the new plans'. I looked at the dates of the three e-mails. They were all backdated and reinforced by the computer's own dating system. I knew I checked my e-mail daily and that none of these had been sent. I also knew that Karl had heard about my plans earlier that week and so he must have been working on this scheme for some days.

'I'm waiting for your thoughts, Mr Armstrong.'

I was snookered. Any attempt to deny the e-mails would be fruitless as Karl had somehow managed to reconstruct the computer software's date facility. And what's more, Karl had just had a meeting with Gee for who knows how long, weaving a story that no doubt had several other pitfalls for me to slip into.

'I don't know what to say,' I ventured. 'Karl has been helping me with this project, but as you can see from the e-mails we haven't actually spoken face to face.' This seemed the best way out. 'I drew up the plans yesterday and as I knew you were waiting for them, I dropped them on your desk last night. Marilyn said you were seeing Karl this morning so I guessed that you would know about who authored them. I'm sorry if you thought I was trying to deceive you.'

'I don't like sneaks, Mr Armstrong,' Gee growled. 'If I thought you were trying to take the credit for someone else's work, especially a colleague more experienced and senior, then I would have you out of this building quicker than shit off a shovel. Now I suggest you amend these plans and add Mr Parker's name to the designer's log, here.'

He pointed to the space at the bottom of the plans where the author initials his work. 'Of course, Mr Gee. I really am very sorry for this confusion.'

'Me too.'

I left the office. Karl was hovering outside, pretending to

read a notice board. Marilyn was by a filing cabinet, but I could tell she wasn't filing.

'Sorry about that, "Sport",' he hissed at me as we passed, adopting Neil's familiarity. I could feel Gee behind me.

'I don't know what to say, Karl. You know I want you to get all you deserve,' I held his hand tightly and looked down at him. 'Just trust me, I'll make it up to you somehow. I won't forget. I've let you down badly and I'll go out of my way to see that you get the justice you deserve.' I smiled at him, baring my teeth, suppressing an overpowering urge to smash the smarmy little grin from his puffy white face.

'No hard feelings.' Karl pulled his hand free and slipped past into Gee's office.

'Fuck you,' I muttered under my breath.

Marilyn looked at me. 'Leave it, Wade. He's got Gee in his back pocket and he's one step ahead.'

'We'll see about that.'

I returned to my desk and sat down, seething. It stuck in my throat that Karl's name would be added to my plans. I was unable to concentrate. Neil got the story from Marilyn and came over to try to calm me, but even his soothing words and the feel of his firm hand on my shoulder couldn't remove the bile from my stomach. I checked my computer for e-mail and there were Karl's three messages, all perfectly backdated and all apparently on my terminal for some days.

At twelve Neil passed on his way to a meeting about Hammersmith. With him was Miles Stone. Neil nodded at me, but kept walking. It was Mr Stone who stopped.

'Wade isn't it?'

'Yes. How are you, Mr Stone?'

'Call me Miles. I'm fine.'

Miles Stone had an electric air about him. Six foot two, he was lean and obviously ruthlessly efficient. His groomed hair, greying at the temples, tanned skin and flawless dress sense increased his sense of power. I shook his hand and for a moment he sat on the edge of my desk.

'Off to lunch?' I asked.

'Yes. Mr Rogers is trying to get me drunk again in order to get me to agree to his designs.'

'I think it would probably take more than that.'

'Correct. I make up my own mind.' He stood. 'Are you working on my building?'

'Not yet, I'm an indian, not a chief.'

'No, Wade. I think you're a chief; but in indian's clothing. I'll have a word with Arnold. I'd like your input on this.'

'Great, thanks.' I didn't know what to say and was flattered that Miles Stone had singled me out.

'I'll talk to you.' He winked and was gone.

I was reading this article about PMT.' Cheryl lolled on my desk. 'And apparently women have this four week cycle thing.'

'Yes?'

'And apparently men have the same sort of thing, only it's over six weeks. Did you know that?'

'No, I didn't.'

'So if we women can work out what your men's cycle is, then we can live in harmony. Interesting isn't it?'

'Yes.' I had little else to do, so Cheryl's philosophy of life was a pleasant pastime.

'And all this is caused by hormones and stuff.' Cheryl crossed her legs. She was flirting.

'What is a hormone?' I asked.

'They're like little tadpoles aren't they?'

'Tadpoles?'

'Yeah, tadpoles, only little.' Cheryl nodded sagely.

'What do you mean?'

'Well, men get their hormones from their bits, you know . . .'

'Oh, like sperm.'

Cheryl blushed. 'You don't have to say it. I don't know. What are you like? You men are all the same, just got one thing on your mind.'

'But you brought the subject up.'

'But I didn't say nothing about, well, sperm and stuff.'

'So what do these hormones do?'

'Well they come from your bits and then they swim about your body and give you moods and stuff. And make babies of course. There are special ones to make you hairy and muscly, and others make your voice break, and some make you want to eat and go shopping, that sort of thing.'

'I see.'

'Course, women have different hormones. We don't get the hairy ones or the voice ones, we get things for ovulation and being pretty and stuff.'

'Where do you get your hormones from then?' I enquired.

'From our fallopian tubes.'

'What about HRT?'

'Oh I know all about that. That's when they give you the tadpoles from a plaster. They squeeze in through the pores in your skin.'

'Right, now I see.' I sat looking at my desk. Cheryl stirred a biro in my desk tidy.

'What was you seeing Baldie Gee for this morning then?'

'The usual; I'm not worthy to work at Allsop and Gee.'

'You are funny.' Cheryl giggled. 'You make Janice laugh all the time.'

'But I hardly talk to her.'

'Yeah, but you look at her all the time across the office. We've seen you!'

'I don't!'

'Yes you do. You were this morning. We all saw. Don't be embarrassed. I think it's nice that you're shy. You've been voted the office hunk of the month, did you know that?'

'I had heard something . . .'

'There you go, you're being all shy again. But we spy on you gazing over at Janice. You go all gooey and doodle stuff on your desk. Look she's over there now, give her a wave.' Cheryl pointed across the office. Janice's desk was just behind Neil's. Now I realised. Cheryl was right. How many hours had I spent watching Neil work, seeing him brush his golden hair out of his eyes or suck on the end of pen, all the time wishing that it was me attached to those lips. How long I had spent nursing an erection while dreaming of him laying me over his desk and fucking me for all he was worth, spreading my cheeks, filling my hole until his balls slapped against my arse. I felt myself flush.

'See, it's true, you're going red!' Cheryl giggled. 'I'm gonna tell Janice.'

Cheryl hopped off my desk and was gone before I could explain. But what would I say ? 'Sorry Cheryl, but actually I was lusting after Neil Rogers?' I was not man enough to admit to that.

Neil returned from lunch with Miles Stone. I watched them stride out of the lift and purposefully enter Gee's office. Gee stood at his office door to welcome them, glistening with oily charm. My view of the proceedings was interrupted by the bulky form of Karl Parker.

'Hello, chum,' he sneered, the whine in his voice grating like fingernails down a blackboard. 'Looks like we're partners now. Let me know when you've completed the latest drawings and I'll check them over for you.'

'Thanks.' I wanted to thump him.

'And then I'll initial them.'

'Don't push it, Weasel,' I warned.

'Listen, buddy,' Karl leaned over, 'you may think that your shit don't stink, but I've got you in the palm of my hand. That lift idea was mine and you stole it. Think yourself lucky that you got off the hook as you did. If I'd been in charge you'd be out on your arse now.'

'If you were in charge, Karl, the entire office would jump from the windows to get away from you. Now, there's a really bad smell around here at the moment, so why don't you fuck off?'

I stared at him. For an instant I didn't care about my job or my future. Violence surged within me, rising in my throat. I towered over Karl, his face puffing like a fish out of water below me.

'Go on then,' he taunted.

'Wade, Karl.' It was Marilyn. 'Mr Gee would like to see you both in his office now.'

Karl strode off. The veins continued to pulsate in my neck.

'Don't blow it, Wade,' Marilyn warned. 'Don't get mad, get even. Now keep your cool. Gee wants to see you. Neil's in there and so is Mr Stone. There's trouble with the Hammersmith project so use some of your charm and earn a few brownie points at the same time.'

Miles Stone stood in the corner of Gee's office tapping the venetian blind with his fingers. Neil stood by the charcoal sofa opposite, his brow furrowed. Gee was behind his desk, a frantic smile smeared across his face. Karl stood lost in the middle of the office, like a stickleback in a jam jar, looking round and around himself, wondering how he got there and what should he do. I was still angry.

'Good afternoon, Mr Stone, Mr Gee, Neil.' I ignored Karl.

'Wade, glad you could join us.' It was Miles Stone. He turned and sat on the sofa and indicated that I should join him. Neil sat on his left, I on his right. Plans were spread out on the low mahogany table in front of us. There was nowhere for Karl to sit. He hovered by the side of the table like an uninvited guest until Gee ushered him out of the way.

'I can't see, Mr Parker.' Gee brushed him towards a large potted aspidistra in the corner. Karl squatted uncomfortably on his haunches and feigned knowledge and interest.

'Wade, these are the plans for a project near completion in Chancery Lane,' Miles said, ticking the plans out with a finger, 'what do you think?'

'An investment property to be let out as office space, I know it, yes.' I had worked on the plans when I had first arrived at Allsop and Gee. It had been my first indication that my job was not to change the world, but to change the tiling in the gents' lavatories.

'And?' Miles looked at me. At any other time I would have been intimidated, but Karl had so angered me I didn't care. I knew that Karl had worked on this project.

'It's functional, practical and will be easy to let and maintain.

The budget was low for a project this size; but it's what I call "bimbo architecture".'

'What?' Miles asked. Neil dropped his head into his hands. I didn't care.

'Bimbo architecture. It's all front. Make the front of the building look great; look here we've got a neo-classical motif, columns, stonework,' I pointed to the drawings in front of us. 'Two statues of no one in particular, but both with laurel crowns to give an idea of corporate power – even though most Roman emperors were murdered by their colleagues. A grand staircase up to the main entrance and then, once you're in, it's the same as any office block you'd find in Coventry; clean, functional, easy to maintain. Hence "bimbo architecture" – great to look at, but nothing going on upstairs.'

Gee laughed nervously. Miles Stone sat back and Neil dropped his head further and threw me a look. I smiled at him, cockily. He shook his head lightly in return. Karl began to bluster about beauty being in the eye of the beholder, but Gee shut him up when, in desperation, he began to compare the building to Samantha Fox.

'Thank you, Karl.' Gee turned to me. 'I think that appraisal is a bit harsh, Wade.'

So now I was back onto first name terms with Gee. It amused me how he alternated, depending on what he wanted and who he wanted to impress. I remained resolutely firm.

'No, it's not harsh, just accurate. Actually "bimbo architecture" is exactly what the clients wanted, had they known to ask for it. First impressions of a building are what will sell it. They wanted low-cost offices that didn't look cheap. That is what we provided, on time and within their budget. Aesthetically it's about as advanced as *The Woodentops*, but it fulfilled the client's remit to the letter.'

There was a silence as I finished. Karl fidgeted. I looked at Neil, who stared back, mouth slightly open. His broad hands were clasped in front of him and I loved him more than ever.

'Now I understand.' Miles Stone turned to me. 'Thank you,

Wade, that is what I have been trying to find out for the last two weeks. I thought these plans were bland because Allsop and Gee were bland, but that is not the case. Obviously I have not made myself clear. The building I wish to commission is to be my headquarters. I want the whole of it to be exciting, a building that represents the values of the Stone Partnership. Something new and something sophisticated, something with brains. I think you understand what I mean, don't you, Wade.'

I nodded. 'Less Pamela Anderson, more Carol Vorderman.'

Miles laughed.

'But not so suburban. Maybe with the chic and class of a Jackie Kennedy thrown in?'

'Perfect.' Miles laughed. Gee laughed too, while I heard Neil let out a sigh of relief. Karl laughed too loud and too late and from behind the leaves of the aspidistra. He was ignored.

It was agreed that I should work with Neil on an initial concept for the building. Karl added that he would check things through. Miles Stone glanced at Karl and then turned to me for confirmation. I could feel Gee's eyes upon me.

'Karl is very good with computers,' I smiled at Karl, 'he can do things with them I didn't know were possible.'

'If you're happy then so am I.' Miles Stone stood to leave. I shook his hand, excused myself and swept out triumphantly. Marilyn was at her desk.

'Did you keep calm, Wade?' she asked.

'You were right. I didn't get mad, but I began to get even.' I kissed a finger and planted it on her forehead.

'Wade, wait.' It was Neil. 'You were brilliant in there. Stone was about to walk and you saved the day. You're amazing, Sport.' He slapped his hands on my arms. I grinned and looked into his azure eyes that so enchanted me.

'Flattery will get you everywhere with Wade,' Marilyn said. 'Now, why don't you two go somewhere and celebrate?' She smirked at me. It was as if she knew what I felt for Neil. At that moment I didn't care who knew; not Marilyn, Janice, Cheryl, Gee, Karl or the whole office; Neil was who I wanted to spend the rest of my life with.

'How about it?' I was jolted back by Neil flinging his arm around me.

'What?'

'How about a drink? We should celebrate. We can work together and with your brains and my charm we should be able to reel Miles Stone in. He likes you, believe me.'

'Sure. I'll get my stuff.'

Neil and I stood by the lift. Neither of us said anything. I could hear the clatter and hum of the office behind me. I felt Neil's shoulder brush against me as we stood together, both watching the journey of the lift towards us, marked out in little scarlet numbers that lit up as the lift ascended. I caught a wave of Neil's scent. This had to be as near perfection as life could be. Neil and I working on the same project for the next few weeks. I wanted to hold him. Marilyn's words echoed in my mind '*Well where you're concerned I think our Mr Rogers thinks everything's perfect . . .*' I slung my arm around Neil's shoulder.

'We're a team.'

Neil returned the gesture. 'I think we are, Sport.' We stood like two thirteen-year-old boys in a school playground, gleeful at having scored a goal.

'You off somewhere?' It was Karl. He waddled in front of us. 'Bit early isn't it?'

'Got some work to do.' Neil responded without looking at him. We watched the numbers flash along as the lift rose higher.

'Shall I get my jacket?' Karl began to leave. It was Neil who replied first.

'Not today, no.'

'Sorry.' I smiled at him. 'I'll let you know when the plans are complete and you can initial them.'

'But Miles Stone thinks I'm part of the team,' Karl protested. The lift pinged and the doors slid open.

'No,' Neil said, ushering me into the lift, 'Miles Stone thinks you are part of the foliage. Bye!'

The lift doors glided shut leaving a red-faced Karl to fume alone.

I giggled as the lift began to descend. 'What about the advice not to offend Karl then?' I asked.

Neil shrugged his broad shoulders. 'Ah, fuck him, I really can't be bothered any more. He smiled at me as the lift descended.

Fourteen, thirteen, twelve, eleven. The floors flashed by in front of us.

'Where we going then?' I asked.

'Don't know. Neil answered. 'Should be somewhere special.'

Ten, nine, eight. 'What do you fancy?' I asked.

'I fancy a lot of things right now,' Neil said, looking ahead.

Then the lift juddered. The lights stopped their cascade through the numbers and the lift ground to a halt. I waited for the doors to open, but nothing happened. Neil leaned across and pressed the lobby button again. Still nothing happened. All was silent. I pressed the lobby button too and still nothing happened.

We stood next to each other, both looking up at the little row of now dark numbers waiting for a sign of life. No matter how many times we pressed the lobby button, nothing happened.

'I guess I'd better press the alarm.'

'No, leave it a minute,' Neil suggested, 'could be just a short-circuit. No need to make a lot of fuss over nothing.'

We waited in silence. Neil rocked slowly backwards on his heels and then forward onto his toes. His face was screwed up with concentration. The fan stopped. I could hear Neil breathing. I noticed him swallow nervously.

'Are you OK?'

'Yeah, fine, fine.' He was lying.

'You're not claustrophobic are you?'

Neil laughed. 'No, no. I'm fine. Just thinking.'

'Good. 'Cause I didn't want you to freak out or anything. Not in a lift this size.'

'No, I'm fine, really. Just thinking.' He paused. 'Everything happens so quickly in life that it's rare you actually get an opportunity to actually stop and decide just where you are going.'

'Well, hopefully, we're going down, to the lobby and then for a drink,' I said flippantly.

'You know what I mean.' Neil looked at me. 'What with Karen and work, this Hammersmith project, dealing with Gee and Karl, you . . .' His voice trailed off.

'I hope I'm not lumped together with Gee and Karl on purpose.'

'You know you're not!'

Neil took a step backwards and sat, leaning against the back wall. The lift was carpeted with a soft beige pile that fitted halfway up the walls to a waist-high mahogany rail that ran round to the silver lift doors. Above that at the back was a large dark frosted mirror, on the sides bronze metal panels.

Neil leaned against the carpet and rested his head on the wooden rail.

'I just sometimes wonder where I'm going.'

I sat next to him. 'You can stay with me as long as you like, you know. You don't have to move out. I know I only said a week . . .'

'Thanks.'

The silence was uncomfortable. Two grown men sitting in a lift. Something was bugging Neil and I wasn't sure that I wanted to know what it was.

'I guess I'd better press the alarm.'

I went to stand, but Neil grasped my arm and held me down. He had a firm grip. 'Leave it a minute yet, unless you really want to . . .'

I looked at him. He continued to hold my arm. His lips were slightly apart, red and smooth. His nose was sharp, tanned brown and the tip just reflected the light in the lift. His too-blue eyes looked at me, the whites clear, the brows curving over, enhancing the colour. His skin was smooth and clear, the delicate shadowing of his beard changing the tone around his chin. His light-brown hair was perfectly groomed as ever, swept to the right. I had never noticed before how sexy his ears were, lightly covered in a down of almost imperceptible hair. He swallowed and I watched his Adam's apple bounce beneath his skin. The cleft in his chin was marginally in shadow from the light above.

I was startled to realise that Neil was examining me too, his eyes flicking from side to side, taking in my face as I was adoring his.

And then he leaned forward and kissed me, lightly, on the lips. It seemed the most natural thing to do. He leaned back and continued to stare at me. There was no judgement in his face, no lust or consideration. It had seemed inevitable that it should happen. And without thinking I leaned over and kissed him back. This time for a little longer, savouring his sweet lips as they hung onto mine, his musk swirling around me like a rich fog that traps ships at sea. I was hooked in this moment, the mist of Neil enveloping me, the taste and sensation of his lips clouding my thoughts. I was lost. I could think only of Neil and this sense of coming home, of belonging. I put my hand up to his face to cradle his cheek. It was as smooth to touch as it was to look at, the down of his beard trickling beneath my fingers.

Neil gently held my head and kissed me deeper. His tongue entered my mouth roughly, the first signs of passion exploding within him. I held his head closer to mine, eager for the moment to continue. We kissed roughly, our lips fighting to maintain a hold on each other as our tongues fought for occupation of the other's mouth. I acquiesced as Neil forced his tongue into me, pushing me backwards on to the floor so the weight of him was on top of me. I could scarcely breath, astonished that this was happening and unwilling to lose one second of this passionate kiss.

I opened my legs and he lay between them, still kissing, forcing himself upon me. My clothes rucked up behind me and we fumbled to remove ties and jackets, to loosen buttons and belts. I kicked off my shoes. Neil tugged at his laces and threw his shoes from his feet, sending them clattering against the walls of the lift. Still our lips and faces were meshed together. Roughly Neil pulled my shirt up. A button popped off. He fought to lift the cotton shirt above my chest. He pulled without success and then yanked each side in different directions. Buttons scattered like a Chinese fire cracker. He pushed me back to the floor with his kiss. He wrestled my shirt from me. I began to fumble with my belt. I felt the buttons from his shirt pebble-dash me with plastic confetti as he ripped his shirt off. Underneath I could see the glorious firm pecs, the chest hair that I at last sank my fingers into. I wriggled from side to side, pulling my trousers down. Underneath my briefs were already alive with pumping man-meat, the blood-engorged head silky with pre-come. I grabbed Neil's head. I wanted more of the kiss, more of him inside me. Neil reciprocated. I could feel him tug his trousers down and kick them behind him. I held his face and pulled him to me, my cheeks wet with his saliva.

He pulled away. We were both panting, hard. Nothing was said. I glanced down. He was wearing light denim boxer shorts, the same clean fresh blue as his eyes that now burned into me like ice. I could see a faint outline of the shaft of his cock in his shorts, but the head was clear to see, transparent beneath a large wet patch, the purple throbbing end waiting for my attention.

We began to fight and kiss again, this time pulling off our underwear. My meat slapped free against my stomach, my balls held tightly upwards as the erection surged through me. I had never believed I could be so hard as I was now. I wrestled my head free and looked down at Neil's cock, now suspended over mine. It dwarfed me, the head the size of a tennis ball, round hard and angry, the shaft long and thick, a rigid vein running the length of it into his balls. It was calling to me, over twelve inches of man-rammer that was pulsating with Neil's ever-increasing heart rate. A drip of his pre-come dropped onto my stomach.

We both paused, breathing deeply, looking at each other, the animal passions that had brewed between us finally free. Neil grabbed my tool and milked it slowly up and down. He stuck two sticky fingers in his mouth, savouring my juice. I groaned. I felt my mind wind down as my passions and instinct came to the fore. I hooked my legs around his tight waist. The muscle rippled beneath his taut brown skin. He rested on top of me to kiss again and for the first time I had the electric shock of feeling his sticky love rod slap against mine. His pre-come was cool as it ran into my pubes. I felt the hair of his stomach and chest rough against mine, his muscles dancing beneath his skin as he rubbed himself against me. I bit his arm. I wanted to eat him, for him to eat me, for us to become one living organism. I traced my tongue along the curve of his biceps, following a thick vein that pulsated with passion just beneath his skin. He tugged my head into his downy armpit, now moist with sweat and rich with his scent. I licked away furiously while his strong tongue probed my ear and his teeth bit at my lobe. I hooked my legs up higher, instinct taking control, eager for his strong cock to tear at my man-cunt. My arse cheeks parted and my sphincter puckered, desperate to have this man inside me. Nothing mattered any more, other than this man and this moment.

I wrapped my arms around him and held him tightly to me. Neil responded, lifting me effortlessly from the floor and pulling me to him. I clenched his strong back between my fingers, pulling at the skin, trying to tear the muscles from his back. Our lips found each other again and my hands grasped the back of his head, his hair in locks between my fingers, pulling his face into mine. Neil shifted upwards, his chest now bearing down on mine, his hips in the air, held up by his powerful, thick legs. I caught a glimpse of his broad feet, the toes spread on the carpet, drained of blood as they strained to push his body higher. Still my legs held onto his waist as I was lifted with him.

Then Neil jerked his torso up and I felt that stiff, come-loaded tool slip between my crack, oiled by the jizz that was already melting out of the piss-slit. I gasped. It was enormous. But I wanted it inside me. I wanted it to be thrust home, to hurt, to sear within me, to bond with my soul. Neil was grunting now like a wild animal, a giant bear with nothing on his mind except a hard fuck and the thrill shooting through the tip of his cock. I rolled my hips back, bringing that great throbbing tool to nestle by my damp cunt.

'Yes, yes, yes,' I moaned and I felt Neil lift himself higher. I closed my eyes, the neon light of the lift disappeared and all I could see was black, the universe before the beginning, nothing in existence, just waiting for the moment when life, matter and the world would begin.

And then he thrust his power tool home. My arse split in two as his great sticky head punched through my sphincter and deep within me. The shaft of his tool continued up inside me, forcing my arse cheeks apart, splitting me like the trail of a rocket scarring the sky. All I could see were stars. The pain at first was shocking and debilitating. My arms dropped from his head and I gasped for breath. It was like a heart attack, my chest pressed beneath Neil's as the full weight of his body followed through to fuck the living daylights out of me. My eyes sprang open, but all I could see were stars. The shaft slid further into me. My legs flailed outwards, fighting to create the space for this intrusion. Still that dick was pushed into me, going deeper and harder than I could have imagined.

And then ecstasy. I felt the fist-like head of his cock slam into my colon and at the same tine felt his stupendous balls slap against my arse. He was in me. Completely. Filling me. I caught my breath and my eyes slowly focused on Neil's head which hung above me. I held it and lifted his face to mine.

Neil's face was red with animal passion, his eyes now a brittle and sparkling blue. He held his cock in me for a moment. It was glorious. For that instant we were as one and the rest of the world would wait while we were suspended, here in time and motion, held in a moment that was the reason for living.

And then I felt him begin to withdraw. I let go of his head and grabbed my ankles, pulling my legs apart to give this monster room to wrestle and fight with my cunt. I felt the tip of his dick pulling my sphincter apart, before he plunged his tool back into me. This time there was no pain, only pure, unbridled ecstasy. I pulled my legs further apart, wanting more of him in me as Neil settled into a hard, regular thrust.

My dick was like a rock, slapping against my stomach while his great tool ploughed at my arse. With each thrust I saw Neil's firm butt reflected in the mirror at the back, the cheeks clenching to push into me. I shoved my arse up, eager for more. Harder Neil pumped, beating my arse cheeks with his bollocks which jangled beneath his man-meat. His rhythm increased, harder and faster he pushed himself. I wanted this moment to last for ever, but this was too glorious a time to be anything other than a moment. He shoved more and more into me, inch upon inch of cock meat filling my hole. I looked at his face, so beautiful, so strong. His eyes were closed in a delirium of frenetic energy.

And then I felt him shoot his load. I saw the look of freedom and relief on his face and felt the warm jism begin to fill me. He pumped his love juice into me and I grabbed at my straining man-meat. One touch was enough and I shot my load too. The come flew from my dick in an arc that flashed across his chest and dropped onto my shoulder and face. Another arc flew free. Neil wiped his fingers through the juice on his chest and sucked on them wildly. Still he pumped, and I could feel his come in my arse, spilling from my sphincter, that valuable pure seed running down my crack and onto the carpet. I ejaculated again. Yet more come cemented our union.

After an age of ecstasy, I felt Neil slowly pull his cock from within me. My sphincter reluctantly let it go while gurgling on the glorious juice it had fed on. His dick was wide, puce and still pumping out come. Grabbing my chance I pushed Neil backwards. He tumbled against the side of the lift and I dived on his cock, eager to drain the last of his jism. It tasted salty and so sweet on my tongue.

Exhausted Neil lay there while I drained his heavy sac of all that love juice. I licked at his balls and at his hole, eager for more. My cock subsided slowly, the last of the monster lot of jism seeping from me.

I lay on top of him, both of us out of breath, our come sticky between us. I kissed him again and he cradled me in his arms.

'There's something I need to tell you,' he began, 'but I guess you already know.'

Chapter Five

We lay exhausted together in the lift for some minutes. It was hot and I was perspiring. I looked at Neil and he had a little row of perspiration on his forehead. I traced my index finger though it, leaving a damp line.

'We should get dressed. This lift may start again at any time and in this state it could be difficult to explain.'

Neil nodded. 'You're right.'

He kissed me and we both began to dress. We used graph paper from my briefcase to dry each other, standing naked together in the left delicately blotting each other's skin while pausing to kiss. Neil had a wonderful body; broad, strong and masculine, covered in a smooth, creaseless, sandalwood skin. The pile of screwed-up paper was then squeezed back into my briefcase and the lid snapped shut. The buttonless shirts were less easy to conceal, with shirt tails tucked beneath tight belts to hold them together. We stood side by side looking in the mirror, our ties tight at the neck holding the top of the shirts together, the bottoms tucked and re-tucked into our trousers. Our clothes were as crumpled as the paper in my briefcase. Our suits had been roughly kicked into the corner and my jacket had somehow found its way underneath us as we had fucked. Neil's hair was especially tousled, mine simply stood on end. We were both flushed.

I checked myself in the mirror. 'How do I look?'

'Frankly, as if you've just spent half an hour in a lift being fucked by a guy who's had a crush on you since he first saw you two years ago.'

I was stunned. 'Are you serious?'

'Yeah, your face is flushed, your hair's a mess . . .'

'No, about the two years of having a crush on me?'

'Yeah. It's been obvious.'

'I had no idea.'

'Oh come on. Those trips to the gym, me leaning over you while you bench-pressed, laying with you in the steam room. I was always having to rush out because I was getting a hard-on. Meanwhile, I seem to remember you were always dreaming of minge.'

'I was thinking about minge to stop me getting hard looking at you.'

'What about you and Janice, then?'

'What about it?'

'Everyone in the office knows you fancy her. You keep mooning at her over your desk. I've watched you. And then, last week at your flat, you looked very cosy together.'

'Me, cosy? What about you and Cheryl? You were just about eating her when I looked up. I never laid a hand on Janice.'

'Wasn't what I saw! I became so obsessed with it that I even moved my desk in the office so I would blot out your view of her.'

'You moved your desk?' I began to laugh.

'Yes. What's so funny about that? I shifted it a few inches every day until she was directly behind me and you wouldn't be able to see her. I know it sounds silly but I really fancied you and it made me jealous to see you eyeing her up.'

'I don't believe this! I was watching you!'

'Me?'

Yes you, you twat! I've played with hundreds of hard-ons while watching you. Anyway, I could still see Janice over your shoulder – it really put me off.'

'That's because the daft bitch kept moving her desk to the right as well so that she could still see you. At the rate we were going by Christmas the whole office would be squashed into the far corner, all so that we could see you play with your hair while you were thinking.'

'What do you mean play with my hair?'

'God, it's so sexy. When you're thinking you swirl your fingers through the crown of your head and your face gets this really concentrated look that's just so fucking erotic.'

I smirked. It was odd to think that while I had been shifting positions around my desk to see Neil, the other half of the office had been doing a gavotte with the desks to keep a clear view of me.

'"The thinker with the sexy arse," that's what they call you in this month's office sex survey. It's no wonder you won. I watched you work out your glutes at the gym and I have been obsessed with your butt ever since.' Neil grabbed my arse with both hands. He stood behind me looking at our reflection in the mirror.

'But I worked out my butt because yours is so great. You're always working it out in the gym.'

'Only because you are.' He held it tightly and I watched him close his eyes in ecstasy.

'Looks like neither of us has known what is going on.'

Neil put his arms around me. 'You are gorgeous, you know.'

'You too.' I turned and we kissed, Neil grinding his cock against mine.

'Not here, let's get this lift started and go home.'

'Sure.'

Neil pressed the buttons again and still nothing happened. He pulled a small silver key from his pocket and unlocked the control panel. Inside he pressed another button and the lift sprang into life.

'How did you do that?'

'Just reset it. Simple.'

I was suspicious. The lift continued downwards. Seven, six, five. 'Did you set this up?'

'Sort of.'

'What do you mean sort of?' Four, three, two.

'Well, I couldn't switch the lift off. I had to get a fairy godmother to do that.'

'What do you mean? If you didn't switch the lift off, then who did and how?'

'Easy, just unlock the panel upstairs and turn the lift to stand-by at a pre-arranged level, say between floors seven and eight.'

'And then jump on me! And who the fuck is this fairy godmother?' Mezzanine, Lobby. The lift doors glided open.

'Marilyn.'

There was a queue of people to get in. There were audible mumbles about the lifts being out of order.

'Marilyn!' I hissed. Neil strode out. I was suddenly aware that we did look as if we'd just had the most terrific shag imaginable. Further, the lift we were leaving was hot and reeked of passionate, animal sex. I stepped out to keep up with Neil as we crossed the sparkling chrome lobby to the exit. Neil's heels tapped against the white marble floor. He brushed his hair back with his hand and swung through a revolving door. I jumped in behind, the speed of the turn spewing me out onto the pavement the other side.

'Taxi!' Neil called.

The wind blew my jacket open and my shirt flapped in the breeze. I fought to hold the layers together while gripping my briefcase with the other hand. I resembled a tatty kite fluttering in the wind.

A taxi pulled up and we jumped in, pulling the rags around me into some semblance of order. Neil gave the address and leant back into the seat next to me. For a moment there was calm.

'What do you mean, "Marilyn"?'

'Marilyn switched the lift off when we were leaving. I arranged it with her.'

'When?'

'Well, she first thought of the idea about six months ago, but it was only today that I thought, "Fuck it, let's go for it".'

'Six months ago?' My mind was racing. I was slowly unearthing a plot that had me entwined for most of my time with Allsop and Gee and of which I had no idea.

'Yes. I had been going on at Marilyn about what a mess my life was and she helped me sort out what it was that I wanted.'

'Which was,' I pressed, eager for more plot and for more flattery.

'You, I suppose. Things with Karen have never been that great, but I didn't realise until I met you just what passion was. I got married thinking, "This is it, this is what people feel, this is normal, I'm doing the right thing", but then on the first day I saw you at Allsop and Gee my world fell apart.'

Neil held my hand. Outside the smoky traffic trundled by.

'By the time you had got out of the lift and walked into Gee's office I was nursing the biggest erection I had ever had. That's when I knew I'd made a mistake in getting married.'

I smiled at him. 'And you know what? I spotted you on my way to Gee's office and made myself look away as I didn't want to be introduced to my new boss sporting a boner the size of a baseball bat.'

The taxi lurched to a halt. 'Watch out, you stupid woman!' The driver yelled through his open window. A prim middle-aged lady in a smart new convertible gave him a filthy look. She adjusted the tight blonde bun in her hair and screeched away as the lights changed. 'Bloody women drivers. Sorry about that chaps.'

'OK,' I called back. Neil gave me a peck on the cheek. I knew that the driver had seen this in his rear-view mirror. I shifted in my seat. Neil snuggled up to me and lay his head on my shoulder. I pressed my head next to his. For the first time in my life everything was still and I was able to catch my breath.

'You two been shagging then?' It was the driver. He asked the question in the same way as if he was asking if we'd just had our hair cut.

'No,' I replied.

'Yes,' said Neil simultaneously.

We looked at each other. The driver let out a roar of laughter and flung his head back. He scratched his messy grey hair and shook his head.

'Well, make your minds up. One has, one hasn't.'

'Yes, we have,' I confirmed. 'Is it that obvious?'

'I should bloody well say so. You two burst into my cab like ferrets on heat and collapse there with your clothes in shreds, holding hands, what do you think?'

I giggled nervously. Neil laughed out loud.

'We shagged in the lift. First time. It's sort of been building up to it.' I was in awe of Neil's composure and his exuberance at telling this complete stranger what we'd been up to.

'Thought so,' the driver replied, steering the taxi at some speed round a roundabout. 'When you've been driving as long as I have you've seen most things. Make the most of it, that's what I say. I remember the wife and me, Southend 1956. Got a bit carried away in a bus shelter during a storm. Thunder clapping all around, lightning flashing and the rain coming down in sheets. Bloody cold too. Still there we was, first time away from the clutches of her mother, and I couldn't restrain meself. Mind you, didn't see her objecting. You want to think yourself bloody lucky your lot don't have to deal with bras. Gawd! It took me ten minutes to undo the contraption she was wearing. We was at it hammer and tongs. Marvellous, all that pent-up passion breaking free. Bloody marvellous. Kept at it even when the bus came. Driver took one look at us and got on his way. Gawd, it was wonderful! Happy days. Missus told me she didn't mind waiting for the next bus; "I know where I'd rather be," she said, "bus comes once an hour but you've come twice already. I'll stick with you!"'

I smiled at the thought of their windswept lovemaking.

'Course, ended up with a nipper on the way and her mother weren't pleased, but I can't complain. At least you ain't going to have to worry about kids after a quick fumble. Lot to be said for being a poof in my opinion.'

Neil snuggled up to me and I put my arm around him. Outside the traffic was roaring, tempers were flaring and jaws were held tightly. Inside the cab, with Neil, it was an oasis of calm.

'You two mind how you go now,' the driver said as Neil paid while I opened the door. 'And thank you very much, sir,' he added when Neil gave him a sizeable tip.

I stood in the living room as Neil closed the door behind

him. It was the same room as I had been in before and yet this time it was different. The furniture was in the same place I had left it. The duvet Neil had been using was still screwed up in the corner where he had left it that morning; and yet it had all changed. From being an ordinary room in which I had sat many times, it now seemed to be full of possibilities. I wanted to decorate, to change it, to move things around, to have some reflection of the almighty changes that were happening in my life. All of a sudden my future was full of possibilities. Gee's moaning and Karl's deception were nothing. This flat, this space was suddenly not just mine but 'ours'; it was shared. There was energy and passion present; there was the chance of something wonderful happening, something fulfilling, something which I had always dreamed of, but never thought would ever happen. I stood in a daze.

I was snapped out of my revelry at hearing the door click shut behind me. Before I had a chance to turn around, Neil had rugby tackled me to the floor. My briefcase clattered to the floor, springing open, sending screwed-up graph paper everywhere and plans sliding over the carpet. Neil grabbed the duvet out of the corner and pulled it under my head. He pressed his lips to mine and we began to kiss. It was easy to pull open our shirts, take off ties and jackets. I sat up and sucked on Neil's nipples. They were hard with lust. I bit them and he groaned in pleasure, the hair on his chest tickling my face. He pushed me roughly back onto the duvet, yanking my trousers down which tore in the process. He threw them behind him and they ended up draped across a corner lamp, hanging like a tattered windsock. My underwear was removed with equal force, my cock already hard and willing for some action. I tried to sit up, to remove Neil's stained boxer shorts, but he held back. I could see his dick was already pumping out more pre-come.

'No,' he instructed, 'let me.'

I leaned back. He gripped each of my arse cheeks in his hands and bent down to my throbbing dick. First he kissed the swollen head, savouring the pecker juice. As he leaned back a string of pre-come stretched out from his lips to my piss-slit. I groaned in pleasure. He ran his tongue roughly down the shaft, tracing the vein that was even now pumping more blood into my already engorged shaft. He took each of my balls into his mouth in turn, pulling on them with his lips, licking the sac that contained them. He tugged at my scrotum with his teeth and it stung with ecstasy. His broad hands gripped my hamstrings and he tilted my legs upwards. At first he only licked and chewed at the skin between my legs, but slowly, gingerly, he edged backwards towards my hole. I could feel my sphincter puckering and opening, waiting for this hot tongue. Then he licked right down my crack, giving a rough brush over my opening. I groaned again, pushing my hips forward to get my arse closer to his face. But Neil was in charge. He held my legs firmly, opening them further, stretching the muscles as the tip of his lips kissed my cunt. I groaned some more. The ecstasy of expectation, sensing him begin to feel his way into me, dreaming of the lust that would follow.

Neil kissed my hole and sucked on it gently. I gave myself over to him. His tongue gently prised my hole open. My nerves rattled with the sensation of his hot moist tongue probing me. He pushed his tongue in further while pulling my arse cheeks further apart with his strong hands. Slowly he lost his initial calm and began slurping and eating me, his tongue darting in and out of my hole, chewing on my man-cunt.

I dropped my legs over his shoulders so that he would be encased in my arse, my heels rubbing over his back and shoulders. I heard him moan in delight and it turned me on even more. I grabbed my aching tool and began to pump, the pleasure too much to bear. But Neil's hand shot up to stop me. More and more he ate me, tongue-fucking my arse. Shivers of delight shot through me every time his tongue plunged into my hole.

And then he was working on my balls, nuzzling them around with his nose, the light afternoon bristles of his beard scratching my inner thigh. I gripped his head, held his hair and pulled his head upwards, frantic that he should taste my cock which twitched and strutted for him above. He pushed my legs apart and took the tip of my dick in his lips, sucking on the ample juice that smeared the tip. Slowly he took my dick into his mouth. As he did he fought with a free hand to remove his damp boxers and that monster cock sprang free. I looked down and saw it pointing straight at me, running upwards along his taut abs, his two goose-egg balls hanging delectably below. They swung as he rocked back and forth on my dick. I dropped my head back onto the duvet and revelled in the sensations his mouth was giving me. Gradually he worked his was down my member, inch by inch taking all nine inches down the back of his throat until my bush was pressed up against his face. Fuck! Neil was one hell of a cock-sucker! He began to work on my tool, his head bobbing up and down, his lips nibbling and chewing on my knob end.

He slipped a finger into my arse and then two. The thrill was too much to bear. I began to wail as the orgasm exploded in my balls. Sensing that this was the time, he dived on my cock and worked the shaft and tip even harder. I could contain myself no longer as my come shot through my shaft and into Neil's adoring mouth. For a moment he gagged at the amount of jizz pouring forth, but he quickly realised that, even after the sex in the lift, I was full of man-juice once again. He slurped and worked the come out of me, as his hand reached down to his own twelve inches of fat, purple meat.

Suddenly, he rocked back on his haunches, my juice dripping from his chin, his fat pecker in his hand, pumping it with all his might. Seeing the orgasm uncoil in his face I leapt forward to receive his jizz. He shot his first load into my face. I felt it fly onto my forehead and closed eyes, run down my nose and drip from my chin. But this was too valuable to waste. I sucked on his bulbous mushroom head while he pumped at his shaft, his love-juice squirting into my mouth like the sweetest milkshake. As his pumping slowed, I rested my hands on each of his quads and went down on his fat, subsiding dick. I took as much into my mouth as I could, which was only about half, and drooled over his tool. His was a dick to worship.

We lay there, spent, me feeling his juice melt on my face.

Neil gripped my hand. 'Come to bed.'

I stood, silently and was led to my bedroom. Neil pulled back the duvet and I climbed in. He got in next to me and pulled the duvet over us. He pulled me to him, hooking his leg over me to hold me tightly. I could feel his fat, hot cock, wet from come and sex, pushing into my stomach. Under the duvet I traced my finger up from his pubes, along the thick creases of his abs and onto his solid pecs, his chest hair soft beneath my palm. I kissed his neck. He groaned and held me closer. His eyes were closed and I shut mine too. All I could feel was the warmth and strength of his body. All I could smell was Neil, that luscious musky smell that I had inhaled so often before, but which was now coiled around me, holding me safe.

'You look like the cat that got the cream!' It was Marilyn. She sat behind her desk, her plump face crinkled into a smile. 'I hear that lift number two got stuck for almost forty-five minutes yesterday, before it miraculously restarted.' Her eyes glinted at me. I was profoundly embarrassed. I stood, mute. 'Morning, Janice. Morning, Cheryl.' A duet of high-pitched 'mornings' echoed back.

''Ere, was you stuck in that lift last night, Wade?' It was Cheryl. She was removing a lime-green overcoat to reveal a shocking-pink lycra miniskirt that was barely wider than a belt.

'Er, no, I don't think so,' stumbled my reply.

'You don't sound very sure,' Marilyn goaded. 'Either you were stuck in that lift or you weren't. I wouldn't think there could be any confusion over it.'

'Er, no. I wasn't. I didn't know it had got stuck. Marilyn was just telling me all about it, weren't you, Marilyn?'

'I had rather hoped you were going to tell me all about it, Mr Armstrong.' She sat upright, her lips pursed into a smirk.

'You leave him alone Mrs Allbright,' Cheryl said, coming to my defence. 'Poor lamb, he's shy, aren't you, Wade?'

'A little.' I could see Marilyn enjoying my discomfort.

'See, he's going red. Look, he's blushing, Mrs Allbright, 'cause of you.'

'Nice when a man goes red,' Cheryl continued, 'shows he's sensitive and shy. You're sensitive and shy aren't you, Wade?'

'Sometimes, yes.'

'Now don't you be so sensitive not to talk to Janice sometime. It's no good you just mooning over her across the office, you want to do something about it.'

'I'm not sure,' I sputtered.

'No you're not, but I am and you'll make a lovely couple.'

'A darling couple,' Marilyn chimed in, thoroughly enjoying every moment. 'You make your move, Wade Armstrong. Don't let it hang around for six months, you get on in there.'

'That's right, you listen to Mrs Allbright, Wade, get on in there.' Cheryl was excited by Marilyn's enthusiasm.

'I've known people dither for up to two years before finally making the move, even though I've told them all along that they were barking up the right tree and should make a move before someone else came along.' Marilyn tapped a pen on her desk.

'But it's not as easy as that, Marilyn,' I urged, wishing she would keep quiet and unburden me of Cheryl's matchmaking.

'But you're wrong, Wade, it's very easy. All it takes is an opportunity to be alone, for say, about forty-five minutes, in a small confined space? Add a bit of gumption to ignite the flames of passion and hey presto!'

'Exactly!' Cheryl chorused, 'Some gumption or paraffin to get the flames of passion burning!'

'Well I don't know.'

'Look, I'll ask Janice to come out with me and Neil and you can tag along. That way you won't be under amy pressure.'

'I'm not sure . . .'

'Oh go on, Wade,' Marilyn interjected. 'If Neil's there he can give you a few tips. I hear he's an absolute animal when he gets going.'

'Really?' This time it was Cheryl's turn to be wound up. 'Where d'you hear that then?'

'Oh, on the grapevine, you know.'

'Oh yes,' Cheryl mused before her face fell in confusion. 'No I don't know, what do you mean?'

'Yes do tell us, Marilyn,' I joined in keen for revenge.

'Well, apparently, and as I say I have no definite proof of this, our Mr Rogers has had his eye on someone in this office for sometime.'

'No!' Cheryl gasped.

'Yes,' Marilyn corrected, 'someone in this office has been the focus of his attention for quite some time now and I'm not so sure he can keep himself under control!'

'Ohmygod!' Cheryl squealed. 'It must be me, it must be me. I knew it, I knew it! I could tell.'

'There's more,' Marilyn said, fishing an envelope out of her top desk drawer. 'I found these.'

Marilyn opened the envelope and several small white buttons dropped onto her desk. They skipped and danced on her blotting pad for a few seconds before coming to rest. I recognised them instantly as mine and Neil's shirt buttons from the lift.

'Buttons!' Cheryl exclaimed and then looked puzzled. 'What about them?'

'I have it on good authority that these are Mr Rogers' shirt buttons, torn from him in a moment of frenzied excitement!'

'I ain't popped no buttons,' Cheryl said picking one up.

'Maybe there not his buttons,' I suggested.

'Oh they're Mr Rogers' buttons, believe me,' Marilyn stressed in hushed tones.

'Ohmygod!' Cheryl squeaked again. 'They must have just popped off him while he was looking at me!'

Marilyn looked incredulously at Cheryl. 'As far as I know, and do correct me if I'm wrong, but Mr Rogers is an architect, not a poltergeist. Nor, as far as I know, is he a victim of "the haunted buttons of Canary Wharf."'

'No, silly,' Cheryl corrected, 'he does all those weights and he must've been looking at me and breathed in one of those really deep passionate breaths, about to sigh sort of thing, and he was just too big for his buttons, so they popped off.'

I gawped at Cheryl. She was serious.

'You're a marvel, Cheryl. Not in a million years would I have thought of that,' Marilyn announced, her eyes wide at me.

'I've got to tell Janice!' Cheryl threw herself away from Marilyn's desk. I looked at Marilyn. Cheryl reappeared.

'You've got to go out with us again, Wade. Say you will.'

I didn't know what to say. I felt insecurity flood into me. What if Neil really did fancy Cheryl? He had been married for three years and I assumed had a good sex life with his wife. Maybe I wouldn't be enough for him? He had been very loving that morning. We had showered together and kissed and made the most passionate love under the steaming water. I pictured the water cascading down his chest, the hairs now thick with water against his skin, those sensual nipples standing out at the bottom of hard pecs. Soaping his back, running my hand down the little bumps on his spine to his coccyx; and then the vision of his butt, those hard glutes standing out like two ripe melons. The water fanning out over his cheeks, the tiny torrent that ran down that dark, hair-lined crack. Slipping my hand between those cheeks, opening them up, seeing his pink puckered hole and the weighty balls hanging between his legs. The water had dragged his pubes into thin ponytails of hair that hung from his scrotum. And the licking and sucking and chewing, the warm water diluting but not removing the taste of him, that spicy hole, that sweet sticky tip of his pulsating dick. Hugging his legs, gripping his hard calves, sucking on his glorious toes that each had a tuft of auburn hair adorning them, while his broad strong feet splashed about my face. And Neil had worshipped my body too; licking my abs, chewing my taut nipples, grasping my biceps and pulling me to him and holding me as if he never wanted to let go.

And those words I had heard him whisper to me through the hiss and splash of water; 'Never leave me, Wade, never leave me.'

But what if he left me?

'Of course Wade will go, won't you, Wade?'

'What?'

'You'll go out with Janice and Cheryl.'

'Er . . .'

'Then it's settled. I'll arrange it with Janice and let you know.' Cheryl slipped off.

'Thanks,' I said when Cheryl had gone.

'Oh you'll be alright,' Marilyn said, picking up the buttons. 'Believe me, I'm a girl who knows about these things and you'll all have a good evening and they'll get the message that it's not going to work out. Then they'll move on to someone else in this office. Although I have to say, from a girl's point of view, you two really are the hottest studs here and the rest do look poor seconds in comparison.'

'Yeah, but you know what it's like . . .'

'Don't you go all soft on me, Wade Armstrong. I've had to listen to Neil Rogers gush about you for almost two years and for the last six months we've both been walking about clutching spare keys to the lift so that he could get you alone. You've stubbornly refused to listen to my hints, so now its time for me to have a little fun. By the state of the lift last night, you've had a considerable amount of fun thanks to my organisation already!'

'Yeah, thanks.' I blushed again.

'And think how much fun it'll be when Neil finds out you've turned the tables on him for a while. I don't know why he strings that Cheryl along. But now you can put an end to it.'

Neil had gone straight to a site survey that morning and I didn't notice him when he arrived. However, I glanced up just after eleven and my heart skipped a beat when I saw him sitting at his desk and grinning at me. I grinned back and gave a little wave. Neil lifted his hand in response. Behind him, Janice waved back too. I nodded and dropped back to my work. Far from being behind Neil, Janice was now clear to his right, her desk having leapt about a foot that morning. I peeked a few seconds later and Cheryl was in attendance. She whispered something to Janice, threw a look at me and then rolled her hips towards Neil. Neil was still grinning at me. Cheryl perched on his desk and petted his hair. He flicked his head away and I heard Cheryl laugh. Marilyn was right, this was going to be something to enjoy. They conversed for a few moments and then Neil looked confused. He turned his head to me, confusion and amazement on his face. I smiled nonchalantly in return and got on with my work. I began to count. By the time I had reached thirty-three, Neil was sitting on my desk.

'Something you want to tell me?'

'Er, no.'

'About tonight?'

'No. Why, are you doing anything?'

'Well, I had planned to spend and hour or two sucking the world's most beautiful cock and kissing this incredible man I've just met.'

'Just met?'

'Well, that I've known for a while . . .'

'The one you planned on giving the most earth-shattering shafting to, but made wait six months while the poor guy dreamed, fantasised and wanked about you?'

'Well I didn't know you were interested, did I?'

'Suppose not. Marilyn seems to be the only one who could see what was going on.'

'So what is it with tonight and Cheryl? You want to palm me off onto her?'

'No! She was desperate and it was Marilyn who set the whole thing up. I think that after six months of dealing with us two she's having the last laugh.'

'I might have guessed. I saw her briefly this morning when I went in to report to Gee and she gave me a big grin, a handful of shirt buttons and called out, "Boys will be boys and girls will be bored!"'

'Watch out,' I hissed. Karl was approaching. He had a sneer smeared across his podgy face.

'Off out again tonight, lads.'

'Yes,' said Neil matter of factly.

'By the way how is Karen these days?' Karl added.

Neil shrank back. 'Is that any of your business?'

'As long as it doesn't affect our business then, no. But if it does, then, quite probably, yes.'

He continued walking. We watched him go, his tread burning into the turquoise carpet tiles on his pilgrimage to the office and temple of Baldie Gee.

I rubbed Neil's forearm. 'Don't let him bother you.'

Neil flopped his hand on top of mine. I glowed with reassurance. 'I'm not bothered about him or this place, but he's right; I do have one or two major aspects of my personal life to sort out.'

I didn't know what to say. I wanted to spend the rest of my life with Neil and I knew that Neil had to make his own decisions about where I would fit in. In the meantime I would have to wait for him to make those decisions.

'I can't tell Karen, not yet,' he whispered.

'I know.'

Marilyn dropped a memo on my desk.

'What's this?' It was nearly five in the afternoon, the light was fading outside and after a good afternoon discussing plans for Hammersmith with Neil I was sketching out some preliminary ideas.

'It's a memo,' Marilyn said curtly.

'I can see that. You don't send me memos.' I was confused.

'Well, I do now.' She stood next to the desk while I read it. It was from Cheryl giving Neil and I instructions for that evening.

'She doesn't waste time does she,' I remarked.

'No. And she was quite insistent that I put it in writing and give it to you personally, so there could be no mistake.' She emphasised the last point.

'So we couldn't get out of it, you mean.'

'Correct. So seven pm sharp next door at the Cork and Casket, or else both you, Neil and I will get it in the neck tomorrow.'

'It was your idea,' I pointed out, 'so don't go all tight-lipped on me.'

'I know it was my idea. I've had Cheryl skipping like Bo Peep over to me every five minutes this afternoon discussing plans. "They're so gorgeous and talented and funny. I can't believe it!" I nearly told her not to believe it. "Gorgeous" "talented" and "funny" just scream out "gay" to me, but she'll learn.'

I shrugged.

'She told me I was her fairy godmother. Can you imagine?'

'Yes, I can. Thanks, Marilyn, for everything.' I wanted her to know that I was truly grateful.

'Oh, don't thank me,' she quipped. 'For you I'm a fairy godmother. For Cheryl and Janice, I'm a godmother who's found them a fairy.'

She dropped a silver key onto my desk.

'What's this?'

'It's the key to Mr Gee's executive washroom I've just mislaid it here so that you and Neil can have a good wash and brush up before seeing the ladies tonight. I thought you would appreciate spending a minute or two alone before the ordeal begins.'

I slid my hand over it and mouthed a 'thank you'. Marilyn strode off back to her desk. I looked up but Neil wasn't at his desk. I pondered for a moment before curiosity got the better of me and I set off for the washroom.

The office was closing down for the evening. Desks were abandoned, bins filled with newly scrunched paper, biros stacked in sharp silver desk tidies. I nodded to a couple of colleagues as I crossed the office. The washroom was in the far corner, perpendicularly opposite Gee's office. Only four staff members on our floor had access to it. To Gee, it was the holy of holies, the corporate temple that acknowledged that he had 'arrived'. That there were similar washrooms on every floor and that the one in the basement was the sole preserve of the building's janitors didn't seem to bother him. And for some strange reason, I had always been curious as to what was in this closely guarded tomb.

I glanced behind me before clicking the small silver key into the lock and twisting it. The door swung soundlessly open. I checked again and slipped inside. Once in, I could hear the lift doors ping outside as more workers were absorbed into the building's gullet to be discharged at the bottom a few minutes later.

The washroom was surprisingly spartan. Three porcelain floor-length urinals were built into the opposite wall. At the far end was a frosted window, the evening shadows cast through it along the grey marble floor. There were two lavatory cubicles, with cheap Formica partitions that didn't reach the ceiling or the floor. Next to this was a wide double sink unit with polished silver mixer taps and a clean mirror reflecting the urinals opposite. In the middle of this scene was a yellow plastic cone with the inscription 'Danger Wet Floor'. It was a huge disappointment. The lavatories in any West End hotel were far more luxurious and if this was corporate reward, I didn't want it.

A lavatory flushed. I stood rooted to the spot. Had I made any noise? Did they know I was here? How long had I been here? Second-rate bog or no, the charges for being caught would be severe. I turned to tiptoe out, when the lavatory door swung open and a great looking arse, clad in dark blue overalls backed out. The figure was hunched over as if he was checking something. The body was good. I paused for a moment. Thick black boots, dark blue overalls which gathered at the waist with elastic and then some broad shoulders. The overalls were open at the neck. The figure turned his back to me, still unaware of my attention. I studied his arse, tight and fleshy in the overalls. I was about to leave when the figure turned.

'Oh, sorry, sir. I didn't realise you were here.'

The voice was gruff, dominant, apologetic, but not forgiving. I looked into his ocean blue eyes and recognised him. It was Neil. I was about to blurt out that he'd scared me shitless when he continued.

'If you want to use the facilities, then please do, sir. Would you like me to leave?'

He picked a wrench up from the window sill. It had been hidden in shadow before.

'Er, no, thank you. Carry on.' I was confused, but thrilled. Neil continued to look at me while he held the wrench. Self-consciously I went and stood by one of the urinals, unzipped and pulled out my already growing cock. It flopped into the urinal and I half looked over my shoulder at Neil. He was motionless, staring at me. I turned back to the urinal. My cock was growing rapidly, the blood pumping in with each beat of my racing heart.

Neil coughed. I turned and looked again. He was gone. I strained behind me to see him standing over the basins, washing his hands. His reflection returned my gaze. I held his eyes for a moment and then looked back. What was going on here? I looked at the white tiled wall in front of me. Maybe I should just speak to Neil, it was him after all, but there was an aroma of sex in the room; of danger; of passion.

I jumped. Neil stood by the next urinal. He slowly unzipped his overall. Underneath he wore a tight white T-shirt that stretched and hung loosely by his midriff. His pecs stood out, straining the fabric, his nipples hard.

My mouth went dry. My cock was now rigid. I tried to force it to point downwards. Horizontal was the best I could manage.

'That's the trouble with these overalls,' Neil grunted next to me, his voice soulless, 'gotta unzip the whole shitty thing to take a piss.'

He flopped his cock over the top of the now open overalls. It rested on the top of the zip and hung like a python towards the porcelain basin. He put both hands on his hips and let his dick hang there. I couldn't tear my eyes away from it. A small trickle of champagne coloured piss shone from the hole. I was paralysed with fear and excitement. I wanted to reach over and grasp his fat dick with both hands and then ram it down my throat. But I wasn't in charge. This wasn't my room and I wasn't in control.

'Taking a long time?' Although it was a question, it was accusatory.

'Yeah.' I couldn't think of an excuse.

'But that's a pretty big dick you got, so I suppose it takes a long time.'

'Yeah.'

What now?

'You've got a pretty big dick yourself.' What a fucking lame thing to say! I sounded like some second-rate actor in a Chi Chi La Rue porn film.

'Yeah? You wanna measure?'

'Yeah, OK.'

Neil slipped the overall off his shoulders and shrugged his arms free. He pulled it down to his waist. The T-shirt rippled over his stomach revealing rows of abs. He hooked his fingers under the waistband and inched the blue cloth over his waist. I gasped as I saw he was wearing nothing but a Wilson jockstrap underneath. The mesh pouch was straining to hold his bulging tackle while his butt stood out from the elastic supports at the back. The overall dropped to his ankles and sat on top of his work boots. He thrust his packet towards me.

'Take a look, pussy boy.'

I gingerly touched his balls. He slapped his big hand over mine.

'Either grip 'em or leave 'em for a man who wants them.'

'Yes, sir,' I replied, grasping the hot pouch. I slipped my hand over the waistband and lifted his cock free. It began to stir in my hand. My dick was still rigidly sticking out of my pants.

'Now measure, pussy boy.'

I lined my rock-hard cock up against Neil's semi-flaccid dick. Mine was longer by about two inches.

'Looks like you win.'

I sheepishly nodded.

'But hold on, I think mine's still got something left in it.'

I saw his buttocks clench, the blood flew into his dick and it leapt an inch in length. Then another and another. It stood out alone now, holding itself up.

'Maybe we're equal.'

'Yes, sir.'

'Hold on, what's this?' His buttocks clenched again. More blood flowed into it. It leapt forward again, now bigger than my nine inches by a good two inches.

'How long is it now, pussy boy?'

'Eleven inches?'

'Then there's still some life left in it yet.'

He grabbed my hand and licked the tips of my middle fingers. He stroked the end of his growing cock with them and let out a low groan. I saw his buttocks clench again. His dick rose into life, the final inch stretching out of him as his dick stood upright, fat, long and proud.

'Twelve inches.'

I nodded.

Neil stood with his eyes closed for some time, savouring his hardness, cupping his balls with his hands and playing with the tightness of the jockstrap around him. I began to undo my trousers. Neil snapped into life.

'Did I say you could do that?' His eyes flashed vengeance at me.

'What? Sorry, no.'

'No what?'

'No, sir.'

Neil grabbed my arms. He kicked off his overalls and stood in his white T-shirt, jockstrap and black work boots. He was tall, mean and fucking big. He frog-marched me over to the last cubicle partition, held my arms above my head and pushed me against the Formica wall. I gasped for air.

'Don't fucking play with yourself with me around, alright?'

'Yes.'

'Yes, what?'

'Yes, sir.'

'If you're going to play with anything, then you can play with this fucking man-meat. It's gagging for attention. Look at it.'

I glanced down. It was pulsating with hardness and staring me in the eyes.

'Now get this fucking poncey suit off and do some real work.'

'Yes, sir.'

I threw my clothes from me, kicking off my shoes and peeling away my socks. I was about to pull down my Calvins when Neil barked at me.

'Leave those, pussy boy. Don't want you playing with yourself without permission.'

'No, sir.'

'Now beg for my dick. '

'Please sir, let me service you. Let me service that monster of a dick you have.' I pleaded to be able to have his tool. All pride left me, all I wanted now was to taste that man-cock. My throat gagged to take it in.

Neil slipped his dick back into his jockstrap. It was an enormous sight.

'Suck it now. But don't touch.'

I clasped my arms behind my back and leaned forward. The pouch was rough, but it was already sweetened with his pre-come. I sucked and licked on his packet, eager for more. Neil stood over me, proud, thrusting his hips towards my hungry face. He leant forward, trapping my head between his cock and the cubicle partition. I writhed in ecstasy as he ground his sticky packet into my face.

As I lapped this up, he peeled his jock down and freed his tool and balls.

'Take it, fuck face.'

I dived on the end of his dick. The head was pounding with blood, hot and desperate, already damp with pre-come and my drool.

'Take it, I said!' He thrust his hips towards me.

I sucked on his dick, lubricating it as best I could, but still it was only half way in. I eased my throat open to slide more in. Another inch entered, the meat sparking my taste buds into life, saliva flooding my mouth. Gently he rocked back and forward, fucking my face. I tried to take it all in, but there was just too much. He eased his dick out of me.

'Call yourself a cock-sucker and you can only take eight inches?'

'Sorry, sir. It's too big, sir.'

'Bollocks! You're made to suck this dick and suck it you will.'

He thrust back into my mouth. My head banged against the partition. I gasped as his meat filled my mouth.

'Now suck that meat, pussy boy,' he ordered.

I gagged to take it in. More meat filled my mouth, saliva and pre-come drooling down my chin. I gripped the hairy globes of his arse and pulled him to me. My tongue worked the underside of his dick, darting around to oil this great piston.

'Come on, you fucker, swallow it!'

He eased forward again. I felt my throat open more, his mushroom head slipped down, filing my oesophagus. With the head through, the rest of his dick followed and within a second I felt his rough pubic bush slamming into my nose and eyes, while his bollocks slapped against my wet chin. My eyes sprang open with delight. He was fully in me. I looked up. Neil had a look of such sweet satisfaction on his face, both hands braced against the partition, his tool buried in my face. I held onto his arse and pulled his groin into me. His pubes were fabulous against my face. I loved the sensation of feeling his balls swing against my chin. I parted his cheeks and thrust a finger into his hole. He gasped and held his thrust for a second before continuing. I finger-fucked him while he fucked my face.

I was gasping for air, but the thrill was too much to relinquish. He thrust harder, two quick humps on my face and then I felt the jism shooting down my throat, it filled my mouth like ocean filling the last gasps of the Titanic. Come burst into my nose and through my cheeks to dribble down my chin in great gobs. Rivers flowed into my hungry stomach. I gasped in delight as I felt my own cock shoot its load into my damp Calvins. Untouched, the head of my dick had been chafing against my underwear as I had rocked to take in this man-meat. It was all that it took.

Neil slowly withdrew, panting. I gazed at him, full of his love.

'Jesus! I was right,' he gasped, 'you really are one hell of a cock-sucker!'

'Fuck!' was all I could gasp. 'I never thought I could take it, but shit, that was fucking glorious!'

He knelt next to me, took my face in his hands and kissed me. 'Twelve inches! Don't tell me you haven't done this before.'

'Once or twice.' I gazed at him. 'But never twelve inches! This was the best by far.'

'Still hungry now, pussy boy?' He kissed my nose provocatively.

'Starving . . .' I gripped his firm thighs, ready for another session, but Neil pulled away

'Good, 'cause we've got an appointment with Cheryl and Janice, remember?'

'But can't we again, just quickly?' I was desperate for more.

'No! We don't want to keep them waiting and, after all, you arranged the meal . . .'

'Oh, come on!'

'No.' Neil's eyes glinted at me and a wicked grin crossed his face. 'After all, remember what Marilyn says, "Don't get mad, get even!" So you'll have to wait!'

Chapter Six

It was seven fifteen by the time Neil and I had scrambled out of the office. Janice and Cheryl were standing outside the Cork and Casket. I flattened my hair and wiped my mouth as we approached; my lips were sore from the friction of Neil's cock.

''Bout time too!' Cheryl scolded. 'We've been out here for hours freezing, ain't we, Janice?'

Janice nodded.

'Just as well you two ain't brass monkeys otherwise we'd be in trouble, wouldn't we, Janice.'

Janice giggled and continued to look at her feet.

'Sorry we're late,' Neil began.

'Yeah, sorry,' I added.

'I've had my hands full,' Neil explained. 'Something came up and I had to deal with it.'

'Yeah, I've had a big project that I couldn't get my head round, but have now.'

'Hope you're not tired,' Cheryl warned.

'Not tired,' Neil calmed her, 'just drained.'

'Where we going then?' Cheryl asked, goose-pimples covering her arms.

'Fancy a drink first?' Neil suggested.

'Thought you'd never bloody ask. Come on, Jan.' Cheryl grabbed Janice's arm and led her into the pub. I stood for a moment with Neil outside. He grinned at me.

'Nice pair of birds,' he said with a cockney accent.

'Yeah. Don't fancy yours much,' I replied.

'What d'you mean? You're not a poof are you?' He grabbed my collar.

'Nar!' Come off it! You ain't no arse bandit are you?' I shoved him back.

'Fuck off!'

'Yes please!' I replied with my best nelly voice.

'Stop pissing about you two and buy us a drink!' Cheryl stood in the doorway, the overhead fan blowing her brunette ringlets over her face. 'Jesus!'

'Coming!' I replied, grabbing Neil and dragging him towards the door.

'I don't know about you two,' Cheryl muttered on her way back in.

We entered the pub still laughing. I spotted Janice perched on a stool by the bar. She had a silver compact in her hand and was prodding a contact lens around her right eye.

'What you want then, Jan?' Cheryl asked.

'Diamond White.'

'Me too. Thanks.'

I leaned on the bar and ordered the drinks. Neil stood behind me and started making small talk. The barman busied himself with bottles of beer. Above me lights shone down through faux-Tiffany shades. The pub was aiming for the panache and complexity of Renoir, but barely reached the level of a lop-sided alsatian painted for the local art club. I squeezed Neil's arse. It was hard. He flexed it in my hand and wriggled backwards so I could have a better feel. In front of him Cheryl continued to chatter about work. Janice blinked furiously, her right eye now bloodshot.

'I nearly told Baldie Gee, he could shove his bloody work where the sun don't shine, but then I remembered I'd seen a nice outfit I wanted and the overtime would be good.'

I leaned over and handed Janice and Cheryl their drinks. Neil grabbed his bottle. 'What are we talking about then?' I asked.

'Shoving things where the sun don't shine!' Neil answered provocatively, a discernible twinkle in his eye.

'What?'

'Don't be silly, Neil!' Cheryl said, draping herself over him.

I felt a pang of jealousy. 'We were talking about Baldie Gee giving us lots of work.'

'Tell me about it.'

'I've gotta go to the bog!' Janice jumped off her seat and beetled off.

'It's her eye,' Cheryl said by way of explanation and promptly rushed after her.

'What was all that about?'

'Don't ask me.' Neil replied, swigging on his beer. 'Let's get a better seat. There's a table over there.'

I followed Neil to an alcove, boxed in on three sides by reproduction wood panelling and overhung by yet another pseudo-Tiffany shade. Neil plopped into his seat and I shoved myself in next to him.

'How long do you think they'll be?'

Neil shrugged his shoulders. 'Who knows. It's one of life's great mysteries what women actually get up to in the loo. Karen would spend hours fiddling. I used to time her and keep a note of the minutes I'd spent waiting for her to come out. I gave up after three hours and something. It was too depressing to see my life trickling away in waiting.'

It was the first time since we had made love that Neil had mentioned his wife. 'Do you miss her?'

'Who, Karen?'

I nodded. Neil looked at his bottle.

'Yes and no. It's difficult. I thought I loved her. I do love her, but not in the way she wants me to love her. I love her company, she makes me laugh, we have a nice life together. But those are not reasons to stay with someone, are they?'

He looked at me. I couldn't return his gaze.

'I don't know. Sounds pretty good to me. Who wants a lover when they can have a best friend instead?'

'But I want both.' He slung his arm around me and gave me a matey sort of hug. 'Now don't go all silent on me!'

'I'm not.' I loved being with Neil, he was my best friend and now I was thrilled that he was my lover too – but was the risk of losing him too much to gamble? 'It's just that you never mention her . . .'

'Be bad taste to have my dick down your throat and say, "Wow, Sport! Karen can't suck cock like you can!" Don't you think?'

'You know what I mean.'

He took his arm off me. He was perturbed.

'Look, I don't know what the answers are. I saw you two years ago, and have dreamed of this moment ever since. I can't believe my luck that I have fallen in love with someone and they are loving me back.'

It was the first time he had mentioned love.

'It's great. I love it. But I also thought that with Karen and yet I now see, or at least I think I see, that that was wrong. That I was wrong. That I needed something more. I can't explain it.'

We sat in silence.

'I don't know what I'm going to do. Whether we'll work out, if we'll drift apart or if I'll end up back with Karen.'

This last comment stung me.

'She's alright.' It was Cheryl, arriving like a tornado opposite and hotching round the seating so she was next to Neil. Her ringlets spun round her head like Medusa's snakes. 'Got a gammy lens, that's all. I told her to take it out, but she's blind as a bat without them in. She'll be here in a minute. Which one's mine?' She held up the two bottles of Diamond White.

'That one.' Neil tapped a bottle. Cheryl held the two bottles up to the light.

'Nah, this one!' She picked the fullest. 'Now what's wrong with you two? It' s like a funeral in here. Who's dead?'

She let out a shriek of a laugh.

Neil perked up instantly and turned on the charm. For him it was the greatest insult to be considered anything but great fun. For to be anything else was not to be the centre of attention.

'Nothing's wrong! We were just talking about work and life, you know.

'Life eh!' Cheryl took a long swig. 'What are you going to

do with your life. Get a divorce?'

Out of the frying pan and into the fire.

'Why is everybody so obsessed about my private life?' Neil said it as a joke, but the underlying tension was obvious.

'Ooh! You're Mr Touchy tonight, aren't you!' Cheryl threw me a look and an exaggerated wink.

'Oh ignore him, Cheryl. He's like a cat on a hot tin roof!' The analogy was lost on both of them.

'I like cats.' Cheryl flirted to get herself out of danger. 'Ain't got one though. Me mom had one and it tore the curtains to bits and poohed on the carpet.'

'Nice. What sort was it?' I kept the conversation going.

'A cat.'

'But what sort of cat. Persian?'

'No, just a cat. Black. We called it Blackie.'

'Original,' Neil piped up.

Before Cheryl could reply Janice jumped in next to me. She was full of enthusiasm and energy. It was an attempt to overcome the fact that her right eye now looked like it had been recently hit by a baseball travelling at a hundred miles and hour.

'OK?' I asked

'Fine. Took me lens out. Bit sore. Can't see a thing now!'

She blinked at me like Cyclops.

I handed her a drink. She swigged from it with a passion, nearly choked and asked what we were talking about.

'Cats, Cheryl informed her.

'Don't like cats. Give me asthma.'

'Do you suffer from asthma then?'

'If I get a cat shoved in me face, then yes.'

'I never knew!' Cheryl chimed in.

'You've never shoved a cat in me face, have you!' Janice was always to the point. 'I like *The Aristocats* though. Got it on video.'

I nodded.

'Do you like *The Aristocats*?' Janice turned her bulging red eye on me.

'Oh, yes. I do.'
'Do you, Neil?'
'Not all of them, no.'
'What do you mean?'
'Well there were those two evil Siamese ones in it. Didn't like them.'
'Oh yes, you're right!' Cheryl added. 'I'd forgotten them. Nasty beggars.'
The conversation dried up. We all reached for our bottles and continued to drink. Neil spoke first.
'So what do you two ladies fancy to eat then?' Cheryl and Janice giggled. 'Italian last time. How about a steak or something?'
'Yeah!' Cheryl shrieked.
'Lovely!' Janice added.
'How about you, Sport, fancy a nice bit of hot beef?'
'I don't know. I've had quite a lot recently.' I nudged him. Under the table he gripped my leg. Slowly he began rubbing it, all the while keeping a straight face and the conversation going over the table.
'You eat a lot of meat then, Wade?' Cheryl asked.
'I don't normally, but in the last few days I seem to have had it at every meal.'
Neil was rubbing my groin. My cock hardened.
'Not good to eat too much. I read it in *Marie Claire*,' Cheryl continued.
'I've just got a taste for it. You know what it's like when you get a fabulous piece of rump in front of you, it's difficult not to dive in.'
Neil played with my balls. It was almost too much.
Cheryl giggled. 'I know all about rump!'
Janice laughed too and drained her bottle.
'I bet you're surprised just how much you can get down your throat, aren't you, Sport.'
Neil tugged at the base of my dick, hauling the foreskin back over my swollen helmet. I shifted sideways, out of his reach. It was too much to take. 'If the dish is right, then I can

always eat it all – as my Grandmother used to say.'

''Nother drink?' Janice nudged my bottle. It was still half full. Cheryl drained her bottle.

'Come on, boys, keep up. What now?'

'Same again,' I began, only to be interrupted by Neil.

'Bollocks, you pussy boy! Get some vodka shots. They've got different flavours here.'

'Yes!' Cheryl jumped up and worked her way out of the booth. 'Come and help me, Jan.'

Janice followed obediently, rubbing her eye as she went.

'That's not a stiffy you've got is it?' Neil said, loudly, while Janice was still in earshot. The two girls stopped in their tracks and began to snigger before continuing their journey to the bar.

'Neil!' I chided. 'Don't go giving them ideas!'

'Well are you hard, or are you hard?' He placed his hand on my packet. My cock was just deflating, but at his touch sprang into life again. He held my chin and brought my head around to his. He kissed me tenderly on the lips. Foolishly, I pulled away.

'Neil! People will see!'

A grey-haired couple who had just entered the bar had seen. They shuffled their feet for a second on the mat before turning and walking out.

'I don't care who sees. You're gorgeous and you're with me. That's all that matters. And you have stubble burn on your chin.'

'And who's that from I wonder?' I rubbed my chin self-consciously.

'Sorry about earlier, about Karen. I didn't know what I was talking about.'

'That's OK.' I snuggled up next to him. He smiled at me and I gazed into his beautiful eyes. They were the same blue as the turquoise in the lamp over the table.

'Where we going to eat then?'

'Pizza.'

'What about all that steak business?'

'I hate steak. But I had to get you back for that *Cat on a Hot Tin Roof* jibe.'

'Didn't think you got it.'

'I'm not as well read as you, but it doesn't mean I didn't wank over Robert Redford when I was little.'

'Paul Newman.'

'Him too.'

'l preferred Burt Reynolds. Or Lee Majors.'

'Yeah – the six million dollar shag. I used to fantasise that he had a bionic dick. I could do with some of that!'

'I've just had a bionic fuck – why would I want another?' I squeezed his packet and he thrust his cock into my hand, a leer on his face.

'What about that guy in *BJ and the Bear*? Remember him?' Neil asked as I pulled my hand away.

'Yeah! Great hairy chests of our time!' I drank some more. 'I guess I'll have to add your name to that list.'

'We have the technology, we can rebuild him.'

'Nah nah nah nah . . .' I began singing the theme tune, 'nah nah nah nah nah . . .'

Neil loosened his tie and began undoing his shirt. I caught a glimpse of his chest and it gave me a thrill as strong as it always had done. I could make out his nipples, hard under the crisp cotton of his shirt. I wanted to suck them. 'How long are we going to stay with Cheryl and Janice?'

'Don't know. We'll eat and then maybe go to a gay club so they'll get the message. Surely the sight of me with my tongue down your throat should give them enough information.'

'You're not serious!'

We were interrupted by Cheryl.

'Can you come and help. It's Janice.'

'What's wrong?' I stood up and saw Janice being comforted by a barman wiping her eye with a damp cloth.

'She got vodka in her eye!'

'Which one?' My heart sank at the thought of her getting it in the one that was already swollen.

'Lemon.'

'Not which vodka, which eye!' Neil interrupted, taking charge of the situation.

'Oh, her bad one. We was getting the drinks and Janice was testing them by putting her finger in each one and tasting it. Anyway, her eye hurt, so she rubbed her eye and she got vodka in it.'

Janice was not in a good state when we got to the bar. Her eye had swollen even more and was now almost closed due to the swelling. Her left eye had also gone red. She looked like a rabbit with myxamatosis. She was sobbing.

'Sorry, sorry.'

'Don't worry!' Neil put his arm around her. 'Come on, let's get you off to Casualty and check that everything's alright.'

Janice continued to weep. 'I'm sorry! This should've been fun, but I've ruined it.'

'Rubbish!' I added. 'Come on, Neil's right, someone should look at that eye.'

'Suppose so,' Cheryl said reluctantly, lacking all enthusiasm. 'Just as we was getting on well too.'

The journey to Casualty was made by black cab. We sat inside, largely in silence. Neil made some jokes about what an unusual night out this was, but Cheryl became spiky and so the subject was dropped. The only sound came from Janice, simpering in the corner, being cradled by Neil.

The hospital was lit brightly in the night sky. The harsh white of the inside a contrast to the cluttered smoky ephemera that filled the Cork and Casket. We sat for two hours before Janice was led into a small consulting room to be examined. Cheryl went with her.

'Well I guess this gets us out of any funny business with them then,' I said after flicking through a four-month-old copy of *Hello!* magazine for the second time.

'Yeah. Left me feeling horny though.'

'What? A gammy eye?'

'No, hospitals. Something about all those men in white coats.'

'You've seen too many *Carry On* films,' I suggested.

'Oh, Matron!' Neil quipped.

Casualty wasn't too busy. It was still early, not quite nine forty-five, and before their main weekend rush. I sat next to a middle-aged man clutching his arm. From eavesdropping on his conversation with his wife, I discovered he had fallen and was waiting for the results of an x-ray. To the right of me an old lady sat slumped in a wheelchair, sucking on her lower dentures, her mind long since tuned out from the decay of old age. Inside she was still eighteen, a girl with opportunity and possibility abounding.

'I think they're depressing.'

'What?' Neil answered.

'Hospitals.'

'Oh, yeah, hospitals are. But not doctors. There's a real cute one in Examination Room Three. You wait till he comes out.'

'You eyeing other people up already?'

'Don't get paranoid!' Neil hugged my arm. 'He's not in your league.'

We sat for a few moments intently watching the door to Examination Room Three. The man next to me was called and disappeared after a short discussion with his wife, who was told in no uncertain terms to stay where she was.

The door to Room Three opened and a boy came out, his hand in a bandage. A woman stood in the doorway.

'Her?' I asked.

'No. That's the mother. Wait.'

The woman came out and took the boy's hand and led him out. The boy skipped at her side, oblivious to his surroundings. The doctor treating them came out and stood to wave them off. Neil was right, he was cute; about five foot ten tall, brown wavy hair, greyish eyes, a strong wide build, a cleft in his chin and a dimple in each cheek. He had a friendly, but earnest look in his face.

'Looks like Will Carling,' Neil commented.

'Now, Will Carling, I could see to him alright.' I was trying to get back at Neil for starting this in the first place.

'It'd have to be a three way,' Neil added. 'If Will Carling's up for a man-shag then I want to be there. And if you are having anyone else, then I definitely want to be there.'

'Why?' I teased him.

'Because you're mine.' Neil touched my cheek with the back of his hand.

The wife of the man with the broken arm shifted in her seat. 'I like Will Carling too. He's got a lovely bum,' she said unexpectedly, pulling a packet of sweets from her blue duffel coat. 'Polo?'

I was startled, but Neil took it in his stride, leaned over me and took one. 'Thanks.'

I took one too and added my thanks. The woman took a sweet, popped it in her mouth and slipped the packet back in her pocket. Her hands rested back on her burgundy pleated skirt. She was probably in her mid-sixties, with greying hair that had been solidly set earlier in the day. By evening, it was just fractionally out of shape and she looked vaguely bedraggled, but her humour was not.

'My husband used to be like Will Carling,' she continued. 'You probably can't see it now, but he was fit and had a lovely bum. Still has got a lovely bum actually.'

'I didn't see,' I suggested diplomatically.

'Oh you look when he comes out. Lovely it is.' She sucked on her sweet, staring ahead. She had about her an air of familiarity and boredom.

'We will,' Neil promised, nudging me. 'Did he play rugby?'

'For years and years. Was very good too. Played for London Irish. Quite a runner he was. If he got the ball you wouldn't see him for dust. You play?'

'No,' I replied.

'Used to,' Neil said.

'Did you?' I asked.

'Yeah, at college and then for a bit afterwards, just a local team. Nice to get out on a Saturday.'

'I never knew that.'

'You two a couple?' the woman asked. 'You know, "partners"

whatever they call it these days?'

'Sort of,' I replied.

'Yes,' said Neil, taking my hand in his.

'Well, make the most of it that's all I'd say. It doesn't last long, believe me.' Her eyes began to fill with water. 'You enjoy yourselves. Don't matter what anybody else says, if you love each other then that's your business and don't let people persuade you otherwise.'

Neil squeezed my hand. 'We won't.'

The woman sniffed and dabbed her nose with a tatty tissue that was clamped in her fist. 'That a *Hello!*?'

'Yes,' I handed it to her. 'Don't know why I like it. It's always full of such bloody good news. Never say anything nasty about people. They'd find something good to say about Hitler I expect; "Adolph and Eva frolic in their new Bavarian summer palace".'

We both laughed.

'Oh, yes, I remember now, that's why I like it. It's always full of such bloody good news. Makes a change!'

Cheryl appeared. Janice was behind her, clutching a sterile pad to her eye. 'Too much protein in her eyeball. Got infected. There's no bloody protein in her brain that's for sure.'

'Sorry,' Janice moaned as she shuffled up behind Cheryl.

'Protein and vodka. You are a silly cow, Jan, you really are!'

Neil put the two girls in a taxi and sent them off home. We stood outside the hospital wondering what to do.

'What now?' I asked.

'What time is it?'

I looked at my watch. It was nearly ten. 'Any ideas?'

'Yeah. You game?'

'For what?'

'Are you game?' Neil gripped my shoulders. 'Say yes. I've fantasised about this for two years and now you can make my dream come true.' The schoolboy in him was jumping on the spot.

'OK. Whatever.'

Neil grabbed me by the hand and hailed a cab. He gave

directions back to Canary Wharf and made me promise not to ask any questions. I sat in the taxi a soft erection belly-dancing in my pants while Neil cackled next to me.

Back at the office, Neil paid the driver and instead of going into the office building, led me to the gym next door. It was still open. We put down our membership cards, took a towel and went in. It was very quiet; at ten thirty on a Friday night that wasn't a surprise. The guy behind the café was rinsing out the cappuccino machine. Neil jumped up the stairs two at a time, me fighting to keep up with him.

'I haven't got my kit,' I pointed out.

'Don't need it,' was all Neil would say.

In the deserted changing room, Neil began throwing his clothes into a locker. I followed slowly, begging him to tell me what this was all about.

'Meet me in the steam room in two minutes,' was all he said as he ripped off his long white boxer shorts and hung them in his locker. The flash of his dick took my breath away even now. The long thick meat hung and swayed between his legs, standing out slightly from his torso, the shaft beating against the hefty balls either side. His golden brown body reflected against the white tiling and the mirrors dotted between the lockers. I watched him jog off; first his pecs bouncing as he left and then I watched that firm thick arse of his, flexing as he dashed off through the showers before turning right towards the steam room and out of sight. My tool was already growing. It was just as well the locker room was deserted as my arousal would be difficult to hide. Mind you, with the beautiful and graceful body of Neil running past them to take their attention, I could have stood with a pulsating rock-hard erection and no one would have noticed.

I threw my Calvins in the locker and pushed it shut, spinning the combination to lock it. I grabbed my towel and wandered towards the steam room. It was eerily quiet. In the distance I could hear funky music playing in the gym above us. The showers were deserted, the heads dripping onto the white tiled floor while water gurgled in the large brass drain in the centre of the wet area. I turned right into the short corridor that led to the steam room. It was dark. The light reflecting from the tiles partially lit the way and I could make out the door of the steam room, but after that, all was blackness. I paused to look for a light switch. There was none.

'Neil?' No response. 'Neil, are you in there?' My voice echoed around me and faded away.

Gingerly I stepped down towards the steam-room door. It was frosted glass and I could see that it was pitch black inside. The door was slightly ajar and steam billowed out in clouds like a cooling tower. I looked behind me, nervous and excited. There was no one there. There was just me, the distant music and Neil, somewhere inside.

I swung open the frosted door and peered inside. My eyes had got used the half-light of the corridor, but the steam-room was like an endless cave. I stepped into this cave, the blackness surrounding me like reams of velvet. The steam outlet was by the door and hissed against my leg. I jumped forward and pulled the door closed behind me. The floor tiles were cold beneath my feet. I looked down, the normally jade slates barely visible. I put my hands out in front of me.

'Neil? Stop pissing about. Where are you?'

Again, my question was answered by my own echo. I took another step forward, still feeling out in front of me. I strained to see in the dark, but it was night around me. I looked behind and from the reflections flashing through the door I could make out the beginnings of the plastic block bench that ran around the outside of the room. I could make out more of the room looking this way. It was no larger in fact than a medium-sized garden shed, lined with dimpled plastic sheets that rose to a curved ceiling. With the lights from outside glimmering, it now resembled a chapel. Above me water droplets hung like a legion of bats ready to dip and curve into the twilight outside.

The steam outlet hissed and gurgled, a faint ringing coming from somewhere within its pipes. The room was warm, but not too hot. I felt myself relax. If Neil wanted to play, then I could play too – and besides this looked like fun.

The sounds of outside reverberated though the thick walls. It was as if we were at the bottom of a huge liner, metres below the surface of the sea with only the pumping and grinding of the engine to keep us company.

I edged to the side and sat down. The seat was damp and warm against my arse. I my opened legs and my warm mantool flopped into the seat. I rested my hands palm down on the seat beside me and waited in the dark. My eyes were getting used to the blackness, but still the back of the steam room was invisible. I groped to make out a shape or a form, but could only see the infinity of night spread out before me.

I had been sitting there for a few minutes and was beginning to wonder if I had got the right instructions from Neil when I made out the breathing of a man somewhere to my right. I looked, but could see nothing. Then fingers reached out and touched mine. My hand flinched first with fright, but the fingers intertwined with mine and lifted my arm into the darkness. I held my hand out, waiting. I felt my middle finger being licked and sucked, drawn in to a warm mouth and massaged by teeth and lips. I reached my hand out to feel the face. I could sense Neil's stubble beneath my hand, the curve of his cheekbone, the soft skin around his eye. His lashes tickled me as he blinked. His eyebrows were thicker, but still soft, like small streams of hair that led out to his temples. His forehead was smooth with tails of damp hair hanging onto it. I traced my finger down his nose and onto the skin above his top lip. His mouth came up and began sucking on my fingers again. I closed my eyes and revelled in the sensation. Pulling my hand out of his mouth I traced the line down through the light cleft in his chin, down his neck and onto his Adams apple. Here the beard was growing through. I swept my hand in the direction of its growth and the skin was soft against it and the stubble impeded my travel like light sandpaper.

There was a groan. I lifted my hand back to Neil's face and he sucked hungrily again on my fingers. He took my hand in his hands and played with each of my fingers in his mouth. My cock began to stir into life. The steam swirled around me, blanketing me and comforting me as my senses took control.

Neil took my hand from his mouth and traced the fingers over his chin, down his neck and into the damp hair on his broad expanse of chest. I gripped the hair and it slid between my fingers as he led me to his left nipple. It was hard and firm, standing out like a beacon on the corner of his left pec. I teased it, toyed with it between my fingers, pulling on the areola, pinching it while a voice moaned with delight. My cock lifted from the seat in front of me as blood poured into it.

The sensation was too much. My mouth watered and I leaned down and put this pert nipple in my mouth. I caught it between my teeth and tugged at it slightly. It was salty from sweat and warm in my mouth. The hair on his chest tickled my face. With a free hand I made a play for his other nipple. Two strong hands came down on my head, running their fingers through my hair and pulling my face into his muscular chest. Now it was my turn to groan with pleasure. I licked at the chest, eager for the taste of the salty sweat. As I pushed my tongue against his torso, Neil lay down. I fell on top of him, shocked to feel his broad, tall frame beneath me. Effortlessly, Neil grabbed my waist and pulled me on to him. The first thing I felt was his arm-sized cock beneath me. It was hard, flexed against his chest and primed for action.

I ran my hands along his body and found his head. I pulled it towards me and we fought for a kiss; our tongues licking and threshing in each other's mouths. The feel of this hot body between me made my man-rammer ecstatic. I straddled my legs over his body and pushed my groin on to his. He reciprocated, pushing his cock between my legs, cleaving my arse and sending a shiver down my spine.

We kissed and writhed together for some time. Alone in this dark cell, while the world hummed and churned outside. Still I could see nothing.

Neil pushed me up and sat next to me. 'Good?'

'The best.'

'It gets better.' He put his hand down to the base of my cock and rubbed my balls in the palm of his hand. He gripped the base of my shaft, his fingers just able to go round. Roughly he pulled down the skin and my mushroom head slipped out from beneath my foreskin. I leaned back against the wall and waited. At first I could just feel two moist lips sucking and kissing the tip of my dick. Then a tongue darted over the piss-slit. I groaned. Then the lips parted and my cock-head slipped inside his hot, wet mouth. Spit oiled the movement as he took my pleasure tool inside. Down he went, licking and sucking, dropping his jaw to take it right down his throat until I could feel his nose rammed into my pubes and his tousled blond hair flopped around my thighs. I gasped as he slowly withdrew, tracing the vein along the back of my dick with his tongue. He teased the end again, tasting the pre-come seeping out before taking in the whole tool again. This tine he was faster, more assured. He kneeled in the dark in front of me and I felt two broad palms grip my thighs as he worked his magic on my cock. I gripped his hair and repeatedly shoved his head down on my love rod. But the more I pushed him down, the more he held back before pulling his mouth off my dick and gently kissing the tip.

'Wait, There's more . . .'

He placed his hands on the inside of my legs and gently parted them. My balls slipped onto the plastic bench. My dick was rigid against my stomach, the tip batting gently with my heartbeat against my navel. I felt Neil slip a finger under my bollocks and feel for my hole. I groaned and slipped my hips forward. Neil took my legs and lifted them into the air so my hole was open to pleasure. He traced his tongue over my scrotum and onto the skin that led to my man-cunt. My sphincter puckered, waiting for some attention. I felt the top of his tongue graze over the surface of my arse, before returning to work on my hole. In it burrowed, while fingers pulled my arse cheeks apart to get more of the honey within. I could hear the slurping above the hiss of the steam as Neil sucked and drank from my hole.

'Better?'

'You bet.'

One hand fell from my arse and scrambled for something on the floor. Still his lips and tongue toyed with my puckered man-cunt. Then I felt something cool and hard against my arse.

'Got something that wants to pay a visit,' Neil whispered.

'Yes, yes,' I urged him.

Neil pushed the dildo against my arse. I felt my sphincter open up as the head probed in. It was wide and I pushed down on it with all my might to get it to slip in. Neil danced it around my hole, teasing and stretching it while the dildo nuzzled its way forward. More I pushed, eager to get this thing up my arse.

'Need a little help?'

'Maybe,' I ventured.

I heard Neil spit on my hole and then felt the sweet touch of his lips against my piss-slit.

'Oh, yeah, that's it.' I pushed down once more and felt the head of the dildo squeeze past my sphincter and glide inside. This was a one hell of a fat man-rammer Neil was inserting. I gasped as the shaft continued to enter me, pulling my arse apart. But there was no pain, only the sense of being filled with Neil's love. My cock-head was now being licked and sucked royally, I bucked my hips upwards for more cock-meat to be eaten and forward to take in more of this love tool. I felt the tips of Neil's fingers brush against my arse, tickling the cheeks as the dildo was shoved home. At the same time Neil dived down on my cock and again I felt his nose brush into my pubes. I grabbed his head, my legs splayed out either side, and bent down and kissed his crown.

I gave myself over to the thrill of the night as my come-shooter was sucked and licked and my arse was pounded with the dildo. My arse cheeks squeaked and ground against the plastic seating and my back banged against the wall as I was pumped for all it was worth. My orgasm exploded within me as the dildo banged against my colon, jizz shot forth and the hungry, willing mouth took it all, pumping and licking the head to get every last drop of love juice from me. I wailed as my arms flailed by my sides and I deflated on to the side of the bench. I was panting for breath, the room now unbearably hot. Neil pulled the dildo from my arse and it slipped out, leaving my legs to close behind it.

I felt Neil's body moving away.

'Don't go, not yet,' I urged him.

'Wait a minute, I'll be back,' he reassured.

Then there was light. I blinked at the dazzle and saw Neil standing on the bench fiddling with the light socket above.

'Easy. All you need is a coin and you can undo the fastening and loosen the bulb.' He turned around. His dick was like a lance, a solid truncheon of meat standing to attention. 'Good?'

'Oh, fucking excellent,' I said, exhausted by the dildo, the sucking and the heat. 'Come here.'

Neil came over and I looked at him again, like someone new, his features imprinted on my fingertips, every contour framed within my mind. He kissed me and gently began to play with his huge tool.

'Let me . . .' I insisted.

'No. This was for you. For your pleasure. For your memories. I've waited to suck your cock for so long in here and tonight my dream came true.'

He kneeled above me, one leg straddling me, and jerked on his pounding tool. He groaned as he climaxed. I leaned up as he pointed his gusher towards me. The elixir flew from his cock, spattering across my face and onto the wall. I grabbed his hips and dived down on his rod. He pumped the juice into my mouth and I drank it thirstily. He had the best-tasting spunk. I slavered to lick around his head as he milked the last drops from his dick. Slowly his tool began to descend. I kissed the head as it passed me and then licked the loose jizz that lay in his pubes while massaging his arse.

'I'm knackered, let's get out of here.'

'It's too hot.'

Neil leaned down and picked up the dildo. It was bigger than I could believe.

'You got that fucker in me?' I gasped.

'Yeah. Knew you could take it. Besides, you're gonna need some practice with taking thick bits of meat. Mine's going to need a seeing to by the time we get home. Your arse going to be up to it?'

I grinned and took his hand as we left the steam chapel of love.

'You bet.'

Chapter Seven

MEMO
To Wade Armstrong
Neil Rogers
From Karl Parker
Re: Stone Enterprises Project

Dear Wade and Neil,
We haven't met for two weeks to discuss how the designs for the above are developing. Mr Gee is keen that we all work together to impress Mr Stone with our designs so that we can seal the contract. I understand that several other partnerships are bidding for the contract (Robson and Fowler being the leading contenders who have just won the Swiss Blue Ribbon for the Gigy Building in Geneva) so I think it is vital that we all get together and brainstorm.
I'm at my desk most days. Talk to you soon.
Karl.

It was no wonder that Karl hadn't heard anything from Neil or I over the previous two weeks. We had barely shown our faces in the office, preferring to work, eat and fuck at home. The relationship we had was amazing – a real synergy that was coming up with some inspired designs that flowed as a constant river of ideas, enthusiasm and creativity between us. What's more we fucked like horses on heat. In the morning, in the afternoon and the evening. No time was a bad time to play with each other. I would wake to find my cock impaled on

Neil's mouth, my tool stirring into life as I did. In the morning while we worked we would design a little, kiss a little, sketch some plans and then fuck over them; Neil thrusting his load up my willing arse, slapping my cheeks and cheering as he filled my hole. Or else I would fix him face down to my design board, fasten his hands with whatever I had to hand; tape, string, clothing; even a chain of paperclips in one instance. Then I would spread his legs and tie them to the feet of the table. With the designs pressed between his taut abdomen like some rare flower being preserved for posterity, I would grease his arse with my tongue, drink deeply from the juices in his cunt before fucking him with all my might; sometimes pulling out so he could drink my juice, other times thrusting home so that my come sealed us together. Afterwards, always, we could collapse on top of each other; two hot sweaty bodies linked by lust, love and intellect, pouring forth our desire for each other or some new design idea that had crept into our brain while we had fucked.

Lunch was more often on each other than at the dining table. Whatever food we had, it always tasted better eaten from Neil's body. Warmed by his smooth skin, seasoned by his sensual presence. Whether it was a prawn cocktail resting in the trenches of his abs or a diced banana to prise and chew from his arse crack, everything I ate inspired me. It was as if my taste buds were linked to every other sensual organ in my body to bring forth all the creativity I had within me. Neil felt the same. He began to think in a new way, thoughts that in the past had led to stale and unoriginal ideas, now led to a vast territory of creativity. It was as if his mind was a savannah after the flood, filled with new growth, new life and new opportunity.

We worked from the moment we awoke to the moment we fell asleep exhausted at the end of the day. Sometimes we would go for hours without speaking, both of us drawing, computing and creating until the touch of his toes would draw me to his body to worship it some more. We rarely went out, unless it was for more food or to make a brief appearance in the office.

Then all we would do would be to collect our mail, make apologies and then return to work. And no one doubted that we were working. The state of both of us was unmissable. We looked exhausted and drained, as indeed we were, but at the same time we had a glow of inspiration that kept questioning at bay. Only Marilyn knew what was going on and even then I don't think she appreciated the significance of what had happened between us.

'You look tired,' she said on one fleeting visit.

'I am.'

'Tired, but happy. You've changed.'

'I have?'

'And it's for the better. You working?'

'Constantly. We're coming up with some amazing stuff.'

'Are we going to see it?'

'Soon. There's so much of it, I don't know which route we're going to follow, but I've never had a creative surge like it before. Things OK here?' I asked, eager to know that our absence wasn't creating trouble.

'They're fine. The usual. Don't worry about him,' she said, nodding towards Baldie Gee's office. 'He's very happy. If you're coming up with great ideas then that's fine. Just as long as you've got something to show him when the time comes then there'll be no trouble.'

'Great.' I turned to leave, but Marilyn stopped me.

'Just remember Karl. He's supposed to be part of it and with you two not being here it's pretty clear he's not involved.' She raised her eyebrows. 'I mean, we all know he couldn't design a lollipop stick if his life depended on it, but with you working from home, everyone knows he's not doing anything on this project. And as I've said, he's got Gee in his back pocket and you need to be careful.'

'Yes, why is that?' I asked, keen to know the truth about Karl and Baldie Gee.

'Never you mind. I'm no gossip – and that's one thing you two should be thankful for!'

* * *

There was another memo waiting for me on my desk.

MEMO
To Wade Armstrong
Neil Rogers
cc Arnold Gee
From Karl Parker
Re: Stone Enterprises Project

Dear Mr Armstrong and Mr Rogers,

Time is ticking by and we need to get together to sort out just what we are going to submit to Miles Stone. I'm worried that it's all being left a little late for the drawings to be assessed and completed. I have spoken to Mr Gee and he is similarly keen that we liaise soon and decide our line of attack.

Talk to you soon – by the end of this week at the latest.

Yours
Karl Parker.

My terminal was stacked with various e-mails. One was from Neil, sent only minutes earlier. It read:

Wade, my hung stud,

Let's not hang around too long. I've got jizz in my bollocks that's just waiting for you. I've never been happier or more alive than when I'm in your arse, or you're in me, your tool in my mouth and your juice down my throat. I never thought I could enjoy sex as much as I do with you. THIS IS THE REAL THING! Hurry, I want to make love to you again and I won't be able to wait until we get back home. My donkey dick is already hard and I am salivating for your creamy cock to be back in my mouth where it belongs. Jesus! How filthy can I be???!! What have you done to me??!! Whatever it is, I LOVE YOU for it!

Yours forever, Neil

I finished reading it, perched on the corner of my desk while sweeping post into my open briefcase to read and file in the bin at home. I was about to leave it when an icy chill blew around my back. It was Karl. He was fatter than before, his face puffed up and bloated while a blush of frustration burned his face.

'You got it then?'

'What?' I replied, amused at the bluster that rippled the pages on my desk.

'My memo. You can't say you haven't read it, I just watched you.'

'Yes, I've read it,' I replied, dropping it casually into the bin and flicking off my terminal to hide Neil's e-mail, 'and the last one as well. You're right we must get together.'

'Oh.' Karl was slightly taken aback at my agreement. 'When?'

'Let me see . . .' I opened my diary and skimmed through the pages while I felt Karl's eyes follow the dates. Playing with him, I put my finger on a time that afternoon before snapping the diary shut and suggesting, 'You'd better ask Neil, he's kind of the dominant one in this partnership – I mean, threesome.'

'I have just asked him,' Karl snarled. I glanced over his shoulder and saw Neil chatting with Marilyn, his coat already on.

'And what did he say?'

'He said he couldn't stop, he had some scatter cushions on the eighth floor that needed rearranging and I would have to talk to you.' A big grin crept onto my face. 'And if that was joke, I don't think it's very funny.'

I pursed my lips and shook my head. 'No, it's not a joke. Neil is planning on pitching for the scatter cushion contract for the eighth floor and he wants to get in some practice.' Karl remained stony-faced. 'Could you just wait here a moment, I think I'll just have a quick word with Neil.'

I snapped my briefcase shut and made to leave.

'Where are you going?' Karl moaned.

'I said, I'm just going to have a quick word with Neil. If he puts those Conran electric-blue cushions with the Laura Ashley South American Indian designs, there'll be murder! Wait here, I'll be back.' I dashed away.

Karl remained behind me, scouring my desk and pouting with indignation.

I didn't return, Neil and I slipping away down the fire stairs, pausing only to kiss on the ninth floor and for Neil to wank in my face on the third, his warm salty jizz sprinkling me with yet more inspiration while I fingered his arse. We escaped some half an hour later, rushing home to work or to fuck; whatever stuck first.

We went out on one night only. We'd had a great day designing, our plans over the past month coming together, and had created a building which was a homage to Frank Lloyd Wright's design for Edgar Kauffmnan's house, 'Fallingwater'. In our design we melded the surrounding land and features within the building, utilising debris from the development of the nearby underground, a natural rock formation as well as utilising intricate brickwork that existed in the deserted warehouse that currently stood on the site. The best part was to integrate a stream that flowed through the site into the actual building itself so that there would be fresh water running though the centre of the building. It was a triumph of balance between the natural and artificial. Every facet of the project complemented each other. As a whole it was greater than the sum of its parts. It was, in fact, a sculpture to the relationship I had built with Neil and our new found happiness. We called it Fallingwater Two. We decided to celebrate by going out.

'Where?' I asked, slumped on the sofa with a coffee to revive me.

'How about The Corps?'

I sat up. The Corps was a well-established military club in the East End. It had a reputation of entertaining the fittest and most attractive men in London. They had a strict door policy only to admit those in uniform and who were strong enough to take the action inside. 'How do you know about The Corps? I thought you were married?'

'I know these things,' Neil replied, sitting next to me and dropping his arm around me. 'Go on! We'll have a laugh!'

'You don't have to convince me, of course we'll go. I'm just surprised you know about it, that's all.'

He gave me a big kiss on the lips. I nearly spilt my coffee.

'What we going to wear then?'

'I've got some stuff with me and we can raid your wardrobe. I've seen you've got some combat trousers, some boots. That and a nice tight, ripped T-shirt and we'll be okay. One glimpse of your hard pecs and the management are going to be falling over themselves to let us in.'

We spent about an hour getting ready. Neil stood in an old faded jockstrap, the pouch stretched from wear. His bollocks hung low and I could see his cock snaking round inside the mesh, finding room to settle. When he turned round I had a great view of his bubble butt, his cheeks split by his hairy crack.

'What do you think?' Neil asked.

'Fucking gorgeous. You sure you want to go out?' I was ready to have sex again.

'Not the jockstrap, which trousers?' He held up a pair in each hand.

'The left,' I suggested. They were a pair of khaki army trousers, with a bondage tie round each ankle. He put them on. The waistband of the jockstrap just peeked over the top.

'Horny!' I said

'Yeah, they feel good,' he added, pulling on the steel toe-capped boots he had last worn in the executive washroom. On top he wore a white vest T-shirt. Even though neither of us had been to the gym for some time, Neil's body looked hotter than ever. He put gel in his hair and slicked it back. He was my very own, full-sized Action Man. His blue eyes flashed at me, stubble on his chin adding to an air of masculinity, his broad shoulders stretched the fibres in the vest which hugged and accentuated his hard nipples. The vest ended halfway down his torso, leaving two rows of hard stomach muscle uncovered.

Meanwhile, I pulled on some dark-blue mottled combat

trousers, boots and a dark navy T-shirt. As I stretched the T-shirt over my chest, I noticed that my body fat seemed to be at its lowest ever.

'Why is it that after not going to the gym in God knows how long, I am bigger and in better shape than I have ever been?'

'Because, stud, you have been fucked into fitness. How many times have we shagged today, let alone over the last three weeks?'

I paused, counting up the sex that day; that morning we did it twice, then again at about ten when Teletubbies started, once while the lunchtime news was on, again in the afternoon having completed the plans for Fallingwater Two. 'Five times.'

'Yup and if we don't do it another three times before we get to sleep I'll be surprised.' He winked. 'That's got to be the equivalent of four hours in the gym. It's no wonder you're the world's most perfect man.'

'How about we make it six times before we leave?'

'NO!' Neil shouted.

I spiked my hair with gel, we called a cab and left.

We sat in silence on the way to the club. We were both big men dressed for action. Neil's thick thighs lay astride, his boots tapping on the taxi floor, his head turned to look out of the window. I stared at his neck, a solid lump of flesh, the sinews twisting as his head turned to the right. I traced a vein down though his neck, onto the top of his chest and which disappeared under his vest. His skin was smooth like sand, reaching a crest of hair that rose as a wave on his chest. His bicep was like a football on his arm, another vein pumping life into this rock of muscle. I gripped Neil's thigh. He put his hand on top of mine and squeezed it.

'I think,' he began, 'that this is the most perfect time in my life. I can't imagine ever wanting more than this; the creativity we had today, the way I feel tonight and the fun we are going to have, and you.' He turned his head towards me. I thought he was about to cry. Instead he put a hand to my face and pulled me to him. We kissed and I knew what he meant. This was life's peak and we were lucky enough to have conquered it.

The entrance to The Corps was subdued – a large wooden door that led into what looked like a warehouse. Above the doorway was one sharp spotlight, illuminating the pavement beneath. A bouncer stood guard, a tall, thick-set black guy, with his arms folded and no emotion in his face. As the cab pulled up, a squat, pasty-faced guy was being turned away. He was wearing jeans and an American football shirt. His fleshy arms were covered in goose bumps. He looked familiar. The bouncer sent him on his way as he was not up to the standard of The Corps. I felt instantly nervous, a fist twisting in the pit of my stomach. Neil strode forward and as he did the black guy reached out and opened the door.

'Evening chaps,' he growled, without opening his mouth.

'Hello,' I offered, while Neil just nodded and walked through.

Inside the half-light I could make out the huge space that The Corps occupied. It still wasn't busy, a scattering of men standing around the outside of the room or leaning against the bar in the centre. The warehouse was as large and square inside as it was out and little had been done to disguise its industrial heritage. Iron beams span a web across the ceiling some twenty feet up. The walls were solid brickwork spaced between iron girders. The floor too was a herringbone of brick. The only addition to the space was the large square wooden bar which stood in the middle and a row of tiny brass hooks which circumnavigated the room. The whole place was lit by a sprinkling of lights suspended from the ceiling by lengths of flex. Music pounded from invisible speakers and the air was heavy with smoke and sex.

Neil walked to the bar. I followed him and I could feel eyes following both of us. We ordered some beer and then we went and stood by the wall to get our bearings. It took some time to adjust to the low level of light and to see who was with us. The guy behind the bar was the only man illuminated, dressed in snug-fitting jean shorts, baseball boots and white The Corps

T-shirt, on the back of which was written '. . . the hardest place, for the hardest men . . .' As I looked around I could see other guys, similarly dressed in military fatigues, some in leather, all very masculine, all were in good shape.

'Some fantastic looking guys,' I commented.

'Strict door policy. But you know what?'

I looked at him.

'No one is a patch on you.' I kissed him. He pushed me back against an iron girder and kissed me back, harder. 'Tonight I am yours. You do what you like, but I am only here for you.'

'And I'm only here for you.'

I felt a sense of relief. So early in our relationship I was worried that he may find someone else, someone who could give him more. I feared that having freed him from his marriage, he would take his liberty and leave me behind. But now I was happy. The nerves in my stomach subsided. I grasped his crotch and pulled on it provocatively.

'Dance?'

'Sure.'

He took my arm and walked to into the central space. He put his arms around me, held me and we danced slowly, oblivious to the men around us, his hands sweeping across my back, clasping my buttocks while his tongue probed my mouth.

Later the club was full, the dance floor pulsating with hard muscular bodies dancing to the electric beat. I was drunk. I held onto Neil and buried my head in his chest as he leaned against the wall.

'You OK,' he asked.

'Fine. You?'

'Never better.'

'You worried about meeting someone you know?' I asked.

'Nah,' Neil's chest surged with a giggle, 'besides, they're going to be here for the same reasons as us!'

'Guess so.' I pulled away and looked at the mass of men

around us. 'Anyway, who are we going to know who would want to come here and would be able to get in. They've got such a strict door policy.'

'Miles Stone?' Neil said flatly.

'Yeah, he's fit enough,' I agreed, 'but he's shifting his arse up the corporate ladder so he'll be off with his trophy wife enjoying bottles of wine that cost more than we earn in a week.'

'No,' Neil repeated, 'Miles Stone.'

'What?'

'Miles Stone, he's here.' He nodded to the bar. 'He's over there somewhere.'

'What?' I exclaimed. 'Why didn't you say something?'

'I tried to, but you couldn't hear me. It was when we were dancing. I saw him come in.'

'Where?'

Neil nodded over to the bar. It was impossible to see anyone through the throng that filled the warehouse. All I could make out were hard bodies, men with men; dancing, kissing, feeling each other.

'What's he wearing?' I asked

'It looked like a lot of leather.' Neil drained his bottle.

'You sure?' I had difficulty picturing the severe leadership of Miles Stone as a leather boy.

'Positive.'

'Did he see us?'

'Look around this place, Wade,' Neil admonished. 'We could have the Queen Mother in here and you'd still not know about it.'

'Was he alone?'

'Seemed so. Another drink?'

I nodded and Neil pushed off towards the bar. I leaned against the rough brickwork and smirked. At our next meeting with Miles Stone I didn't know how I would look him in the eye.

A short, fit-looking skinhead came and began dancing slowly in front of me. He had a wiry frame, was pretty good-looking and was wearing long Doc Marten boots. He smiled at me and I returned the gesture. He stopped dancing and strolled towards me. He had strong white teeth and rough skin.

'Dance?' he asked. His voice was much lower than I had expected.

'No, thanks. I'm with someone.'

'Boyfriend?' the skinhead growled.

'Yeah,' I said filing with pride.

'Could make it a three-way?'

'Thanks, but no. We're fucking like rabbits at the moment. One more would confuse everything.'

The skinhead nodded and melted into the moving crowd. I was alone again. I kept my eye-line lowered to avoid amy further propositions. The last thing I wanted was for Neil to see me chatting to a variety of men when he returned with the drinks.

I was tracing a circle with my boot in the sawdust at my feet when I was approached again.

'Come here often?' the voice asked.

I smiled at the ridiculousness of the chat-up line. I looked up, about to reply with something equally banal, when I was met with the leather-clad form of Miles Stone. My mind blanked. He was wearing thick leather boots, leather trousers which were held up by a belt with a thick silver buckle. Over his chest he wore a leather waistcoat, held together by three silver buttons. He had a great body. My eyes were drawn to the packet in his trousers, the leather creasing to give it room. His skin was smooth, his weighty pecs pushing his waistcoat forward, his shoulders big round mounds of muscle, tapering before reaching the globes of his biceps which gave way to strong, ruddy forearms. One of these arms was extended. I shook it.

'Hello,' was all I could think of to say.

'You look surprised.'

'Er, yes, I am, kind of.'

'Didn't expect to see me here?'

'Well, I'd heard you were here.' I wished I hadn't had those two last bottles of beer, my mind was hazy and I couldn't think of what I wanted to say.

'Heard? From whom?' Miles confidently swigged from a beer. My hands twitched for something to do.

'Neil Rogers, he said he'd seen you.'

'He's here to. What is this; an Allsop and Gee office outing? Am I going to have the pleasure of seeing Arnold Gee in a jockstrap?'

I laughed while I tried to think of something witty to reply with. 'No, he couldn't come. He's washing his hair . . .'

Miles laughed. 'So, you two together?'

I nodded.

'Thought so.' My brow furrowed in surprise. 'It's pretty obvious, the way you two were flirting with each other that something had to be going on. I just didn't know if you were two of these corporate types who are so busy looking at their cost flows they don't realise the cock fun they are missing with each other.'

'Well, it took some time, but we're together now.'

'Good. I don't think I could stand another meeting with the air as charged with sexuality as it was in Gee's office last time.'

My eyes widened.

'Your brilliant explanation of Bimbo Architecture had us all mesmerised, but when I looked at Neil's face, I just thought, "Go on, my son, for fuck's sake, give him one," he was so apoplectic with desire for you.'

'Well, he did, very shortly after that.'

Miles grinned.

'About fifteen minutes after that, in fact, I was plugged up the arsehole by him in the office lift.'

Miles threw his head back and laughed.

'Something funny?' Neil approached. He handed me a bottle of beer and then one to Miles. Miles took it, a surprised look on his face. 'I saw you two talking from the bar so I asked the barman if he knew what you were having.'

'And he remembered?' Miles was astonished.

'Sure did. I said, "Cute guy, early forties, a little grey at the temples," and he said, "Dressed in leather, silver buckled belt, smooth skin and sexy butt, yeah, he's having the same as you." Looks like you pulled, Miles.'

'Which barman?'

Neil pointed through the crowd. 'There, tall, blondish.'

'Irish, with green eyes,' Miles confirmed. 'I'll have to have a chat with him before the night is out.'

'So what were you talking about?' Neil stood next to me. He put his arm round my waist and gave me a gentle squeeze.

'Wade was just telling me how you fucked him in the lift.'

I felt Neil give a little start, but not so his composure was lost to anyone around us. 'He is always to the point.'

I tried to explain what Miles had been saying about the chemistry between us when a siren went on. The lights dimmed further and the music became an overwhelming pumping beat. Smoke swirled about our heads.

'What is this?' I asked. 'The blitz?'

Miles Stone was undoing his silver buckle. 'That's the cue for the underwear party to begin. The doors have been locked,' he shouted above the melee around us. He began unlacing his boots and peeling down his leather trousers. He popped open his waistcoat and his firm contoured torso flashed into view. He certainly was in very good shape.

'How about it?' Neil asked, turning to me.

'I'm game,' I replied, pulling his head towards me and planting a big kiss on his lips in front of Miles. Neil dropped to one knee and began untying my laces. Miles already had his boots off and was just taking off his waistcoat. His skin was completely smooth, the only hair being the little tufts of black that sat under his arms. His torso was taut – each muscle clearly defined, all of them rippling gently as he peeled down his trousers.

I shook off one boot and Neil began untying the other.

Beneath the leather, Miles was wearing a pair of black Speedo trunks. After witnessing the bulge in his trousers, seeing his packet held within the thin material of his trunks was no disappointment. Miles turned and hung his clothes on one of the little pegs that surrounded the room. His arse was tight and firm. Casually he tugged on his balls. I could make out the thick shaft of his dick. His stomach was smooth, his tissue thin skin papier-mâchéd over hard muscle.

I shook off the second boot. Neil stood and began unbuttoning my navy trousers. My cock was already struggling into life, despite the action it had already seen today and the alcohol I had consumed. He pulled them down gently, revealing my white Calvins and already bulging dick. All around us men were undressing. I could see men in jocks, in Speedos, in lycra shorts, in G-strings and thongs; some in big tatty underwear, holed and ready for action, others in tight rugby shorts, undone at the waist as their erections came up like a periscope to see the action around them. A black guy stood in nothing but a pair of white lycra pants, his coffee brown torso bursting out of the waistband. Inside his pants I could see his big black man-tool powering up, stretching the fabric as it geared up for a drilling. I shook my own trousers clear and pulled on my dick to clear it from curling round my pubes. It stuck out like a coiled spring.

'Someone's in luck,' Miles said, his thick cock similarly strengthening.

I squeezed my groin and my ramrod grew some more.

Neil kicked off his boots. I grabbed his waistband as he was about to pull his combats down and took over. I wanted to see Miles' face when Neil's equipment came into view. I knelt and inched his khaki combats to the floor. I gasped as I saw his dick inches from my face. I could feel the heat burning from it, smell the testosterone in the sack beneath and see the blood surging into his fleshy tool. Already the mesh packet was straining to contain his thumping cock.

'Fuck,' Miles gasped. 'They should call you two the donkey brothers.'

Neil laughed, gripped the back of my head and pulled my face into his groin. I licked the hot meat through the pouch and hung onto his arse hungrily. My delight was broken by Miles.

'I'll see you guys later, maybe. I think Irish eyes are smiling at me and this pillar needs some action.'

I turned to see Miles striding through the crowds towards the bar where an eager looking barman was sucking on a finger. As Miles went, the crowd of butt-hungry men parted, his natural authority clearing his way. I hung our clothes on the pegs that surrounded us.

Neil led me to the middle of the dance floor. We were surrounded by naked and semi-naked men with the most beautiful bodies I had ever seen. Tall, fit, muscular frames, some hairy, some smooth, all with hard arses and throbbing dicks. Some danced alone, in their own world, playing with themselves whilst they fingered their arseholes. Others were in two or threes, exploring each other's bodies. Nothing was out of bounds. One guy was already handcuffed to the bar, his legs spread and cuffed to the brass footrest. Men were licking at his man-cunt, pulling on his dick. One guy knelt on the bar and shoved his dick in his mouth. The cuffed guy sucked on it hungrily. The black guy I had seen was having his white lycra worked over by the skinhead – whose body was a maze of tattoos. The skinhead mauled into the black guy's groin, desperate for the length of fat black pecker inside.

Neil pulled me to him. He kissed me and began to tug my Calvin's down. I didn't care that I would be naked. I wanted to be naked, to be open for Neil to do with me as he wished. I kicked off my pants and my prick sprang free. I ground my manhood against Neil's packet, reaching my arms round to finger his arse. The ocean of men around us melted into the distance. Their groans of pleasure and the pounding music gave way to bliss as Neil worked his hand over the tip of my dick, pulling back the skin and teasing my helmet with his wet fingers. I kissed his neck, then his broad shoulders, tracing the vein down through his bicep to suck longingly on his fingers. Unable to withhold himself Neil pulled off his jock. I took it and stuffed it into my mouth, sucking on the damp pouch while Neil pulled himself into me. I could feel that huge dick of his push against my belly, up to my button. I pulled on his hard nipples and he threw his head back in ecstasy while he fingered my man-cunt.

'Yes, yes,' I murmured. 'I've got to have you now.'

Neil kissed me to silence me. I pulled my head away. I had an overwhelming urge to be plugged again by his thick shag-stick. I pulled him back to where our clothes were.

'Fuck me. Fuck me,' I begged.

Without another word, Neil turned me to face the wall. He pushed me against it and I spread my arms out. Feeling the rough brick beneath my fingers, I spread my legs and soon felt Neil at my hole, licking, pulling, fingering. I moaned. Neil was now an ace rimmer – he knew just how to get his tongue inside my cunt and fill me with thrills. He stood and pressed his chest against my back. I could feel his power rod upright against my crack. I pushed my arse towards it, the cheeks eager to give way to my gagging, puckered hole. He grabbed a bottle of beer and began to pour it down my back so that the cool fizzing liquid slipped between him and me. It flowed down, spreading over my cheeks and pouring in a torrent into my crack. The beer felt good. Neil stood back and took a mouthful of the alcohol before returning to rim me. The booze was squirted into my hole. I felt the icy rush of it deep inside me, followed by the rough lick of his tongue. I turned to see him stand again, pour more beer over his thick chest and them massage it into the end of his rock hard cock-head.

'Need a bit of lube tonight. It's bigger than ever.'

I looked down. His ramrod was purple. It had to be over twelve inches of thick hard cock. My mouth dried. I wanted it in me more than ever. Neil put the tip of the bottle at my hole, swilling more beer into me, fucking me gently with the head of the bottle.

'Fuck me!' I wailed and felt the bottle disappear and the tip of Neil's shaft position itself on my launch pad.

'This is what you want?'

Blast off. He pushed against me. My hands dropped to my

cheeks, pulling them apart to get his love inside me. I pushed down on the intruding Polaris missile as it flew to its destination. The head crashed through my sphincter which was no barrier, rode up through my inside before effecting a direct hit on my colon.

'Yes!' I screamed out.

Neil began to fuck me harder than he had before. He was an animal beating submission out of my tight pussy. I was crushed against the wall as he rode his throbbing cock into my arse. I reached down to pull on my tool, milking my own pre-come. Neil continued to fuck me. Sometimes he paused to hold his dick within me and to angle his shaft around inside. This was almost too much to bear. Then he would pull his dick out so that the head stretched my sphincter before plunging himself back into me. Harder and harder he thrust. He took my hands in his and stretched me out on the wall, impaling me at the same time, thrusting and banging me against the brickwork. I used my arse cheeks to hang onto his tool, to fight his serpent and keep it inside me.

His fucking became faster and harder. I felt his hands push against mine, his fingers stretching outwards as he came in long hard bursts, filling my arse with his seed while my hole sucked and squelched for more. His rhythm slowed, his body hot and smeared with beer and sweat. But I wasn't finished. As he withdrew and my man-cunt breathed a sigh of relief, I turned and began beating my meat to relieve the tension in me. Neil dropped to his knees and took hold of my hips. It didn't take long for me to shoot my load and to have Neil thirstily drink me. My hot love juice filled his throat and mouth, shooting arcs of white jizz over his face, through his eyebrows, over his forehead and into his hair.

After I had come we were both still for a while, exhausted and shocked at the passion spent between us. Neil stood, his face still moist with my come. He pressed against me and we kissed.

'Fuck!' he said. 'That's the best yet.'

'Telling me.'

Around us men were in a frenzy, eating the meat they longed for. The skinhead was being face-fucked by the black guy in the middle of the dance floor. He had the whole of the tool inside him while guys cheered, wanked and fucked around them. Behind the bar I saw Miles Stone fucking the living daylights out of the barman who was spread-eagled over the bar with his Speedos gagging his mouth. The barman pulled with abandon on his own dick. Miles had his head thrown back in ecstasy as his fat cock pumped the barman's butt.

I touched Neil's thick member and he smiled at me. I traced my finger around the outside of the head, feeling the ridge between his helmet and the shaft. His meat was still hot and I could feel it begin to stir into life.

'Home?' he asked.

'You ready for bed?'

'Yeah.' My finger smeared through the come and beer over the tip of his bulbous dick head. 'But not ready to sleep.'

My Calvins were lost in the crowd. I wore Neil's jock, eager to have some part of him next to me until we could fuck again. We slipped out into the cold night, the air chilling the alcohol still on our skins. The journey home was quick through the silent streets. We fucked again and then again, not making it to sleep until dawn was breaking through the night sky.

The next day's post brought the real world back into focus. Neil and I received identical summonses.

MEMO
To Wade Armstrong
From: Arnold Gee
Re: Stone Enterprises Project

Dear Mr Armstrong,

Despite repeated requests for a meeting on the Stone Project, neither you nor Mr Rogers have obliged us with your presence. Mr Parker has informed me that it is probably too late now to secure the deal.

I will see you both in my office, Monday morning at 9.00 am sharp.

Arnold Gee

Partner Allsop and Gee

The honeymoon was over.

Chapter Eight

Both Neil and I were in early on Monday. I carried the sheaf of designs and in particular our plans for Fallingwater Two. I wasn't worried about the meeting with Baldie Gee. Although nothing had been drawn to scale or submitted into the Allsop and Gee design process, I knew that when Miles Stone saw our plans he would jump at them. They were inspirational.

Marilyn was not at her desk. I saw her briefly come out, get two mugs of coffee and return. I tried to catch her eye, but she was intent on her work. She appeared again, grabbed the box of tissues on her desk and vanished back in to the office. I arranged the plans in draft order, starting with the earliest ones to give Gee an idea of the amount of work Neil and I had done, as well as the progression of ideas, leading up to the flash of insight that led into Fallingwater Two.

Just before nine I gathered up my paperwork and looked for Neil. He wasn't at his desk. I scanned the office. Janice wasn't yet in, but Cheryl was just hanging her short lime-green jean-jacket on a hook.

'You seen Neil?' I asked.

''Ello, stranger,' Cheryl replied. 'You back now?'

'I haven't really been away; work,' I said by way of explanation.

'Janice'll be pleased. She was saying yesterday—'

'Sorry, Cheryl, have you seen Neil? We've got an appointment with Gee at nine sharp.'

'Nope,' Cheryl replied.

I stood in the middle of the office, scouring for a sign of Neil. Nothing. Outside thick dark clouds scudded across the grey skies. The city beneath was pensive, waiting for the rain about to strike.

At nine I gave up and went and sat on the low sofa outside Arnold Gee's office, waiting for his current appointed to leave. I was joined by Karl, who sat next to me and tapped my file of plans.

'Bit late for that now, Wadey boy.'

'The name's Wade to you, and I don't think it's too late. Work depends on quality, not quantity, but I wouldn't think that's something you'd understand.'

'Oh I understand a lot of things, you fucking pervert.' I said nothing. 'These plans aren't gong to save you.' He slapped my dossier again.

'Don't worry, you fucking little slug,' I hissed, 'you can put your initials on them when we're ready.'

'Initials?' Karl scoffed. 'The only initials you'll need to know now are "P45".'

I felt uneasy. Something was wrong. Where was Neil? And why was Karl so confident and cocky? My worry was broken by the office door opening. Marilyn came out. She glanced at me but made no reaction. In her eyes I saw hurt and anger. Her lips were tight.

'Well, thank you for coming in,' said Gee. 'I just hope that we've managed to sort something out, to maybe set everyone on the road to recovery.' A woman's hand stretched out and shook his. I heard Neil's voice.

'I'll see you tonight.'

Then there was the sound of a kiss. My throat dried and the blood drained from my face. Outside there was a distant rumble of thunder.

Karen appeared in the doorway.

'Wade, how nice to see you. How are you?' She was speaking to me.

I staggered unsteadily to my feet and shook her hand. She offered her cheek and I kissed it lightly. I had forgotten how attractive she was, slender with alabaster skin, pale grey eyes and fiery red hair. Under her arm she carried a small brown handbag. I couldn't tear my eyes away from it, the smooth kid leather, the delicate silk stitches, the little brass clasps to keep it shut.

'I'm fine,' I replied on autopilot. 'How are you?'

'So so, you know. Thank you for being so good to Neil.'

'Oh, it was nothing,' I heard myself say, while my mind was in a whirl of confusion.

'Well, I must be off. I've taken up more time than I should have done already. Thank you, Arnold.'

'All part of the service,' Gee replied, kissing her cheek. 'See your good wife to the lifts Neil and then come back when you're ready. No rush.'

Then I saw Neil in the doorway. He half-smiled and then took the arm of his wife and led her away. The smile melted from Gee's face.

'In here, now,' he said bluntly and strode into his office.

I followed, Karl clucking at my heels.

'Sit,' Gee instructed. I sat, but Karl went and stood by Gee.

'I've just about had it with you, you fucking little weasel.' Gee began, taking my breath away with his ferocity. Behind him rain spattered the office window.

'Ever since you've been here you've done nothing but take the piss out of this company and I've just about had enough of it.'

'But, sir,' I began.

'Keep quiet,' Gee barked. It shook even Karl.

'You steal other people's ideas, you fuck junior members of staff, break up marriages and then lead the errant husband on a goose chase of drink, sex and God knows what else. Have you read your terms of employment recently?'

I was silent. What did Gee know? What was he going on about?

'You must behave in a way that is in accordance with the best interests of this company and I haven't seen you do that for one day in the entire, miserable two years that you've had your lousy little brain in this office.'

'That is not true,' I started.

'Not true? Not true?' Gee taunted. 'You stole Mr Parker's ideas, you encouraged Mr Rogers to leave his wife, you toy with the affections of Janice Wainwright, do God knows what with her and then dump her like a forgotten crisp packet. You lead Mr Rogers to every bar in town picking up any second-rate slag that takes your fancy and encourage the break up of his marriage. This is a family company, Mr Armstrong. What do you think Miles Stone would make of what you've got up to with Mr Rogers?'

I withheld saying that what I'd done to Neil is probably nothing compared to what Miles Stone would like to do to both of us. Now was not the time.

'You've been absent from this office for almost a month and I suppose that little portfolio of sketches is supposed to make up for it. Mr Rogers was a fine architect until you turned up. I could swear that from the moment you came out of that lift his attitude has changed as you wove your little spell over him.'

Well, at least that much was true.

'I won't stand for it, Mr Armstrong.'

No, he was sitting for it.

Neil came in. His face was strained. No doubt he could hear Gee shouting across the office.

'Ah, Mr Rogers, come in. Mr Armstrong and I were having a little chat.' Gee nodded for him to sit.

'Mr Gee,' Neil said without sitting, 'Wade is not responsible for any of my actions over the last two years. If anything he has been very understanding about the problems Karen and I were going through and has been the major force in trying to bring us together.'

'Your loyalty is admirable, Neil, but this e-mail suggests another story.'

Gee dropped a sheaf of papers on his desk. Karl smirked, triumph on his porcine face. I didn't need to see them, I knew that Karl had been up to his old tricks with the computer. I had asked for trouble in ignoring his requests for a meeting. Marilyn was right, he was dangerous and it was only now, too late, that I realised just how dangerous he was.

'Look at them, Mr Armstrong, these are letters from Janice Wainwright pleading that you don't ignore her after your night of "passion".'

'There must be some mistake,' Neil interjected. 'I've been with Wade almost constantly while we've been working and he hasn't seen Janice.'

'Ah yes, while you were working, but what about at night? You haven't kept up with his movements at night have you?'

'Most evenings, yes,' Neil protested. 'We stayed in his flat and generally worked.'

I knew that arguing was pointless. Karl would have stitched up this loophole already.

'Yes in the evenings, Neil,' Gee continued, 'but here he talks about sneaking out after you had gone to bed to see Janice. Now you couldn't possibly know that, unless you were in the same bed as Mr Armstrong and I take it that his flat isn't that small. I mean, you weren't sleeping with Mr Armstrong were you?'

And there it was, Karl's *coup de grâce.* Either we admit that we were sleeping together, in which case Gee would be on the phone to Karen telling her all that had been going on and I knew that Neil wouldn't let that happen, or else I admit that I was sneaking out behind Neil's back. It was a fruitless situation. How Karl had found out about us I didn't know, but I did know that he was now going to twist and wrench everything out of our relationship to his advantage. That was the way he worked.

Neil was silent. He looked at the printed pages of e-mails, but I could tell he wasn't reading them. I spoke first, saving him the agony of making a decision.

'I'm sorry, mate,' I said, slapping him on the back, 'I just snook out when you were asleep.'

Neil looked at me, his eyes filling with tears.

'It was nothing to do with Neil,' I said to Gee, 'he's nothing to do with this.'

I was happy to take the blame for the situation. It was still just possible that both of us would escape Karl's scheming. If there had to be a fall guy, then I could take the shit, resign and at least one of us would be in work while I looked for somewhere new. It was time for a change after all.

Neil dropped the paper back onto Gee's desk.

I spoke to try and remedy the worsening situation. 'If my behaviour has bought Allsop and Gee into disrepute than I apologise Mr Gee. It was never my intention. However, I would point out that during our absence we have been working on the Stone Project.' I unzipped my portfolio and took out the first sheaf of designs that led up to the breakthrough of Fallingwater Two, but left the plans for the finished building in my portfolio. I dropped the plans on his desk. 'This is what we have been working on.'

'The dirt cannot just be swept under the carpet because you have some pretty pictures to show me, Mr Armstrong,' Gee said, looking at the papers on his desk. 'If Janice were here I'd have you apologise to her now for the way you've treated her. But I think that would embarrass her. I trust that you will do the gentlemanly thing when you see her next and apologise for your shoddy behaviour.' I nodded. 'She's not in this morning as Mr Parker has had to send her on an errand.'

Karl really was ahead of the game; weave the story and send all those who could contradict it away. However, it looked as if I had contained the fallout from Karl's bomb once again, but Gee continued.

'Mr Rogers, what are your plans for the future?'

'I shall move back with Karen this evening. We've decided to give it a second go.'

I turned to Neil. He was staring straight ahead. I knew instantly that this was no joke, that Neil was leaving. But why?

'Good. Maybe we can get some semblance of order back here. Now, I'll look over these plans with Mr Parker. Mr Rogers, please return to your desk and compose yourself. I'll call you back once Karl has cast his expert eye over your work.'

I looked again at Neil. He was trying not to cry. A big tear rolled down his cheek. He nodded to Gee and stood up. I saw his perfect blue eyes shot with blood and tears. I went to hold him and comfort him, but Gee interrupted.

'Not you,' Mr Armstrong. I haven't finished with you.'

Neil turned and left, the door clicking shut behind him. Over Gee's shoulder the rain was pouring. Grey cloud now blanketed the horizon as a thick eiderdown of condensation smothered the city beneath.

'You're suspended for two weeks from today. No pay, no perks, no nothing. I hope you use the time to consider your actions carefully, Mr Armstrong.' I was about to speak when Gee continued. 'That is all. Thank you and goodbye.' I went to collect up my plans, but Gee interrupted. 'Thank you, leave those.'

It was pointless trying to say anything. Behind him Karl lifted a hand and gave me a little wave, smug triumph wiped across his grotesque face. I left the office with the world collapsing about me. Marilyn was at her desk. She handed me an envelope that contained my suspension notice, freshly typed, the ink still wet from Gee's signature.

'What's going on?' I asked bewildered. 'Where's Neil?'

'He's gone out for a while. Go now, Wade,' Marilyn advised. 'You'll see him tonight after work. Don't hang around here, it's dangerous.'

I tucked my portfolio under my arm.

'I'm sorry. I tried to warn you about Karl,' she added as I walked away.

'I know you did. Thanks. I'm sorry.'

Numb, I entered the lift and was hurtled to the ground to be thrust into the deluge outside.

I spent a pensive day at home. I was unable to concentrate on anything. Everything reminded me of Neil. Programmes on the television reminded me of the times we had made love, his mug was still in the kitchen with the dregs of his coffee; his breakfast bowl stood in the sink, half filled with soapy water. In the bedroom his smell permeated everything. I remembered how I had longed to possess his scent, and now here it was everywhere; in the bathroom, in the wardrobes, in my bed, over my sheets and strongest on his pillow. I held the pillow against my face and inhaled. It was as sweet as ever, his musk filling my lungs. Outside the rain poured, but with his smell I felt safer. I slept for a while, curled into a ball around his pillow, clutching one of his jumpers which had lain on a chair. In the afternoon I paced, waiting for him to return. I wandered up and down wondering what had got into him, why he had been so quiet in Gee's office. I played and replayed his comments about going back to Karen in my mind. What did he mean they were going to try again? Had I misheard him? Was he just saying it to get Gee off our backs? Why would he move back in with Karen when this was his home, where he belonged?

It was dark by the time I heard his key in the door. It had rained all day and showed no sign of abating. I jumped up as I heard the door latch click. He would explain himself I knew, all would be clear and we would be safe to get on with our lives. I would get a new job and we would be back to normal. I wouldn't see him so much, sure, but it would be alright; we'd manage.

Neil stood in the living room. He was soaked, his face bedraggled with his blond hair. I could tell he was crying, the salty tears swirling with the rain on his cheeks. His broad shoulders were sodden from the storm. Water dripped from the hem of his coat into a pool on the carpet.

'Hi,' he said, not moving.

'You're going aren't you?' I knew it was true.

'Yeah.'

'Why?' I had to know. It made no sense. 'You don't have to.'

'Yes, I do. Gee's right, I need to calm down, get a grip of myself.'

'Bollocks,' I muttered, tears now streaming down my face. How could I let him go? Why didn't I fight? Had I always known that this moment would arrive?

'It's not bollocks. What we have is great, it's wonderful, but it's not right. I have a wife and responsibilities and I need to give that a try, not just throw it away when something better comes along. Do you understand?'

I didn't. I shook my head. And yet in a peculiar way I did understand. It was all too perfect, too easy, too clear. It wasn't meant; fate had bought us together to teach us something, not to give us an unlimited ticket on life's merry-go-round. I began sobbing. Neil stood awkwardly in front of me before turning into the bedroom to collect his belongings. I could hear him grabbing at things and throwing them into his holdall. I heard my soul being shredded as he did it; the fabric of my life being torn away, strip by strip. My home became just somewhere to sleep and live again. I hung on to every note he made as he packed; he even made the sound of leaving seem unbearably sweet. Upstairs I could make out the faint tune of Schubert's *Ave Maria* playing on the radio. And then he was standing in front of me, his bags in his hands, his face sodden with tears.

'It's for the best. I won't forget . . .' His voice broke off. He held out his arms to me. How could I refuse. I stood and held him and he cried like a child in my arms. Deep painful sobs shattered his lungs. He held on to me as if his life depended upon it.

'Come on. You can't go home like this.' I lifted his head and held his cheeks in my hands. Gently I wiped the tears from his face. 'There, that's better.' He was panting now with despair. I fought to keep control of myself. I picked up his bags and handed them to him. 'If you've got to go, then go. My heart is broken, please don't stay to see me cry.'

He took his bags and went to the door. He opened it. It was as if I was watching it in a film and as an audience member I heard myself wanting to shout out 'don't go' and 'stay' or 'stop him leaving you fool'. But as in a cinema, I said nothing, just watched the film reach it inevitable climax as Neil stepped outside into the rain.

'Neil,' I called after him. He stopped and turned to me, the lights from the house illuminating his face like an old master's oil painting. 'It was good wasn't it? I mean, what we had, it was something special . . .' Tears streamed down my face.

Neil smiled at me and nodded. 'The best,' he said and walked off into the night. I ran to the door, but he was already gone.

There was only the rain, the night and me. I pushed the door shut and sank to the floor. I found myself sitting in the pool of rainwater Neil had bought in. It was rainwater and his tears; and I was drowning in them.

The next days melted into one another. With no work and no Neil there was no point in getting up. I would sleep fitfully, dreaming of Neil's beautiful body, of him holding me; of his smell permeating my heart. And when I woke everything was beautiful and calm and serene until the knowledge of his loss seared through my mind like a scalpel and I felt the weight of it drag me down and rebreak my heart. The effects of this continual loss were devastating. I stopped eating and washing. I drank water and Coke. When the Coke was gone I turned to drink. That's what you did when your heart was broken, wasn't it? I emptied the drinks' cupboard, making myself ill on a concoction of gin and milk as there was no other mixer. Mostly I slept, defeated by the battle of losing Neil.

After two, three, maybe four days, there was a tap at the front door. I was laying in bed and ignored it. Insistently the knock continued. Eventually, I pulled on some sweat pants and shirt and answered it. It was Marilyn. She held a flask in her hand.

'Chicken soup?' I opened the door, sweeping a pile of mail to the side and let her in without speaking. 'Looks as if you could do with some nourishment.' I slumped on the sofa and for the first time realised that he flat was trashed. 'How are you?'

'OK.'

'You don't look it.' She was right. I hadn't shaved or washed. Drink bottles fought for space on every surface in the kitchen and living room. The carpet was stained in three places with blackcurrant cordial. Outside, the sun wasn't shining, the air wasn't fresh and I wasn't a welcoming host.

Marilyn busied herself in the kitchen, I heard pots clatter in to the sink and the sound of running water. I knew I should get up and help her, but I didn't care. I gazed outside. How colourless the view was, my glassy eyes focusing on an old crisp bag being blown intermittently by the wind until it landed in a puddle and was still.

'Drink this.' Marilyn handed me a bowl of soup and a spoon. I held them tentatively, the action of eating being unfamiliar. 'Well, it's all going on at work. It's a pity you're not there to witness it. I think you'd rather enjoy it.'

I slurped at the hot soup. It was good. I thought of Neil at work and instantly felt worse. Whatever I thought reminded me of him. This flat, my work, walking down the street all linked me with my former life and Neil.

'Neil hasn't been into work since he left to come and collect his stuff and go back to his wife. A doctor's note has arrived, something about nervous exhaustion, so Karl has been left to work on the Stone project by himself. Janice got a copy of the e-mail she is supposed to have sent you; can't think how that happened . . .'

'I can.' I pictured Marilyn dropping it on her desk with the hissed instruction to 'read this'.

'Oh good, you're listening then. Well, Janice showed it to Cheryl and you can imagine what happened. Our Cheryl is never one to hold back in coming forward and demanded to see Mr Gee to correct any illusions he may have about Janice's purity. Actually,' Marilyn said with a smile, 'she screamed and shouted so loudly that the office resembled the fall of Cuba with staff rushing to take an early lunch. More soup?'

I nodded and Marilyn refilled my bowl with a saucepan from the kitchen.

'Anyway, where was I? Oh, yes, the fall of Cuba. Well, Mr Gee has our own little Fidel Castro, Karl Parker, in charge of the investigation into who and how this e-mail was sent. It's our own Watergate. I've taken to calling it Fornigate, since it's an almighty fuck up about who's been fucking who. And, as with all corporate enterprises, you can guarantee that the truth will never out. Is that your answer machine there?'

I nodded. The light was flashing furiously. I hadn't answered it since Neil had left, unwilling to change the message which announced that 'Wade and Neil aren't in . . .'

'Mr Gee has been trying to contact you to ask you to return to work. I'm sure if you were to open some of this mail then you'd find a letter from him.'

'I can't work. I can't go back in there.'

'Karl Parker has come thoroughly unstuck with your plans. He's trying to make sense of the ideas, but twice now I've heard Mr Gee shouting at him that his designs are, how did he put it, "Not fit to wipe the shit from his arse." Karl of course, being a legend in his own wing-mirror, is falling to pieces.'

'My heart bleeds for him. Trust him to fuck up a brilliant idea.'

Marilyn continued talking, going on about Karl's attempts to get things right and the fact that Mr Stone would be visiting in two days and how important it all was, but my mind was elsewhere. How could he fuck up the plans for Fallingwater Two? There were fully realised sketches for him to copy, and then I replayed the events of that day and remembered: I had only got out the initial designs that led to the building's creation. All I had given him was a jumble of ideas without their resolution. With Karl's sponge-like brain, they would be useless. I began to laugh.

'What's funny?'

'This,' I said, leaning over Marilyn and grabbing my portfolio where I had left it. I unzipped it and sure enough, there were the designs for Fallingwater Two, together with Neil's colour sketches. 'This is what Karl needs to complete the Stone pitch. I didn't get them out in Gee's office and then I was suspended and Gee wanted me to leave, so I left.'

A smile crossed Marilyn's face. 'Oh dear, it's so cruel to laugh at other's misfortune. But in Karl's case, well, fuck him!'

My euphoria subsided when I realised that this was a hollow triumph. I had still lost Neil and would gladly trade any conquest of Karl to have Neil returned to me. A tear dropped onto the designs. The water colours melted in dots; aqua and green pools of despair.

'Come on.' Marilyn hugged me and I wept. 'I know, I know. It's not fair.'

Marilyn stayed the rest of the day. It turned out to be Saturday. It had been five days since Neil had gone. Together we tidied my flat, did a little shopping to restock the fridge and began the process of rebuilding my life. The letter from Gee revoked my suspension, restored my pay and requested that I return to work as soon as possible. I knew that it was desperation rather than goodwill that was driving him. I could have raped and murdered his wife, but with a big project in the offing he would drop charges to get me to submit anything to win the contract.

'What time is Miles Stone due in on Monday?'

'Ten o'clock,' Marilyn replied. 'Why?'

'I think I need to be there to see Karl hit his iceberg.'

I was in the office by nine thirty on Monday morning. Karl had been in at seven and was already clucking around like a chicken with its head cut off. He threw his designs at me.

'Is this what you mean? Or this? Or how about this?' He flung his plans on my desk. They were all uniformly terrible.

'Karl,' I said leaning back in my seat, 'you may have forgotten that you dropped shit on me from a great height, but I haven't. Take your designs and good luck. Miles Stone is a man of taste and I'm going to be there to watch him crucify you when you drop this crap in his lap.'

Karl rolled up the plans. 'You think you're cool, don't you? You and your little bum chum Neil. Yes, I saw you going into The Corps. If you don't back me up I'll tell the whole fucking world that you're a pair of arse bandits.'

'Be my guest. Better to be queer than a liar, a cheat, a scum bag; shall I go on?' I stood and left him fuming in front of my desk. It no longer mattered who knew about me. I had good friends who cared about me regardless. What I had found with Neil was wonderful and no one could take that beauty away.

'Morning, Wade,' a familiar voice said as I crossed by the lifts. It was Miles Stone. 'Recovered from your night out?'

I half smiled. 'Sort of. You?'

'Just recovering. That barman's been with me all this weekend. I'm one hundred per cent top and he's one hundred per cent bottom, so we're a match made in heaven. My dick's raw from shagging. You OK?'

'Nah, not really.'

'Where's that hunk of a boyfriend of yours?'

'Back with his wife.'

'Miles' face dropped. 'What? How did that happen?'

'I don't know. Work, his conscience, nerves, who knows?'

'I'm sorry. Really I am.'

'Thanks.'

'If there's anything I can do then call me.' He handed me his card.

'You could give this geek a hard time today if you feel like it.' I nodded towards Karl.

'Is that this Mr Parker that Arnold's been telling me so much about?'

'Yeah. He helped spilt us up and now is giving me hassle about going to The Corps.'

Miles Stone's face hardened. 'This I will enjoy.' He strode ahead without saying anything further.

Karl spread the plans out on the desk and began going through the designs with Miles Stone. As expected they were pretty shoddy. He had one or two interesting suggestions, all of them creamed from the designs I had left, the rest was just packaged in a new-age glass box that would land in the site, crushing everything beneath it. Having completed his speech, Arnold Gee looked nervous.

'Mmmm,' Miles began, examining the plans. 'Interesting. Well, gentlemen I think I can safely say that my six-year-old nephew could have come up with something a little more imaginative than this. In fact, maybe these plans should be submitted in crayon to fit the intellectual level they aspire to.'

'I think that's a little harsh,' Gee began.

'Harsh? Harsh!' Miles Stone exclaimed. 'I haven't even

begun yet. These plans are the sort of thing I would expect from a first-year architecture student having flicked though a book called *Build your own Bungalow.* Have I wasted all my time explaining what I want to you? Is anyone listening to me? Am I wasting my time now, sitting here while I regurgitate what it is, yet again, that I am looking for?'

'I think Mr Parker does have some other ideas for discussion . . .' Gee began. Karl stuttered a little to explain more, but Miles was having none of it.

'No! What these plans need is a good vet to quietly put them to sleep. Arnold, who is responsible for this?'

'Mr Armstrong had the initial designs for the project,' Karl began.

Miles face blackened. 'And for how long has your name been Arnold? Yes the rats always leave the sinking ship first. Well, where are these designs then?'

Karl fumbled with a sheaf of drawings and dropped them into Miles' lap. He flicked though them, pausing on one or two. 'Now this is interesting, this has possibility, what happened to them after this?'

'Mr Parker got hold of them,' I muttered.

Karl was now shaking on the spot. Gee's jaw was clenching with irritation and anger.

'I'm sorry, Miles, there have been some personal problems in the department over the last couple of weeks that have rather taken their toll on company morale. I'm sure that given time we will be able to present you with something a little more inspiring.'

'Let me give you some advice, Arnold.' Miles Stone rose from his seat, pulling on his coat. 'Personal issues are personal, that is why they are called that. Unless they bring them into the office, leave well alone. Don't question your staff's personal lives since it is very probably the essence of those lives that makes your business such a success. J Edgar Hoover dressed up in women's underwear and had rent boys suck him off; but that didn't make him any less effective as head of the FBI. If anything, it made him better. I'll speak to you later this week.'

With that he swept out. Karl turned to me, anger flaring in his eyes.

'You miserable cunt. You fucking cock-sucking poof.'

I didn't have time to respond as Miles Stone reappeared in the office doorway, magnetic with hate.

'And do me a favour please, Arnold.' He pointed a long straight arm and stark white finger at Karl. 'I never want to have that fucking talentless, piss-poor, butt-ugly, arse-licking bigot in my sight again. Is that clear?'

No one spoke. All three of us just stood there, mouths open as Miles Stone swept out. Arnold Gee sighed and dropped his Mont-Blanc pen onto his desk, the clatter as it fell ringing around the suede comfort of the room.

'Coffee for three is it now, Mr Gee?' Marilyn asked, popping her head around the doorway, eyebrows raised.

'Ooh go on, say that last bit again,' Cheryl urged as I sat at my desk that afternoon.

'He called him a "fucking talentless, piss-poor, butt-ugly, arse-licking bigot" and then left.'

She squealed. 'I think I'm going to have to write that down so I can remember it.' She grabbed a sheet of paper and scribbled the sentence down.

'That's "bigot" at the end with a B not with a P.' I corrected her spider-like scrawling.

'You sure?'

'Yeah.'

'U thought it was an animal, you know like a little pig, a "piggot".'

'No, that's a piglet.'

'Oh.' She scratched the pencil in her hair. 'What's a bigot then?'

'Someone who doesn't tolerate anybody else's ideas or life styles. They're racist, hate women, hate gays, that sort of thing.'

'Oh, well, he's right then isn't he. He is a bigot. He's always horrible about me and Jan. Anyway, bigot or not, he's got a fat arse and no one's gonna love that are they?'

'Probably not.'

'You know what, Jan and I think he was responsible for that e-mail what got you in all that trouble,' she whispered to me, looking over her shoulder.

'I'm pretty sure he did,' I agreed. 'He's fiddled with my computer too, but there's not much we can do about it.'

'Yes there bloody well is!' she exclaimed. 'I've got the computer man in today to sort out me software. Shirley in accounts gave me the number and Gee said it was OK to call him in. Apparently he's lovely, bit rough, but very good at sorting out problems. He could stop Karl pilfering. Shall I send him onto you when he's finished with Jan and me?'

I was going to say no, but something about the way her eyes sparkled when she mentioned him made me change my mind. 'OK. Send him over. Let's see what he can do.'

'Yeah!' Cheryl whooped. 'We'll show that piggot what we're made of!'

I spent the afternoon sorting through the mail that had accumulated over the last month while I hadn't been in the office. Karl and Gee had a long discussion in the afternoon and I waited to be called to give my account of things. The call never came and at six I saw them leave together. I was about to pull on my coat when I became aware that someone was standing in front of me. My first glimpse was of a hefty looking cock-packet crammed into a tight pair of jeans that stood in front of my desk. I could make out the curve of his dick upwards along the inside of his button flies. Looking up, I saw a guy standing in a white short-sleeved shirt. He was obviously a body builder. The shirt was wider than it was long, thick muscular arms fought to hang over his overdeveloped lats. His face was round and cute. Blue eyes, like Neil's only lighter, shone at me. He was roughly shaven, the light beard falling into creases as he smiled. I guessed he was about thirty and had been working out for some time. He dropped a metal tool box on the floor beside him and looked at a scribbled note.

'You Wade Armstrong?' he asked. His voice was gruff with a strong south-London accent.

'Yeah, that's right.' I sat upright, interested.

He looked at a scrap of paper again and scratched his crew-cut. '"Wade", funny name. Anyway, Wade, I'm here to look at your computer, see if I can sort out any bugs.'

'Be my guest.' I pushed my chair back and stood to allow the repairman access. He pushed by me and I watched his bubble butt as he went. This man did some serious working out. He was only about five ten but had to be solid with fifteen stones of muscle. His chest had to be over fifty inches to start with. He had a tight waist and then quads that flared out with years of pushing hundreds of pounds.

'My name's Matt, nice to meet you,' he said, offering me his hand. His grip was solid, his hands slightly calloused. 'What's the problem?'

'Someone's accessing the software, adding documents and then changing the date they were added.'

'Yeah, possible,' Matt said, his thick fingers tapping on the keys. 'It's OK. It's gone six, you don't have to stay, I can work it out myself.'

'No, I'll hang around, got nothing to do . . .' I said, pulling up a chair so that I could see Matt's fat dick outlined in his jeans.

'Fine by me,' he replied, giving me a wink, 'love a bit of company when I'm working late . . .'

Chapter Nine

For two hours Matt typed away, loading various disks into my terminal and regularly referring to two thick manuals which he took from his tool box. Sometimes he looked up to scribble notes on the paper pad by his side. He never looked at me. I sat, reading at first and regularly flicking my eyes upwards to examine the shredded definition of his body. As he leaned forward his arm would bend at the elbow and his bicep would be squeezed beneath his skin, the thick muscle fighting for space beneath the tight cuff of his short-sleeved shirt. I examined his crutch, which was thick with man-meat. His legs were award-winning solid muscle. When he stood to reach round the back of my terminal I could see that his quads were so thick he was unable to close his legs properly. His arse was a solid globe of butt meat protecting the sweet man-cunt buried within. I thought about Neil during this time, where he was, what he was doing, but he had made his own choices and now I had to make mine and go on living. Matt was the opposite of Neil – shorter, wider, with a shock of black hair over his clear white skin; pure animal passion. But he was also similar in as much as he turned me on. He had great muscle definition and took care of himself. He had an easy going attitude, light blue eyes, was overtly masculine and I was sure he was a damn good fuck. After the initial wink, he had ignored me for the two hours he had been working. I was wasting my time. Sitting opposite him with my legs open was a pretty obvious come-on that he had chosen to ignore.

Around us the office had emptied. There was only Matt and I and a security guard present now. In the background I could hear the guard scuffing his feet as he wandered around the office, pausing to nod at me. He was a tall, black guy with a goatee beard. I had seen him regularly, but never spoken to him. He had a winning, confident smile. After a while even the sound of his feet faded, leaving Matt and I alone. The lights shone brilliantly in the office whilst outside the night sky was streaked red as the sun gave its last gasp before settling below the horizon.

It was gone eight before Matt spoke.

'Done it!'

I had almost dozed off. 'Yeah?'

'Yup. You're right, This terminal has been tampered with. This print-out shows the dates and times the entry was made via terminal forty-three. Let's see.' He stood and counted the desks around the office, turning like a weather vane slowly until he came to face Karl's desk. 'That one there. That's forty-three, that's where the trouble came from.'

'Karl Parker.' It was no surprise.

'Am I right?'

'Yeah. It's who I thought it was. Been giving me trouble for some time.'

'He's the same one who intercepted the secretary's terminal too. I'll give the boss a report about it all.'

'Good. Get rid of the little fucker.'

'He work at two desks, or just one?'

'Just over there.' I pointed to Karl's terminal. 'Why?'

''Cause terminal eighteen has been doing a lot of work sifting through people's files, changing shit, all sorts.'

'Which is terminal eighteen?' I wanted to know who the other office snoop was.

Matt held out a blueprint of the office computer wiring. He began tracing the lines around the floor and I followed. He took me to Marilyn's desk. It all made perfect sense. This was how she knew what was going on. I couldn't wait to challenge her the next day and reveal that I knew the truth about her 'grapevine'.

Then Matt said, 'Not out here, not this one.'

'Not Marilyn?' I asked.

'Nah, the biggest snoop has the terminal in there.' He pointed into Gee's office.

'You sure?'

Matt tried the door. It was open and he led me in. 'Yeah, here, this terminal here. Been reading all your mail, the secretaries' mail and terminal twenty-four's mail a lot.'

'Which terminal is that?' I asked. Matt took me to the doorway and pointed towards Neil's desk and the computer which stood on it.

'So Gee's seen all the internal mail that's been between me and that desk?'

'Yup. Made copies of it too by the look of it.'

I shook my head. The floor-length window showed the city outside, carelessly flickering while the surrounding level of betrayal descended around me. So, Gee had been in on this all along. He must have read my e-mails to Neil and his to me – particularly the last one he wrote when we were in the office together. He knew about our relationship and called in Karen to split us up. That's how he did it. That's how they knew.

'You OK?' Matt asked.

'Yeah, just surrounded by shit-bags that's all.' I sighed.

'Yeah, the guy on terminal twenty-four sent you some pretty raunchy stuff.'

'You read it?'

'Yeah, couldn't help it, mate, I'm afraid. It's all held on the hard disk for three months.'

'Great.' I sighed, embarrassed.

'Still, can't blame him. You're fucking horny.'

I looked up at Matt. I could see that his thick cock was stirring into life. He winked at me again.'

'I still am,' I said, casually stroking my dick. 'I thought you weren't interested. You've ignored me for the last two hours.'

'Yeah, I thought I'd see how long you'd hang on before I tried to find out if you wanted to stay for some extra-curricular activity. But you never got up to leave.'

'I fell for that one. If you didn't have such a cute-looking dick, I'd have gone hours ago.'

Matt stroked his growing cock. 'You wanna go somewhere?'

I was about to agree and go wherever he wanted when I changed my mind. 'Nah. How about here, on this spying bastard's desk?'

Matt grinned and sat next to me. 'Sounds good. You've really got it in for him 'aven't you?' He stroked his thick tool.

I leaned over and kissed him. 'You bet.'

Matt put his strong hand between my legs and began rubbing. He didn't need to, my mind was clear except for the thought of this slab of muscle in front of me. I ground my dick into his hand and returned the favour. His tool was hard, the cock-meat vacuum-packed into his jeans. I pushed him down on to the sofa and straddled above him. Roughly I pulled open his belt and button-fly jeans, the metal studs popping as I tugged his dick free. Here was another boxer-short man; crisp white linen containing delights beneath, like tissue-covered white chocolates. Matt undid the belt on my trousers. I began to undo my tie. This wasn't love, it was lust. All I wanted was to have this stud on top of me, to worship his perfect form and to swallow his pecker. Matt undid his shirt and pulled it free. His body was square and chunky. I rubbed my hands over the mounds of his chest. His torso was waxed smooth, the nipples hard. His abs were almost painfully well formed, sharp slashes in his skin to define his six pack. I stood to pull off his jeans and boxers. His boner bobbed upwards in front of me, his white, hard, smooth stomach giving way to a burst of jet-black pubes. His cock was a good seven inches long, but this baby was thick and hard like its owner. I had never seen a dick as solid as this, purple veins pulsating into life, thicker than a fist. His bollocks were drawn tightly up to his tool, his nuts shaved, his black pubes waxed off into a crescent above his pole. Beyond this were his legs, wide layers of muscle upon muscle cascading down from his hips, building upon each other. I gripped them. Two hands wouldn't go round one leg; four hands wouldn't even begin to make a mark on holding his thighs. They were smooth to the touch, my hands sliding over them as I cupped his balls and grabbed his thick come-shooter.

'You like a bit of muscle?' Matt asked.

'I like all muscle, but particularly this one.' I dived on his cock, dropping my jaw to get its huge girth in my mouth.

'You're not so bad yourself,' Matt groaned as I licked and teased his helmet. 'You know I was going to come and see if you needed help anyway. When that secretary told me you wanted to see me, I thought it was my lucky day.' I slipped the whole of his dick down my throat. 'Whooa! Now I know it is!' he groaned. 'Where d'you learn to suck cock like this?' he asked, bucking his hips into my face.

I let his dick slip from my mouth. 'I had a great teacher.' I took him by the hand and led him behind Gee's desk. I pushed the papers to one side and sat facing him. I linked my legs around his waist and pulled him close to me.

'The whole of London can see us,' he noted.

'That a problem?' I asked.

'Nah. Let 'em watch. They'll learn a few things . . .'

He kissed me hard and his tongue drove into my mouth. I ran my fingers through the crop of his hair, pulling his head towards me. My heels dug in to his hard butt and I felt his solid dick push against my bollocks. My arms hung over his wide set shoulders and I dug my nails into his back. He groaned and we kissed some more. He inched forward and I fell backwards along Gee's desk, sending pens scattering from the upturned desk-tidy. Matt leaned on top of me. I could feel the weight of his body pressing down; his smooth skin gliding over mine as he climbed on to the desk with me. For a moment he just ground his hunk of a body on top of mine. My dick was trapped beneath his hard physique, the foreskin wrenched down by the force of his frottage. His nipples, hard as tacks, drove grooves into my chest as he pushed himself upwards. I groaned and grabbed the blocks of flesh on his chest and toyed with these delicious nipples. His eyes closed and he pushed himself against me with increased force, his face a picture of ecstasy.

I could feel his thick man-rammer between my legs, the

pre-come from both our cocks oiling our organs. Matt stopped thrusting and kissed me.

'This his pen?' I nodded

Matt picked up Gee's Mont-Blanc ink pen. He stuck it in his mouth and sucked on it while pulling my foreskin slowly back. I straddled my legs open as he bent down to my cunt. He placed the rounded tip of the chubby pen at my cunt lips and eased it in slowly. I giggled. As he did this he took the tip of my dick in his mouth and began to swirl his tongue over my glans. Pre-come seeped from my piss-slit and Matt lapped it up.

'Tasty boy-gravy. I like that.'

'Plenty more, if you hang on a bit,' I replied.

Matt took the length of my dick in his mouth. The nine inches glided down his throat effortlessly. I leaned back and sighed, pushing my pubes into his nose while he gently fingered me with Gee's pen. I put my hand behind my head and relaxed to the motion of this muscle stud sucking my member. I heard the pen drop on to the desk and then felt a finger wiggle into my hole. I writhed to let Matt know I thought it was good. Then two fingers slipped in. Still I could hear him slurping over my dick, his head gently bobbing over the shaft while his lips and tongue worked my bulbous head.

Matt sat up, his chin wet with the work. He knelt back and his thick dick stood out like a missile shell. We were perfectly silhouetted for the world outside. Far below people were making the last of their journey home but here Matt was about to drive his man-hungry rammer home.

He spat on my man-cunt and licked around my hole. I could feel his tongue lashing inside me, oiling my chute. He grabbed a condom from his trousers and tore the packet. I sat up, took it from him and then bent down to worship again the girth of his cock. I kissed his piss-slit and tasted the salty juice that was greasing his piston. I took his dick once more into my mouth to enjoy the flavour and warmth of his tool. He groaned and I slipped a finger under his nuts to feel for his hole. I found it and my finger slid in. I felt more blood surge into his cock. It was really tasty now, the head riding on the roof of my mouth, the salty pre-jizz dripping onto my gagging taste buds.

I kissed the tip of his dick and slipped on the condom, sucking it a final time to give it more lube. While I had been ready to take the humungous length of Neil's schlong, this was a fat mother-fucker and needed all the help I could get. I leaned back and Matt grabbed my legs, tilting my eager sphincter towards him. He tried to push his cock down to my hole, but it was rock hard with blood and passion. He stood on the office floor and swivelled me round so that my desperate cunt was in his line of fire. He positioned the head of his ramrod against my hole and I felt him begin to push. My man-cunt practically sucked him in it was so desperate for some hot beef inside at. Pain appeared for a split second, but quickly gave way to the presence and pleasure of seven inches of pounding hard man-rammer.

Matt fucked me hard, I rode around on Gee's desk loving every minute of feeling him inside me. At last I was alive again. I groaned and wailed as he plugged me, his nuts slapping against my arse. I didn't care about anything any more. I was Matt's to do with as he pleased.

The door clicked.

I tilted my head over the end of the desk to see who had come in. My vision was upside down, but I clearly saw the cute black security guard standing and watching.

Matt stopped pumping, but left his boner buried in me up to the hilt, a smile of delight passed across my face. 'Now just don't ask, "What are you guys doing?"' Matt said very casually,. ''Cause this ain't a trick question.'

'I can see what you doing,' the security guard said, his hand running down to his crutch. 'What I want to know, is can I join in?'

I let out a howl of laughter and Matt groaned in ecstasy as my sphincter tightened around his thumping dick. 'Sure! Come on in!' I bawled. A fuck-fest was just what I needed.

I clambered round onto my knees, keeping Matt's thick tool embedded in my arse. When I was on all fours on Gee's desk,

I turned to take another look at the security guard who had already taken his shirt off and was readying himself for a man-fuck. He was a good six feet tall with beautiful ebony skin. Age? About thirty. He had a small goatee beard and short wiry hair. I watched him kick off his shoes and pull his trousers down. He wore no underpants and a long banana, semi-erect, cock sprang out in front of him. His balls were big and low slung, a crest of black pubes topping off his wonderful organ. He walked slowly to the desk, slowly rubbing the end of his circumcised dick. He spat on his fingers and ran them around his pecker-head. Matt was gently starting to pump my arse again. I gave the guard a lascivious look and reached a hand out for his cock. It was warm in my palm when I slid that curved black boner into my mouth and began sucking. As the long curved dick slid down my throat I got a whiff of his masculinity as his wiry pubes fuzzed against my face.

We found a rhythm pretty quickly, with Matt working my arse over with his thick schlong and the guard bucking to fill my throat with his fat black cock. I slurped and salivated over both bits of meat, eager that I should be filled with their jizz. The guard leaned over me and I heard him kissing Matt. Then he slipped his cock from my mouth and climbed onto the desk, straddling me. Still he was kissing Matt, as eager for a taste of this muscle man as I was. I flipped over and the guard squatted on my face, his tart man-cunt spread for my eager lips. I worked on his hole and it was a delight to lick and suck out his juice while I could still feel Matt inside me, pumping my willing butt lips. The guard ground his cunt into my face. I fought for air as the aroma swamped me and I burrowed deeper into him. Matt's fucking was exquisite, every thrust of his thick ramrod powering into me, sending me riding across the desk while he snogged the guard. I felt a hand pulling on my dick, but whose it was I didn't know. It yanked my foreskin back and then I felt a hot mouth enclose it. From the angle of the guard's arse, he was now going down on me, sucking, his rough goatee chaffing my stomach while his fabulous mouth worked around my pulsating cock-head.

Still Matt fucked me. His slow strong, controlled rhythm was orgasmic, pumping my arse while my cock was thrust down the throat of this fit guard. Then the guard eased off my dick and turned around, still sitting on my chest. I got a better look at him this time. He had great definition in his pecs, hard nipples, that he now stroked for my enjoyment. Over his shoulder I could see Matt angling his dick round in my cunt, sending coils of delirium through my body. The guard bent down and kissed me, groaning with delight as Matt slid a finger into his wet arsehole. I put my arms around him and held his hot body tight to mine. It was good that my dick was free for a while as the sensations running through my body were about to explode.

Matt began to fuck faster and harder, each thrust pushing into my colon, fiercely and with more determination than before. The guard sensed the change of rhythm. He clambered from my chest and scooted around behind Matt.

'Ok, muscle boy, you first.' I watched the guard bend down behind Matt and begin tonguing his arse. 'You got fucking strong cheeks!' the guard said, as he prised them apart to slip in a finger to taste Matt's sauce. Matt was beyond speaking. I lay back and watched the orgasm uncoil in his face. He was fucking me harder than ever. The desk utensils were sent flying to the floor, papers scattered and the computer on the desk bounced in time to the pounding of my arse as Matt screamed out his orgasm, thrusting into me, his bollocks slapping against my butt cheeks, my legs splayed to their maximum to allow his fat man-tool entry to my hole. As he came, he pulled his dick out of my cunt, pulled off the rubber and began spraying his jizz over me. I was happy to receive it, the white ribbons of come flying across my chest, streaking my face. Behind him the guard continued to work on his arse, obviously enjoying the tasty juice he had found. Matt's ejaculations waned. He collapsed on top of me, his hot muscular body pinning me beneath. I hooked my legs round him to hold him tight, his come bonding us together. My hands gripped his vast biceps and pulled his face to me for a final kiss.

Our kiss was interrupted by the arrival of the guard's fat curved dick which was slapped between us. Together we licked it, slurped on it and teased it with our teeth. Matt and I crouched on the desk like hungry lap dogs to service this meat. Matt took the shaft down his throat first while I bent underneath to suck each of the fat black balls in my mouth. The scent was overpowering and I prised a finger into his hole. The guard groaned. I felt his balls tighten towards his sensational shaft and then heard Matt gag as his mouth filled with come. He gasped , jizz streaming from his chin. Unwilling to waste a drop, I dived in and caught the next flow of his boy-gravy as it shot out and hit the back of my mouth. But Matt was unwilling to let me have it all. I felt his salty lips fighting with me to suck the contents of the guard's sac. Together we slavered over the pumping curved boner in front of us, our faces grinding together, smeared with man-juice, sharing the salty jizz between us. The guard massaged the final drops from his cock, holding our heads in each hand to guide us towards his come. I felt spent, but my dick was still as solid as a rock.

'And now, the best for last,' Matt said, a glint in his eye.

'Sure thing,' the guard added.

Matt grabbed one of my legs and swung me round. My head fell over the edge of the desk. Through Gee's floor-length window I could see the whole of London spread out before me. Two fingers were plunged into my arse and I gasped. Then a mouth worked round the tip of my dick as the two guys began working me over. My legs were splayed to give them room to get more fingers inside me. Someone pulled on my balls, yanking them down. My cock hardened further. Lips and mouths fought over my engorged shaft while fingers fucked into my hole. My legs were forced apart further and my cock hardened some more. Outside the city was lit like a model town. In the night sky a sprinkling of stars were just beginning to glimmer. Four fingers were now in my man-cunt and it felt as if Neil were in me all over again. I closed my eyes and gave myself over to the sensation of these fit men fucking me. I came in great arcs, the guys fighting to taste my come like dolphins jumping for fish. My jizz flew from me as their hot tongues worked my piss-slit.

Eventually my juice subsided and I felt the fingers eased from my hole. Exhausted, we lay naked together on the floor, our dicks subsiding, collapsing onto bodies smeared with each other's love.

'Fuck me!' I gasped, remembering what it was we had done. We had been fucking for almost two hours.

'I think I just did,' Matt laughed. 'And it was the best; a tight hole and a great rhythm.'

'Why didn't you call me earlier?' the guard asked. 'There's nothing better than a midnight snack.'

He was the first to leave. After we had dressed I sat with Matt in Gee's office.

'That guy's fucked you over, ain't he?' he asked.

'Yup. Royally.'

'Well, let's see what Muscle-Matt's got that can make it better. What you want is a nice virus to upset things a little.' He flicked open his tool box and rifled through some disks. 'This is the one. Follow me!'

He led me back over to Karl's terminal and flicked it on.

'What's it going to do?'

'This is a simple programme I found on a job I was doing a few months ago. Been desperate to give it a whirl somewhere. What it does is infiltrate any word-processing programme and slips in a few extra words and phrases.'

'Such as?' I asked, a smile crossing my face.

'The old dear I rescued it from kept getting "suck my tits you fat mother fucker" in her letters. And she worked for Age Concern, so you can imagine the reaction from her clients.'

I howled with laughter as Matt loaded the virus onto Karl's terminal. 'Now I'll leave it a few days before it becomes active to cover my tracks. Three days should do it.'

'Will it spread?'

'Well it can do, but at the moment it will be specific to documents created on this terminal.'

'Perfect. Thanks. I only wish you could be here to see the results.'

'Oh, I expect I will,' Matt said, dropping the disk back in his box.

'How?' I asked.

'Well, who do you think they'll call out to repair it?'

I got home late feeling elated from my three-way fuck and from the knowledge that Matt had sabotaged Karl's terminal. I reviewed the situation. Gee had obviously known about my relationship with Neil and had called in his wife to break us up. Karl was nothing more than his gofer. Marilyn had been right when she said they were a team and I shouldn't cross either of them. The meeting with Miles Stone had been a disaster for Allsop and Gee and I was sure that Gee would want to talk to me soon about revising Karl's useless plans in order to persuade Miles Stone to place the order with the company. This I wasn't going to do. I knew enough that once my plans had been accepted I would be out of a job. The only point which still confused me was Neil. This confusion was increased when I listened to my answer machine. There was a message from him:

'Hello, Wade, are you there? Pick up the phone, please? Hello? Hello?'

He had called while I was being fucked to kingdom come by Matt and the guard.

'I guess you're not there. Look I need to speak to you. I want to explain. I'm staying with Marilyn, you know the number. Call me, please. Take care, mate. I love you.'

My heart told me to phone him and my mind told me to ignore him. My mind won. I had been deceived and let down at every turn and I wasn't ready to forgive – or trust – anyone for some time.

The phone rang several times that evening – each time I screened the call and each time it was Neil pleading to speak to me. I sat, curled up on the chair listening to him wail down the phone that he was sorry and had made a mistake. I was immovable, cold to his pleading. I slept fitfully on the arm chair, my mind a whirl of plans and ideas for revenge.

It was about three in the morning when I was awakened by the sound of scratching on the front door. The television was still on, the snow from the screen bathing the room in an eerie half-light. I switched it off and listened. The scratching continued, followed by a gentle knocking at the door. I tiptoed over and listened again,. I could hear a faint whimper followed by a deep soothing voice.

'Who is it?' I demanded.

'It's me. Open up.' It was Neil.

'What the fuck do you want?'

'Just to talk. Look, Sport, open the door. We're fucking freezing out here.

'We?'

'Yeah, I've bought someone for you to meet.'

I sighed, hooked up the safety chain and opened the door ajar. What good was it trying to send him away? After the thirty-two phone calls he had made that evening, he was going nowhere.

'Hello.' Neil stood clutching a small collie puppy in his arms. 'This is Spike.'

'What the fuck is that?' I asked.

'It's a puppy.'

'I can see it's a fucking puppy. The question is, what are you doing with it?'

'Can we come in? Spike's cold. Treat me like shit, but have some thought for the dog.'

'Jesus! You try every trick in the book.' I unhooked the door and let them both in.

'Thanks,' Neil said, 'and Spike says thanks too.'

'Right, now you're in say what you have to say and then go. It's late and I expect I'm going to have to be crawling up Gee's butt tomorrow morning with a Davy lamp strapped to my head in a vain attempt to save my job. So, what do you want?'

'We wanted to say sorry.' Neil said, waving the dog's paw at me.

'We? We? What is all this fucking "we" business. What has the dog done? What have you brought a dog with you for anyway?'

'It's for you.' He thrust the animal at me. It was like a small black and white powder puff, its big brown eyes gazing at me longingly. The dog gave a little yap and tried to lick my face. 'I thought we could have a dog.'

'Again more "we" business. There is no "we" since you dropped me without any explanation and went back to your wife.' I turned my back on him, angry at the emotions of forgiveness that were surging through me. There was nothing I would have liked more than to take him in my arms and hold him. But I could no longer trust that he would be there for me.

'But there could be a "we"; there could even be an "us"; you me and Spike. Think of the fun we could have.'

'Neil,' I explained, 'a dog is for life, not just for manipulating someone so you can fuck 'em up the arse again! Take it back to the shop and get something for yourself that's a bit more suitable; like a rat.'

Neil sat and hung his head. I felt mean. The dog yapped with glee.

'OK. I asked for that. Look, I didn't buy the dog. It's Marilyn's sister's and Marilyn's just got it for tonight. I thought it would help to get us in—'

'Which it bloody well did.'

'Yes.' Even now Neil's charm was irresistible. 'I just wanted to tell you face to face that I'm sorry about walking out on you. I was wrong. I didn't know what I was doing. Gee had me in his office and showed me some e-mails from you which showed you arranging to go on blind dates with different guys. He didn't say anything about us. I didn't think he knew about our relationship and thought maybe you were seeing other people. He said it bought the company into disrepute and that something would have to be done about it.'

'After what I'd said you meant to me?' I was aghast at Gee's deception.

'I know now that they're not true, that he set me up. I'm sorry. There was so much unresolved about my situation. I'd tried to explain it to you and couldn't. I have a wife and a life and I'm not sure I'm ready for the change. I needed to think, to talk it over with someone.' He stopped speaking and began stroking the dog. The silence was deafening.

'And?' I asked.

'And now I've thought. I love you. It's as plain and simple as that. I love you and no one else. I've told Karen everything.'

'Everything?' I felt embarrassment creeping up in me.

'Yup, everything; you, the lift, how we make love in here; going to the club and fucking you against the wall; fucking in the washroom.'

'OK, OK, you've told her everything. I think you could've spared her the gruesome details of The Corps.'

'Well, I did actually. That would be pushing it a bit too far.' He smirked at me and I couldn't help but smile in return. 'But I've told her about you, about how I feel for you, about what a wonderful lover you are.'

'Oh God! She's gonna hate me.'

'No, no.' Neil held my hand. I squeezed it. 'She said that if you were any other woman she would fight for me; but if I'm gay then all she can do is gracefully concede.'

I held his hand in silence for some moments.

'Does this mean I'm forgiven?' Neil asked.

'Oh fuck! Of course it does. I don't know why I even bothered to fall out with you; you're impossible to hate for more than five minutes.'

'Then kiss Spike and we're all made up.' I kissed the head of the dog and it licked my face. It was disgusting.

'I'm more of a cat man myself. Can we get a cat instead?'

'OK.' Neil laughed and pulled me next to him on the sofa. I snuggled up to him.

'And now it's my turn to confess.' I took a deep breath. 'I got fucked by the computer repairman on Gee's desk this evening.'

'I forgive you. It's not as if we were still going out.' Neil hugged me. 'Just don't do it again.'

'And I had sex with a security guard on Gee's desk.'

'Fucking hell! You don't hang about do you?'

'It meant nothing. I was angry and they were there, and cute, and available.'

'Alright, alright. Is that all? You didn't get to shag anyone in Sainsbury's or on the bus home?'

'No.'

'OK. I forgive you.'

'Thanks. Now kiss the dog.'

'Why?'

'Hey, I had to kiss the fucking dog when you were forgiven!'

Neil took Spike's head in his hands and gave it a big kiss. The dog jumped and yapped with delight.

'Trust you to bring a fucking dog . . .'

'Can I spend the night?' How could I resist? I nodded agreement. 'I'll be back in a minute.'

'Where are you going?'

'Marilyn's in her car out the front. My stuff's in it and I can give her Spike back. She's worried you'd do something to it in a rage and she'd have to explain it all to her sister. Hey, you haven't got a black and white fluffy rag so I could pretend it's dead, have you?'

'No I haven't. Take the dog back, get your stuff and come to bed. We've got some catching up to do.'

I fucked Neil hard. He had always played the dominant role in our relationship, but the past week had taught me something about myself and that night I was in charge. Neil crouched on all fours while I licked at his cunt. I welcomed the return of his tasty hole as I worked around it with my tongue. With liberal amounts of lube I plunged three fingers into him. He groaned with delight and opened his legs to give me space. With my cock-head hard and greased I forced my way in to him and began ramming my nine inches home. He yelped more than Spike to begin with, but quickly settled into a rhythm as I pounded his arse. With my hands gripping his haunches I shoved my load home again and again. Underneath I could feel that twelve inches of thick salami being beaten by Neil's eager hand.

Before I came I flipped him over and gazed at his fantastic form. His abs were as tight as ever, his chest rose with deep breaths, the hair sheer against his skin. Laying between his legs I sucked on his nipples, pulling them with my front teeth while he groaned in pleasure. I gripped his thick tool and tasted again that sweet pre-come on the tip. With his head on a pillow, Neil watched as I worked my tongue and lips over his pulsating mushroom head. I took all his dick down in one go.

'Hey, take care!' he groaned as my nose bumped into his pubes. His man-rammer was as great as ever. I disengaged and crashed onto him for a kiss. We wrestled for supremacy, rolling over the bed while the neighbours upstairs banged on the floor for us to be quiet. But tonight was not their lucky night. Whether Neil was being kind I don't know, but I ended up winning, pinning his arms beneath him as my tongue gouged out his mouth.

From the wardrobe I grabbed my old vibrator. It was eight inches long, black with a ferocious motor inside it. I had bought it whilst still a student to calm my pent-up lust. I tried the batteries and the vibrator buzzed into life. Neil began to laugh, but as I slipped it into his arse he began to appreciate just what it could do. He writhed and wriggled his way down onto it, taking in all eight inches, his sphincter threatening to swallow it whole. I fucked him with it and worked the tip of his greasy cock with my mouth.

He came with yards of thick white jism. My mouth licked and swallowed as his organ pumped out yet more elixir. It must have been days since he had come, for the juice kept flying out of him while Neil yelled in delight at the supremacy of this orgasm. Every finger, every toe, every muscle was driven almost to insanity by the ecstasy. I finished by straddling his chest and pumping my cream out onto his face. Hungrily his hands fought to bring my jack sauce to his eager mouth.

We lay together afterwards, exhausted as a new day dawned. It was gone six and soon we would both have to be in work. However, there was a lot that Neil needed to know before we both stepped back into Allsop and Gee to wreak our revenge and I set about filling him in on what I had found out.

Chapter 10

I was in work by eight and even although I should have been exhausted from the previous night, I had never felt so alive. I had told Neil about Gee's scheming and manipulation. He was speechless. And yet, as we reviewed the events of the past two months, it all made complete sense. Karl was nothing more than Gee's rent boy, finding out information and then reporting back. On the other hand, Gee was the real power in the office, reading and reviewing all the internal mail and memos stored on the computer's hard disk. I was pretty sure that the phone conversations were also tapped. I sat at my desk and planned our line of attack. We had three days before the bug in Karl's computer would become active; three days to bring Arnold Gee to his knees.

I had been at my desk for only a few minutes when I saw Cheryl hurtling towards me like a Transit van racing to beat the traffic lights. She slammed into the front of my desk.

'Wade!'

'Hello, Cheryl.'

'You're back! How are you?' She leaned over my desk and gave me a big kiss on the lips. I was slightly taken aback.

'I'm fine,' I stuttered. 'How are you?'

'All the better for seeing you, big boy!' she gushed. 'Janice'll be so happy to see you back here again. We didn't know if you was coming back or not. Janice has been really upset. Look.' She pointed to her friend who was sitting at her desk and acting as if she was trying to dig a small hole in the surface of her worktop with the tip of a biro. 'Notice anything different?'

I studied Janice hard. To be honest, it was the first time I had ever done so. She was a nice girl, but so painfully shy around me that whenever I was present I usually only saw the crown of her head whilst she looked at her feet. 'Er, no, can't say that I do. Give me a clue.'

'Face, face,' Cheryl urged. 'Look at the face.'

I looked at Janice's face, what I could see of it. It was obvious that Cheryl was here with a mission and that Janice was painfully conscious of it. Then I spotted it. 'Is she wearing glasses?'

Cheryl jumped of the desk like a party-popper and clapped her hands. 'Yes! You win lots of points! And you know what points make.'

'No . . .'

'Points make prizes! And your prize is Janice!'

My heart sank. I had enough on my mind without this. 'Oh, leave her alone, Cheryl, stop matchmaking.'

'I'm not, I'm not,' she protested. 'Just be nice to her, Wade, that's all.'

She turned and drove away at an alarming speed, slaloming her way round the other work stations in the office. I watched her arrive at Janice, clap her hands again and begin to whisper instructions. I could feel the heat from Janice's embarrassment twenty feet away. Then Janice stood and began the long walk to my desk. I dropped my head and waited for her arrival.

I waited and waited and still nothing. I half looked up to sneak a look at her. She was nowhere in sight. And then, from the side of me, she spoke.

'Nice to have you back, Wade.' I turned, startled.

'Hello, Janice.'

Her head ducked towards me, her lips pursed as she planted a kiss on my face. Unfortunately at the speed she was travelling she missed my lips and caught me in the eye. I tried to hold her to realign her for a second approach, but she was already pulling away. I managed a rather lacklustre squeeze of her elbows as she stood up again. 'Hello, Janice. It's nice to see you again.'

'Is it?' she asked, unsure.

'Of course it is. I wouldn't say I've missed being in the office, but I've missed having you and Cheryl around.'

'And Neil,' she added.

'Yes,' I agreed. 'And Neil.' She was nearer the truth than she knew. She stood looking at me awkwardly. 'How's it been whilst I've been away?'

'Oh, fine, fine . . .' She twisted her fingers together.

'Your glasses look very nice,' I offered.

'Do you think so?' Janice gushed. The next six sentences rushed out as a prerehearsed line: 'Me eyes are so bad I can't see a thing without them on and if I don't wear them I go cross-eyed if I'm not careful 'cause my contacts were no good which is why we had that trouble in the bar and I hope that we can maybe possibly go out again sometime when I won't wimp out do you think?'

'Yes, whatever.' There was no other response. I was rewarded with a big smile and Janice left me to report back to Cheryl over at mission control.

The lift pinged and Neil stepped out. He was taller than I remembered, dressed in his long grey Paul Smith overcoat, his shoulders were broader, his face more devastatingly handsome and his eyes bluer than a Caribbean summer sky. However, it was time to put the first part of our plan into action. I glowered at him. He stared back menacingly and walked to his desk. I returned to my work. The reaction was noted by Cheryl and Janice. For a second their gossip ceased, they looked at each other and then slunk back to their desks. I knew that the rumour would spread; Neil and I were not on speaking terms.

Mid-morning and Marilyn paid me a visit.

'Nice to have you back, Wade. Mr Gee would like to speak with you at eleven about the Hammersmith project. I do believe that Mr Rogers will be present at the meeting,' she paused for effect, 'and I do hope that this will not be a problem?'

'Why should it be?' I couldn't conceal a smirk.

'Because I hear from one of the many vines which constitute my grapevine that you two are not on speaking terms.'

'We're not.'

'Fine, just as long as I know. Peculiar though . . .' She made to leave.

'Why peculiar?'

'Oh, it's just that I drove Neil to your flat last night with Spike yapping all the way and threatening to piss on the seats of my new Nissan Micra, and he ended up spending the night with you. And what's more,' she swept her forefinger along the edge of my desk for dust, 'you both have the sort of glow on your face this morning that I had for most of the 70s – that just fresh-fucked feeling that you only get from a good dose of cock!'

'Don't say anything, please,' I begged.

'My lips are sealed.' She glided away.

At eleven I found myself in Gee's office sitting next to Neil. My heart was pounding. Would we be able to pull it off? Our plan depended upon Gee thinking that we weren't speaking to each other. If he thought we were in cahoots then it would all fall apart.

'Gentlemen,' Gee began. This time his calculation seemed to be obvious. Had I been so blind before to his skill of playing us off against each other to his own advantage? 'Miles Stone has agreed to give us an extension on the deadline for the Hammersmith site. We need a fresh approach and we don't have very long.'

'Who exactly is working on this project? Neil asked.

'The team has not changed.' Gee knew, as I did, that Neil and I were the only two staff members sufficiently briefed and talented enough to pull in the commission. What Gee didn't know was just how well we knew Miles Stone.

'But I though that Mr Stone had requested that Mr Parker not work on the project.' I addressed the question to Karl, who sneered in return from behind the security of Gee's desk.

'You are wrong, Mr Armstrong,' Gee countered, his temper brewing just beneath the surface. 'Miles Stone didn't want to see Mr Parker again; his involvement has not been questioned. Besides, Mr Parker has just been promoted to Head of Development. You will now report to him.'

This took my breath away. Neil sensed my alarm and interrupted. 'Congratulations, Karl, and about time too!' They shook hands. I remained firmly seated. 'Arnold,' Neil continued, easing his charm into full gear, 'for personal reasons I would prefer not to work with Wade. I don't want to bore you with it all, but it would be very difficult for me personally, especially as things are beginning to go so well with my wife . . .'

'No need to explain, Neil, I understand.' Gee patted Neil on the back. 'However, Miles Stone has asked specifically for Mr Armstrong's input and I'm afraid that for the sake of appearances he will have to be involved.'

Neil slammed his fist down on Gee's desk. We all jumped.

'But once the project is competed, Mr Armstrong will be leaving us.'

I was taken aback. The plan was going very well up to this point, but losing my job hadn't been a part of the bargain.

'What about my contract?' I blurted out.

'Null and void. Don't fuck members of staff. And before you fuck up this project, I suggest you think about your references. You work well on this and I'll give you a decent reference and you may just be able to get another job and take your randy little cock somewhere else.'

I got up and left the office, white-faced. As I went I heard Neil whisper, 'Bye-bye, you creep . . .'

I met Neil that afternoon at the site in Hammersmith to review the location. I was still reeling from Gee's declaration. The site was about two acres in size and still retained the ruins of a Victorian furniture warehouse. The warehouse had been a listed building but had fallen in to such a bad state of repair the preservation order had been revoked. Around one side of the land ran a stream, hidden from view by tall reeds and dense grass, not to mention several shopping carts, old bikes and various angled shards of scrap metal. The land was marked out by the road on three sides and the Piccadilly tube line on the fourth. Once inside the perimeter wall it was like being in Dresden. The grounds were spattered with rubble, the warehouse a formidable black-windowed monolith. In the distance the traffic thundered by, the monotony of the sound broken only by the diddly-dee of a passing tube train. I twitched with nerves and walked on ahead. Neil strode out to catch me up.

'Calm down. Look, it was going to happen. We just have to step up our tactics that's all. We've got the plans for Fallingwater Two at home. Gee doesn't know anything about them. If Miles Stone chooses that then we can take our business anywhere we want and fuck Gee and Parker; we'll both leave.'

'I suppose so. I'm worried.'

Neil gave me a hug and kissed me. For a moment I felt a little more secure. 'Let's take a look inside and see what we can salvage.'

The blue wooden door to the warehouse lay open, the top hinge rusted away. Inside was a mess. We examined the derelict ground floor. Much of the flooring was an elaborate mosaic of different coloured and styled bricks. It was worth incorporating. It could be lifted, new foundations laid and then replaced. The same was true of a large tiled mural at the south end which declared, 'Croft's Original Linctus – The original pick-me-up'. Many of the white backing tiles were chipped, but the elegant writing made in terracotta contoured tiling was in perfect order. That too would stay.

After taking some photographs, we ascended the central wrought-iron staircase to the upper floor. The railings were a fine example of the early industrial revolution and although the staircase had been replaced, probably around the turn of the century, elements of it could be incorporated into our design.

At the top of the staircase I stopped. I could hear grunting and voices. Neil paused too. He looked at me, brow furrowed and cautiously we tiptoed on. Much of the top floor had been partitioned with plasterboard and used for storage. We snaked our way round the rooms following the guttural groans. The closer we got, the more it sounded like fucking. Neil stopped in front of me and peered around into one of the rooms. His head whipped back and he nodded for me to look.

Two guys were standing in the middle of the room kissing. Their jeans were round their ankles and their boners pressed together. I was going to creep away but something made me want to stay and watch. Neil looked at me; he felt the same. We crouched and looked around the partition at the two hungry lovers. One guy was about six feet with short dark brown hair, gelled into a side parting. He had deep brown chocolate-button eyes. His muscle definition was clear, although his body wasn't too pumped. He couldn't be more than about twenty. His skin was smooth and tanned, a white tan line from bikini briefs wrapping around his waist. I caught a glimpse of his stiff dick, bolt upright, rigid with boy-gravy. He had a classical face, strong jawline and straight nose. He resembled a Greek statue brought to life. His dick was about seven inches long, but what it lacked in size it made up for in sheer power. The thrill from his fuck-stick gave him the stamina of a young stallion on his first day out of the ranch.

His partner was a younger guy, probably about eighteen. He was a typical cute boy-next-door; white-blond hair, tanned body, and a smaller frame. He was about five ten with no body fat and smooth skin. He had a tattoo of a large yellow sun at the top of his arm that nestled into his bicep. He turned and pressed his arse against the other guy's cock. I saw his full fat dick spring tightly upwards to his chest. He had a great pair of balls, large and low slung. The taller guy brought his hands round and began playing with the cute one's nipples, twisting them so that the younger guy would grind his butt into the other's thick ramrod. Framed by the broken industrial windows behind them and the trash around their feet, they looked utterly beautiful.

'Jesus!' Neil muttered, opening his legs to let his cock swell. 'Look at that. It's fucking gorgeous!'

'Telling me!'

Mesmerised, we continued to watch. The taller guy now pumped gently on the cute guy's dick. It sure was fat and he milked the pre-come from it slowly, taking the delicious jizz from the tip and sucking it from his fingers. Both had their eyes closed, savouring the moment.

'You got a condom?' I asked.

Neil nodded. 'Want to join in?'

'I've fucking got to do something. I've got a tool the size of a donkey's hard-on between my legs and it isn't going to wait until we get home. I want it now!'

We stood up and Neil motioned me to take off my clothes. I needed no second asking and soundlessly stripped away my city veneer to show the powerhouse of manhood beneath. Neil did the same. Over his shoulder I saw the two young guys still exploring each other's bodies. In front of me stood the solid, hairy frame of Neil, his twelve-inch dick rigid with desire. He took my hand and together we walked around the corner to where the young guys were making out.

For a while they didn't see us, they were so engrossed in each other. The cute younger one turned and began sucking eagerly on the taller one's hard cock. His head bobbed in and out, keen to get the task of the pecker inside him. He crouched, fingering the taller guy's hole, lapping up the tasty jizz. It was the taller guy who noticed us first. He opened his eyes and was taken aback to see two mid-twenties hunks, naked and hard, watching their action. His brown eyes widened as he smiled at us. He tapped his friend on the shoulder and he looked up then around. His blond fringe was damp from perspiration earned from sucking cock. He smiled too.

Neil took me by the hand and led me across the floor to stand in front of them; four naked, well-hung hard studs greeting each other, their weapons primed for action.

Neil said our names and I smiled at them. The taller one with the classic handsome face replied, 'I'm Tom and this is Dan.' I nodded a hello. Neil reached out and took Tom's shaft in his hand. Tom closed his eyes and sighed. I felt Dan reaching for my tool, his smooth palm gripping my thick shaft and milking it slowly. I looked into his blue eyes and thought he could be Neil's baby brother. I pulled him to me, bent my head down and kissed him. His taste was so sweet; a young man's mouth peppered with the salt from Tom's jizz. I ran my fingers through his blond hair and felt him crumple beneath me. He fought back, his tongue invading my mouth with passion. I felt him hook a leg around me and grind his thick tool and soft blond pubes into my leg. One hand pulled at the muscles on my back while the other gripped the flesh of my buttocks and searched out my hungry hole. He may look like a boy, but his desires were definitely manly.

I looked at Neil next to me. He had already gone down on Tom, desperate for a taste of this boy-gravy. Hungrily he was working over the young stud's tool. Dan fell to his knees too, eager to try out his cock-sucking techniques on a thicker, longer piece of meat. He had no worries. His hot mouth worked around my tip, lapping up the squirts from my piss-slit, finding my hole with his fingers and then fucking me up to the knuckles with his hand. Tom thrust his hips into Neil's face. I heard him gag, but he wouldn't relinquish the fight to drain his man-rammer of its jack sauce. Tom looked at me, he had an arrogant, cocky look as he sensed his victory. This arrogance turned me on even more; he was a hard man in more ways than one. I pulled his head to me and rammed my tongue into his mouth. He fought back and our mouths battled for conquest of each other.

I felt Dan's mouth slip from my cock, but I was busy kissing Tom. Then I felt my arse cheeks parted and the same hot mouth probe my hole. Tingles filled my spine, I weakened and, sensing victory, Tom pushed my head backwards and thrust his tongue in further. I crouched slightly, happy to relinquish power to Tom as well as open up my cunt for Dan to fill with his tongue. I held my position for a moment, tongued by these two Adonises for a while at each end. I felt an orgasm bursting to break through, but held back from touching my dick so that the encounter would last.

It was Neil who broke the spell, spitting Tom's dick from his mouth and plunging a finger deep into Tom's arse. Tom pulled away from our kiss and gasped in ecstasy. Neil stood up, gripped Tom by the hair and pushed his head down to his throbbing dick. I saw Tom gaze at Neil's huge tool. He took the head into his mouth and oiled it with his tongue. Saliva dripped from his mouth at the thought of the pleasures to come. Slowly he worked his mouth down Neil's shaft, taking the majority of it down his throat. Only I could take it all. On all fours he had his white rump shoved into the air. It was an opportunity too good to miss. I dropped onto my knees, spread his hard white butt and looked at the caramel hole inside, his man-cunt tightly closed. I sucked on a finger and pushed it in. I felt Tom pushing backwards onto me, eager for the intrusion. I bent down and breathed in his musk. His arsehole was hairless, the skin smooth as ice. I curled my tongue onto his sphincter and my fingers felt goose bumps come up on Tom's arse. I probed into his hole, licking and slurping out all the goodness, whilst behind me Dan had his tongue in me up to the root. We worked on each other; Tom on Neil's fat oozing dick, me on Tom's tight boy-cunt and Dan on my willing hole.

Tom broke off first. He jumped to his feet, his face wet from Neil's pumping man-rammer, his cheeks greased with my spit. 'Wait.' He tiptoed away. Neil looked at me and then at his rigid boner. I didn't need a second invitation. I crawled forward, Dan following behind, still working his lips over my cunt. I plunged down on Neil's thick tool. It tasted as delicious as ever, lubricated by his ample pre-come and by Tom's eager mouth. Behind me I felt Dan slip from my arse and lay on his back below me. With his hands on my arse, he pulled my cock into his face. I pushed down, feeling my tool slide into Dan's anxious mouth. He tugged on my arse hard to get the whole length of my man-meat in him until my bollocks were draped on his chin and my pubes bashed into his nose. As he did this, my lips reached the base of Neil's hot dick. There was no one who could suck cock as well as I could, all twelve inches lodged in my throat, my fingers toying with his hot cunt. We held it there for a moment, my hips fucking Dan's face as I worked over Neil's steaming meat.

Behind us I heard the sound of a metal cylinder being rolled into the room. Dan wriggled from under my dick and Neil's hot tool slipped from my mouth. Tom had brought in a large red gas cylinder. I looked at it for a moment, unsure of what to do. But Dan recognised its value. He draped himself over it, his arse thrust up into the air, his cunt begging for attention. Neil kissed me and then turned to Dan. He bent down and spat into his hole, oiling it with his lips then spitting again and stretching it with his fingers. Neil was one hell of a hung stud, but Dan was desperate for the conquest. He lay over the cylinder, groaning with expectation and delight as his arsehole was lubed for action. I looked at Tom. He beckoned me over, the arrogance still on his face, his thick hard man-rammer rigid with blood and held vice-like flat against his stomach. He put his hands on my shoulders and pushed me down. For a moment I was going to resist. Why should I let this boy fuck me? Who did he think he was? But as I descended I caught a close view of his sticky red, cut boner and I couldn't resist. The smell of this flame-thrower was irresistible. I lay on the cylinder next to Dan. He turned his head and smiled. I kissed him and he draped his arm around me; brothers together while the men oiled our cunts with their spit and fingers.

I heard the sound of condoms being slipped on and braced myself. Dan looked scared for a moment as I saw Neil begin to penetrate him. He struggled to take in all the fat man-meat that was being thrust into him, but that was the last I saw. I felt Tom position his hard man-cunt fucker at my hole and begin to push. He was brutal, shoving his thick shaft deeply into me. I gasped and spread my legs. This boy certainly knew how to fuck. My arse pushed upwards into the air to give Tom's tool the space it needed and then I felt Tom settle into a rhythm. It was the same as Neil's. Behind me they had an arm draped over each shoulder and were pistoning together. I put my arm around Dan who was practically splitting from the meat inside him, and he gave me the biggest grin I have ever seen. He kissed me again as the force of the meat being pumped in behind us thrust us clanking into the gas cylinder beneath our chests.

We were fucked long and slow and hard. Tom used every

muscle he had to power into me, spreading my cheeks and filling me with his hard salami. Next to me Dan was in a frenzy of ecstasy as Neil fucked his little-boy butt for all he was worth. I felt their beat getting faster, each plunge of their rammers going further and harder into me, slamming against my colon which caused me to gasp continually with delight. And then I felt Tom begin to come. He cried out in wonder as his juice was freed from him into the rubber deep within my willing butt. I turned to see Neil coming too, his face twisted in a contortion of delight as he shoved every inch of his man-rammer into Dan. I watched Dan take it all, delirious with excitement, his blond hair tousled, his blue eyes sparkling.

Tom withdrew from me and I turned to see his athletic body near collapse with exhaustion. I pulled the rubber from his dick and tasted his delicious boy-gravy. Some fresh come pumped into my face and I licked at the salty goodness eagerly. Dan had done the same and his face was covered with Neil's jizz. I cranked on my shaft and Neil did too. Neil pulled Tom down to kneel in front of our tools, awaiting the fountain to come. Dan pumped hard and shot first, the white ribbons of jizz flying onto Neil and Tom who lapped it up like cats before bowls of cream. I shot quickly afterwards, the orgasm unwinding in my legs and then blasting from my piss-slit like water from a fireman's hose. I sprayed down Neil and Tom. It was then that Tom lost his arrogance and cool and dived onto my pecker, his face covered in jizz, as my ramrod shot the white elixir to the back of his throat.

Neil began to laugh. We knelt together, drenched in each other's perspiration and come and hugged. It had been a fabulous afternoon. As we dressed, Neil gave Dan our phone number.

'If you ever need a hand with anything then call us,' he said as they left. Dan nodded.

'Might do,' Tom added in a non-committal sort of way, adding with a smile, 'I think we just might do . . .'

Through a broken window frame we watched them leave the

site. They jumped and half ran to get over the debris outside. They looked like two boys who had just got fabulous Christmas presents. Dan turned and waved back at us. We waved in return and then Tom joined in before they slipped out of a hole in the wall and into the world outside.

We were still at the window when I saw a larger form moving hurriedly across the wasteland. It was Karl. Although he was covered in a vast green parka jacket, I knew it was him.

'We've got company.' I leaned out of view and nodded to Neil who peeked through a broken frame.

'Well, we'd better make it look realistic.' He pointed. 'You go over there and we'll meet up and have a row in a couple of minutes.' I nodded and we separated.

Creeping around the upper floor I heard Karl enter downstairs. On the other side of the staircase I could hear Neil stomping around. Karl began to tiptoe upstairs, I busied myself with making a useless sketch of the current floor plan. I wandered away from the stairs to give Karl access to the upper floor.

'Armstrong? Where are you?' It was Neil.

'What?' I replied, returning to the centre of the warehouse. Neil was waiting at the top of the steps. He winked and his head gave just a slight tilt backwards to indicate one of the partitioned rooms behind him.

'Have you finished?'

'Just about.'

'Yeah, well I have, and anyway you're finished as far as I'm concerned. Get a move on, I want to go.'

'I've just got to finish this sketch.'

'Don't waste your time. You're going to be out of Allsop and Gee in two weeks anyway.'

'Yeah, but I want decent references and, as you know, I'm the brains here.'

'Don't fuck with me,' Neil warned, moving menacingly toward me. Over his shoulder I caught a glimpse of green jacket and a prying eye. I ignored it. 'You've led me into all sorts of fucking perversions already, I'm not looking at your fucking plans. Parker and I will deal with it.'

'Good luck, cunt breath.'

'Cunt breath is better than dick breath any day, faggot.'

'Oh piss off, arsehole.' I made to leave.

I heard Neil mutter 'Forgive me.' I paused for a fraction of a second and then I was lost. The world turned about me, my eardrums pounded with noise and I went tumbling to the ground. Then there was pain in my cheek. I lay dazed for a moment, the white paint on the ceiling peeling above me, the floor beneath my back. Neil had just thumped me. I was decked, winded and totally confused. I heard his footsteps stamping down the iron staircase. I lay there, rubbing my cheek. It was already swelling. Fuck! The bastard had just hit me!

'Fuck you!' I called after him, meaning it too. 'Fuck you, you fucking second rate lousy fuck! Go back to your fucking wife.' I found myself becoming tearful. 'Fuck off back to her. Fuck you! Fuck her.' I was sobbing. Whether it was the strenuous fuck we had just had, the pressure of stitching up Gee, or the trauma at losing Neil, I didn't know, but big tears rolled down my cheeks. I regained my composure, certain that Karl had seen what had happened, before leaving, running and tripping over the debris outside to get away. The bastard had hit me!

'God I am so sorry and I love you, I love you,' Neil cried when I got home. He was waiting for me, an ice pack ready for the bruising.

'What did you hit me for?'

'It had to look real,' Neil pleaded. 'Think about it. I was acting away and I realised that I would have to hit you if it was going to look plausible.'

'So you thumped me one.'

'I'm so sorry, but I had to, really, Karl was there. They'll know about it in the office tomorrow and from now on no one will believe we're friends. That way the plan will work. Do you forgive me?'

He was right of course. I was just angry that I hadn't thought of it first and hit him. Even though he had pulled his punch it was fucking painful and I would have one hell of a black eye the next day. 'Sure, I forgive you.' Neil kissed me. 'But tonight, I ain't going to forgive your arse. Tonight, your hole is mine.'

'If that's the case,' Neil taunted, 'I'll have to think about treating you roughly more often . . .'

Chapter Eleven

'So, are you going to tell me what you're scheming or not?'

It was Marilyn. She stood in front of my desk whilst I tried to hide my damaged face. My right eye was swollen, with bruising along my cheek in puce, plum and burgundy. It was sore to the touch, the skin grazed across my cheekbone.

'I told you, it was at the tube station, someone hit me and I didn't see.'

'Poppycock,' Marilyn retorted, now visibly hurt by my lies. 'You're six foot two and built like a brick shithouse; no one would be able to reach your eye, let alone dare to sock you one. No, the only way you'd get hit like that was if you didn't see it coming; and that would only be if Neil thumped you. Now you told me yesterday you were planning something, what is it?'

I fought for something to say. As always, Marilyn had seen right through me. I felt bad cheating Marilyn, but Neil and I had decided that the less people knew, the better.

'And what's more, Karl is crowing like a cock on an electric fence. Now, are you going to tell me or not?'

I acquiesced and told Marilyn everything that had happened the previous day. I explained that Neil and I were trying to derail Gee and Karl's chances of winning the Hammersmith project, but that this would only work if they believed that Neil and I had fallen out, hence Neil had hit me. I also explained Gee's thorough spy network which shocked her.

'So he snoops though everything I put on my terminal? The letters to my gynaecologist, my notes to my mother?' I nodded. 'That's unforgivable.' She clasped her hands in front of her.

'Don't you worry about me, mum's the word. However, I think that Arnold Gee has got a few surprises coming his way.'

Shortly after that I was called into Gee's office. Neil was already present. We barely acknowledged each other.

'Goodness me, Mr Armstrong,' Gee exclaimed as I entered his office, 'what on earth happened to you?'

'Got hit on the tube last night.'

'On the tube?' Karl echoed as he entered the office behind me, a grin smeared across his face as he skipped with glee behind Gee's desk. A faint waft of the smell of fish followed him in.

'Yeah, the tube. Now can we drop it? I don't want to discuss it.'

'Fine, fine. You should be more careful who you come into contact with, Mr Armstrong. Bad deeds always get their comeuppance.'

'I know.' That much was true.

Neil began to explain some thoughts for the design of the Hammersmith site. It was a new post-modern homage to Le Corbusier – vaulted concrete ceilings, thick stone walls, few windows. It would look like a latter-day pillbox. It would be modern, avant-garde and Miles Stone would utterly loath it. Gee and Karl on the other hand, seemed genuinely interested.

'But how will all this work?' Karl questioned, suspicion in his voice.

'It's a post-modern minimalist use of space. From our last meeting with Miles Stone, it is clear that glass boxes are out. That last design would be great in Stevenage, but not for a central London headquarters.' Karl bristled behind the table. 'This is new, innovative and, although it is pricey, Mr Stone has said that cost is not a contributing factor at this time.'

Gee and Karl studied the plans. The design did look grotesque, a vast cement dome on a stone box, with arrow slit windows, few floors ; a waste of space that would be impossible to heat. Its cruel and forbidding exterior would break all sound requirements as it would reflect every noise from the traffic and railway and be a wholly unacceptable face for the Stone Partnership. However, Gee and Karl weren't convinced.

'I would hope, Mr Gee, that should Miles Stone commission the project, you would maybe see your way to include me in its development . . .' That tipped the balance. Karl stepped in first.

'Your position in this company is very precarious, Mr Armstrong, but should this commission be accepted there is a chance that your termination date could be extended, but that will have to be decided in the future.'

I nodded and looked at the floor. Neil stepped in.

'I'll discuss that with you, mate,' he said to Karl. 'I came up with this plan, I know how it works, I'm not so sure there would be a place for Armstrong on the team.'

I kept quiet. Gee finished the discussion with an announcement that all crew for the project would be decided in the future. I stood ready to leave.

'Karl,' Neil slapped Parker on the back, 'how about we do a mail-out to major clients telling them of the reorganisation in the department, your promotion and new role as Head of Development now that Mr Armstrong's days with us are limited.'

I paused in the doorway, my back to the office. It was Gee who spoke.

'Good idea, Neil. Get on to it, Karl. Draft something and let me have a look.'

'Yes, sir!' Karl said smugly and pushed by me to get out. There was that smell of old fish again. Karl smelt as if he'd been eating fish for breakfast. It wasn't a strong odour, but it was definitely present.

I left Neil and Gee alone to 'bond'. Outside Marilyn was talking to the cute black security guard I had sucked off earlier in the week. I smiled at him and blushed at the thought of us fucking on Gee's desk and the taste of his lovely long curved black dick shooting its juice down my throat. He winked at me.

'Now come on, Antony, all I want you to do is reposition

the camera for a week at most. It would be a great favour to me.'

'I can't really do that, Mrs Allbright. They're fixed in place for a purpose.'

'Yes, well, I want it fixed in another place for another purpose.'

'Everything OK?' I offered.

'Fine thank you, Wade,' Marilyn said, clearly irritated that someone was ignoring her pleas.

'I'm OK, you OK?' the guard asked.

'Yeah. What's going on?'

Antony explained that Marilyn wanted the security camera by the lift to be refocused on to Gee's office. He wasn't keen to do it.

'Oh, go on,' I urged, putting my arm around him and giving his muscular shoulder a squeeze. 'I could make it worth your while . . .'

Antony grinned at me, his white teeth flashing a devastating smile. 'OK, for you, Wade. But for one week only. OK?'

'Fine, fine, yes, yes. Just do it today, thank you.'

Antony left. Marilyn gave me a quizzical look. 'I don't believe it! The place is crawling with your lot!'

'What?' I attempted innocence.

'Don't give me that, Wade Armstrong. Your face may have remained innocent, but believe me when you arrived at my desk I saw a marrow grow in Antony's trousers where there wasn't one before.'

'It was after Neil and I broke up . . .'

'You don't have to explain, thank you. You make the most of it while you can. If Antony repositions that camera I think it'll be to all our advantage. Now get on with your work.'

I returned to my desk, aware now that there were two plots being hatched. I couldn't concentrate and felt jumpy, excited and nervous all at the same time.

'What happened then?' Cheryl arrived.

'Got hit on the tube.'

'Nasty.' Cheryl pulled out a nail file and began brushing the tips of her fingers absent-mindedly. 'Funny though, I heard Neil saying that he had bruised his hand last night. You two have a row?'

Jesus! Was it completely impossible to keep our plans a secret or was every other office in the country as knowledgeable about everyone else's goings on as ours was? I gave up trying to conceal the truth. Cheryl would whittle away until she was satisfied she had found out what was going on.

'Look, alright, Neil hit me in Hammersmith yesterday. We had a row. OK. But please, don't talk about it.'

'Oh, I knew that. I saw Karl this morning and he told me everything. Why did you row?'

'Why were you talking to Karl?' I countered.

'Keep a secret?' Cheryl giggled. It was clear this was the reason she was here in the first place. 'Well, me and Janice have been pissed off with the way you've been treated so we stapled an old smoked haddock under Karl's desk. It's gonna make him stink!'

'I've already smelled it.'

Cheryl went off into peals of laughter. She waved at Janice who was at her desk watching the conversation, nodded wildly and then held her nose between her fingers to indicate that the haddock was already smelling. Janice clapped her hands and waved at me.

'He's coming over. Gotta go.' Cheryl picked up some papers from my desk and left. Karl approached and the smell of fish was pungent.

'You wanna check this?' He handed me a letter. It was the announcement of his promotion and offered Allsop and Gee's services whenever the client required them. I glanced over it.

'Not really, no.'

'Thought so. I'll give it to Neil, bum-chum.'

As Karl left, the trail of decaying smoked haddock followed him.

I met Neil at lunch time in the basement. This was the only safe area in the entire block where we could speak in privacy.

We stood in a long corridor with dark metal lockers either side and strip lighting running the length of the room. At each end were double swing doors. The floor was grey marble linoleum which shone from the harsh lighting above.

Neil had advised Karl not to send out the mailshot until Friday, that way it would be on every client's desk on Monday morning at the start of their week. We were seeing Miles Stone at 10.00 am on Monday and would be able to gauge the response. It was Friday that the bug on his software would become active and infiltrate the letter with the foul language Matt had promised, giving him yet another headache. Hurriedly, I told Neil about Cheryl and Janice and the haddock stapled underneath Karl's desk.

'I could smell fish, but didn't know where it was coming from. But you're right, it is Karl.'

It was then that Antony appeared, smart in his navy uniform and peaked hat. I had told Neil about Matt and the guard, but Neil didn't know which guard it had been.

'Hi, fellas,' Antony said, dropping his hat into his locker. 'What you doing down here?'

'Not much,' I replied. 'How are you?'

'Done the camera as Mrs Allbright asked.' He rubbed his crotch with his hand. He took his jacket off and hung it in his locker. Beneath he wore a crisp white shirt, his coffee skin rich and dark against the bright white cotton. He scratched his goatee.

I introduced Neil to Antony. Neil grinned, catching on instantly to who this guy was.

'You have great taste, Wade. He's cute.' Neil flirted. Antony turned to face us, his erection straining in his tight navy trousers. 'I think Wade and I owe you one, Antony.'

Neil stepped forward and unzipped Antony's fly. Underneath I could see the hard man-meat curving within his white underwear. I stepped forward and Neil and I knelt in front of his temple of cock. I undid Antony's belt and together we pulled down his trousers and underwear. Antony's fat black cock sprang free, curving upwards like a scythe, the tip already creamy. I felt my cock straining in my Calvins. Together Neil and I flicked our tongues over the tip of this great dick. Neil reached his hand round and began toying with Antony's hole. I pulled down on his pendulous black balls whilst running my tongue up and down his thick shaft. His wiry pubes fuzzed into my face. I kissed Neil with this fat cock between us. The pecker juice was oiling the tip, cementing our kiss as we serviced this proud man-rammer.

We batted the cock between us as we kissed, both Neil and I pulling down our own trousers to free our hard dicks. Neil sunk his lips around Antony's cock and began giving the best head he could. I manoeuvred around the back to make my way into Antony's man-cunt. I felt him open his arse cheeks with his hands and push his hot steamy hole into my face. My head banged back against the lockers so that my face was sandwiched between his cheeks, his strong musk filling my nostrils. In front, Neil worked over his hard dick, taking the length of that rich black tool down his throat, pressing his face into his pubes and pressing Antony's arse onto my face.

I felt Antony pumping his dick down Neil's throat. His hands gripped my head behind him and pushed my tongue into his sweet arse. I licked and tongued furiously at his tasty cunt while all I could hear were Antony's groans and Neil salivating over the tool in his mouth. With my tongue in his sphincter, I could feel Antony come, his hole tightening with every pump of jizz from his balls. I heard Neil slurping at the juice that spat forth.

Antony collapsed to his knees. 'Jeez, guys, you sure know how to give a fella a good time!'

I stood next to Neil, whose boner was pressed flat against his stomach. He stroked the tip slowly. 'Fancy some boy-gravy of your own?' he asked.

'Oh, yeah, give it to me, man!'

Neil and I stood in front of him and pumped our tools. Antony's drained cock grew back into life as we pumped over twenty inches of fat cock into his face. We came together, the pecker-juice flying from our tools in fat ribbons onto Antony's face. He lapped it up and at the same time came again. I yanked my cock hard, the tension of the day being released in a fanfare of jizz. When we finished, Antony was covered in come. He sat with a sweet smile on his face.

'Never can get enough,' he said, wiping it from his face and sucking on it hungrily. 'Always loved a nice mouthful of jizz, you can't beat it!'

'I know what you mean,' Neil added, milking the last drops of love juice from his cock, letting it drip from his fingers like paste.

I took Neil's finger and tasted his salty come. It was good. I smiled. 'It just tastes so good!'

That evening at home I took Miles Stone's card and noted his address. I put the plans we had for Fallingwater Two in a hard-backed envelope and sent it off; they would arrive Saturday.

'But what are we going to call our company?' I asked Neil.

'How about Great Erections?'

'Seriously.'

'Armstrong and Rogers?'

'Bit dull. Too like Allsop and Gee.'

'How about The Donkey Brothers?'

'We might just as well call it Fat Cock Designs!' I teased.

Neil jumped on top of me, pushing me down on the settee. He ran his fingers through my hair. 'I don't care what we call it, as long as I'm with you.' He ground his crutch in to mine. He was hard.

'God, you make me so horny, but I don't know if my cock or my arse can take another shag!'

He kissed me. 'How about we call it Bumping Fuzz Productions? 'Cause when I bump my fuzz against your hole I have great ideas!'

'No, I've got it!' I sat up pushing Neil backwards.

'What?'

'How about we call it Shaft?'

'Shaft?'

'Yeah, 'cause it's your shaft that thrills my hole, you love to shaft me and in setting up this company we're going to shaft Gee and Parker, not to mention a load of their clients?'

'Shaft.' Neil pondered it. He rubbed his hard twelve inches that now stood out of his sweat pants begging my attention. 'Yeah, I like it. Shaft it is. Now, how about you spread your butt cheeks and let me show you just what shaft means?'

I pulled off my shorts and span round on the sofa. My two hard buns flexed in Neil's direction. 'I thought you'd never ask!'

Friday at work and I was on edge. Karl had written his letter to the major clients and it had been agreed by Gee. It was short and to the point announcing Karl's promotion and asking if any clients needed any architectural advice then they knew where to get it. I was nervous that Karl would inspect the letters before sending them out, but Neil had intervened. He had suggested that Karl put the entire mail-merge onto a disk and send it to the postal room, to be printed, merged enveloped and then posted. Karl had been reluctant because he wanted Gee to sign every letter, but when Neil pointed out that there would be over two hundred of them and that Gee was very busy, Karl gave in.

Karl's desk was a real no-go area. It reeked of fish. I noticed that he had put two plastic air fresheners on his desk. Cheryl was beside herself with glee.

'It serves him right, nasty bit of toe-jam. Shouldn't mess with Janice and me, and,' she added, 'he should change his suit more often. No wonder he stinks. Anyway how are you? How's your eye?'

It was still sore. The bruising had come up more. 'It's OK. Looks worse than it is.'

'So why did Neil hit you then?'

'Oh, nothing much.' I couldn't think of a plausible excuse.

'Must be some reason,' Cheryl continued.

'Oh we had a row.'

'Oh. Lovers tiff?'

I paused. What should I say? Had Cheryl guessed or been

told by Karl? I was fed up of lying to friends. 'Something like that, yes.'

'I knew it!' Cheryl slammed her palms on my desk. 'I knew it. That's why you weren't interested in me and Janice weren't it!'

'Yes. Look, I'm sorry, we didn't mean to lead you on . . .'

'Why didn't you just say?' Cheryl appealed. 'We wouldn't've minded, we're very cosmopolitan even if we do come from Hatch End.'

'Well, it didn't start until recently so . . .'

'Oh, don't explain to me. I told Jan, plenty more fish in the sea.'

'Well, I hope we can still be friends.'

'Course. Don't think about it. Honestly, men, ha! You are funny.'

'I suppose so.' I marvelled at how well Cheryl was taking all this. Something didn't quite add up.

'"Nowt so queer as folk" as my gran says.'

'You could say that.'

'So who is it?'

'Who's who?' Now I was lost.

'Who's the other woman that you and Neil had a fight about? It weren't Sue in accounts was it? 'Cause I can tell you, she puts it about. She photocopied her fanny and sent it to Mr Beavers on the twelfth floor. "A beaver for Beavers," Jan said.'

'No, it's not Sue. I think we've got our wires crossed.'

'Well as long as it's not her we don't mind. Just don't beat each other up. Anyway, Jan's still gonna work on you, only more subtle like. She don't give up easy!'

'No, I'm sure she doesn't.'

'She's like an old dog with a rubber ring; she won't let go!'

At three thirty Neil walked by and dropped the final plans for the Hammersmith site on my desk. The design looked like a cross between a cement castle, a second-world-war pillbox and a municipal bus station; it was hideous. On the cover was a yellow Post-it note; 'Karl has sent his disk to the mail room for printing and posting.' My heart sang with glee. All we needed now was for Matt's computer virus to work and every major client of Allsop and Gee would receive a letter on Monday morning the likes of which they would never have read before.

I added a few touches to the Hammersmith Fort and took the plans to Karl. He perused them, his brow furrowed.

'You sure about the arrow slit windows? Gonna be dark in there.'

'It's cutting edge design, Karl, do you know what that is?'

'Yes,' he snapped defensively. 'You don't have a monopoly on innovation.'

'It's a homage to the Heinrich Cack house in Vermont.'

'I can see that.'

I was amazed, since I had only just invented the building, but Karl seemed to know everything about it.

'Thank you, you can go. Ten o'clock Monday morning for the presentation.' I nodded as I left. Karl added, 'And I should think by eleven you'll be on the streets looking for another job. As head of this department I won't be keeping you on.'

Although I knew this was coming, it hit hard. Why did he have it in for me? What had I ever done to raise such animosity in him? I was worried because I knew that from Monday I would have no income and no job and would need to find something fast. My hopes lay with Miles Stone and my design, but would he commission a project so large from a new company? The length of time it took to get a new commission accepted would mean that if Miles Stone didn't commission Fallingwater Two either Neil or I would have to work to support the new company while it got of the ground; if it ever got off the ground.

I threw on my coat, grabbed my things and wandered to the lifts. Marilyn was anxiously waiting.

'It takes forever for these bloody things to arrive.' She pressed the down button again.

'You going too?' I asked.

'Yes, got to get a video of *One Hundred and One Dalmatians* for my nephew's birthday. I always leave it to the last minute.'

The lift arrived with a stark ping. Marilyn hustled in among the four people in the lift. I stood next to her, watching the doors close.

'You don't look a happy bunny,' Marilyn said.

'Nope. Karl's told me I'm out as of Monday morning after the meeting.'

'What about your plan?' she asked cryptically.

'Working slowly, but it's not necessarily going to earn me a job.'

'Well, I may have something up my sleeve, you never know.' She winked at me as the lift reached the lobby.

'What?'

'Never you mind. I can't guarantee anything, but I always go home early on Friday, and I've set the bait, so we'll see what happens. Bye!'

She span off through a revolving door and into the Friday afternoon mayhem outside.

Saturday was unbearable. I sat by the telephone waiting for Miles Stone to call. He didn't. He would have received the plans for sure, but didn't call to find out more.

'It is Saturday,' Neil comforted me, the length of his muscular arm around my shoulder holding me tight.

'I know, but the plans are so good, I thought he would've called to find out more,' I protested.

'He's a business man, so he'll play it cool. Come here.'

He pulled me into his big chest and his rich musk billowed through my lungs. With Neil I felt safe. I hugged him tight, his broad hairy chest pressed against mine. I slipped my hands up the inside of his T-shirt and stroked his back. I moved my hand round to his chest, feeling the curly hair soft beneath my fingers. I tweaked a nipple and Neil groaned. I lifted his T-shirt above his head and began to suck lovingly on his hard areolae, pulling the nipples between my teeth as he ground his hard man-meat into my stomach. I brushed my face through the hairs on his chest, down over his taut abs and to the rigid pole that was stuffed into his sweat pants. I pulled the elastic waist down to reveal his boner. Every time I saw it, it never failed to take my breath away, the long thick veined man-rammer, with its bulbous head held erect on his furry stomach. Gently I traced my tongue down the vein in the shaft until I reached his nuts hanging below. I pushed my nose into his sac to feel the weight of his balls on my face. The scent from his arse permeated my nose. I inhaled it deeply as I licked between his legs. I grasped his arse and pulled his groin into my face. I worked my way up his dick again. All the anxiety I felt melted away as my lips reached his mushroom head and I savoured his sweet pre-come. I delicately licked his piss-slit, the juice moistening my lips and mouth. I felt Neil caress my head. With the tip of his dick in my mouth I looked up at him. He stood tall and powerful above me, his face a picture of ecstasy as my mouth swirled around his plump cock-head.

Gently he began thrusting his hips towards me, his thick tool sliding into my mouth. I felt it reach my tonsils. I breathed in and his throbbing man-rammer slid down my throat with my breath. I felt his nuts swing against my chin as his soft pubes bristled into my face. With one hand to guide his thick tool into my mouth and one hand pumping my own hard dick, I worked my magic on Neil's cock. In and out it slid, the pre-jizz dribbling down my chin, my mouth filled with salty wonder. Neil held my head gently and developed a rhythm, bucking his hips away so that his cock-head would ride to the tip of my lips and then pulling my scalp towards him as he rammed his fat man tool down my throat. This was what life was about. Not work, not Parker or Gee, but Neil, his fat cock and my throat soon to be filled with his boy-gravy.

There was a knock at the door. Neil didn't hear it, continuing to thrust into me. I didn't care any more. Didn't care if the visitor came in or left; all I wanted was more of this glorious meat in me. I pulled hard on my own dick, feeling it damp with jizz and hard with passion.

The door knocked again. Still Neil thrust his load into me and still I swallowed his hot member, his bollocks swinging like two demolition balls against my chin. I gripped his arse and fingered his hole. I was almost delirious with delight.

I felt a breeze against my face. I opened my eyes to see that the front door had opened and the figure of Miles Stone was standing watching Neil fuck my face. I felt as if I was in limbo. I could see what was happening, but didn't care. I had this hot stiff cock rammed down my throat, my own hard member in my hand and the promise of all that jizz to come. That was all I cared about.

I watched Miles silently come into the living room. Put down his bag and slip off his coat. Underneath he wore a white T-shirt and leather trousers. He rubbed his crutch. My eyes widened, desperate that he should join in. At this point I wanted as many hot men as possible. Silently, he pulled his T-shirt over his head. His smooth tight tanned body glowed beneath. He kicked off his boots and yanked down his leather trousers. He wore no underwear and was rock hard. Neil slowed on my face-fuck and turned to see Miles.

'Glad you could join us,' he said casually.

Miles pulled back on his Doc Marten boots and stood looking at us with his hands on his hips, his dick pushed solid and outright, like a branch from an oak tree.

'So you think you can suck cock?' he asked, his voice deep and gruff.

With Neil's dick still in my mouth I nodded. He strode over and stood next to Neil, his boner pointing straight at my face. I could see the skin on his body smooth from waxing, his pubes cut into a short bristle around his shaft. Neil turned and kissed him hard. I watched their tongues lap over each other but my attention was drawn back as Miles' fat glans bumped into my face.

I gripped both dicks in my hand and pressed them together. Neil's shone from the spit already on it and I set about working my saliva over Miles' shaft. Above I could see Neil's and Miles' fit hard bodies pressed together, the hair on Neil's torso contrasting with the silky smoothness of Miles'. I wrapped my arms around their butts and felt for their holes. Neil's I recognised – hairy, wet and hot. Miles was different; tight and smooth. I spat on a finger and took it back to his smooth man-cunt. I pushed a finger in and I heard Miles groan. In response he pushed his dick towards my face. I sucked eagerly on the hard, hot shaft, flapping my tongue over his head to lubricate it before working my way down his thick pecker. I could feel Neil's dick pressed against my chin. I began to alternate, first taking Miles' dick down my throat, then Neil's longer thicker tool. I looked up to see the two of them admiring my work, stroking my hair and pulling my head down on their cock with each alternate thrust.

'Take both,' Miles pleaded.

I opened my mouth and worked both cock-heads into my mouth. Their saltiness whisked together in my mouth as my tongue darted over the two tools. Together they thrust gently into my mouth. There was too much meat to get down my throat, but the two heads and pre-come in my mouth was delicious. I jostled the dicks around in my mouth, having them side by side and on top of each other, all the while licking the hardness and milking the pre-come from their seeping piss-slits. Above me Miles and Neil kissed. I fingered their holes as hard as I could. Neil took my fingers willingly and although Miles' hole had taken some time to loosen up, I now had three fingers buried within him.

Miles was the first to come. I felt hot salty jizz fly into my mouth. I looked up to see Miles with his head rolled back in ecstasy. Neil pressed a kiss to his face as I worked my tongue over his cock-head. More jizz hit the back of my throat. I was awash with it, jism down my throat, up my nose and spilling from my chin. I pulled my hand free from Miles' man-cunt and pumped on my own tool. With the taste of all this pecker-juice in my mouth I didn't take long to come. The orgasm exploded within me, cock cream flying, my prick pumping like a soda siphon.

I lapped at the come on my chin. Neil pulled me to my feet, my cock still semi-erect, Neil's huge tool swinging with its own weight beneath his legs whilst Miles milked his prick slowly with his thumb and forefinger.

'Hi, Miles,' I said grinning. 'Glad you could come.'

'Yeah, I must return the favour sometime. It's difficult to decide which of you two is the more gorgeous.'

'He is,' Neil said, pulling me to my feet and kissing me, stealing the milkshake from my chin with a lick.

'Well, I came round to talk business, but I don't think I need to now.'

'No?' I asked.

'No. You're both hired.'

'You liked the plans?' Neil exclaimed.

'Liked them? I loved Fallingwater Two. It's perfect. We're going to make a good team.'

'Great!' I whooped. 'Shaft is in business!'

'You bet your arse it is!' Miles confirmed.

Chapter Twelve

I arrived at Allsop and Gee for my last day at work in a Prada suit. With Miles Stone ready to give Shaft the commission I wanted to look as good as I could as I gave Gee and Parker the finger.

The first surprise of the morning came from Karl. He bounded up to my desk with the remnants of an old fish held in a sheet of computer paper.

'Is this you, you fuck wit?'

'No, it's a dead fish, Karl.'

'Don't get clever with me, you cunt, did you stick this under my desk?'

'No,' I answered firmly, 'but I wish I had.'

'Look what it's done to me!' He stood back. He had obviously been sitting at his desk when the rotting piece of haddock had dropped onto his lap. It had left a wide greasy stain over his crutch. He reeked of fish.

'I expect that's the nearest your cock has been to a bit of fish in years!' I quipped.

'A damn site nearer than yours has ever been certainly!' Karl retorted, livid, his puffy face blue with rage, his piggy eyes practically out on stalks.

'Yes, I am a cock-sucker, Karl, and I'm pleased to say I'm a very good cock-sucker. As you are not very good at anything, I don't think you're in a position to criticize. Now, do you mind? I have a presentation to prepare for.'

'Don't you fuck off yet!' Karl growled, getting hold of my lapels. Effortlessly I pushed him away. He stumbled backwards and fell, the old haddock in his hand dropping onto his shirt to imprint yet another stain.

'Don't you fucking touch me, you weasel!' I bawled.

'What did you do to my mailshot?' Karl yelled in return.

'What?' I pleaded ignorance and, after a week of lying about everything else, I was now very good at it.

'Some bastard's sabotaged my mailshot!'

'Who wrote your mailshot, Karl?' I barked in return, the entire office now standing silently around us.

'Me.'

'On whose computer?'

'On mine, you know that.'

'Who was responsible for taking it to the print room?'

'I took it.'

'Then you only have yourself to ask what went wrong with it.' I adjusted my jacket and lied a little more, for effect. 'So, what did go wrong with it?'

'I'm not sure, something with the printing.'

'Well, either way, sad boy, sort it out yourself, 'cause I couldn't give a fuck!'

Karl's phone was ringing; another customer wanting an explanation for the letter they had received.

I met Marilyn at her desk by Gee's office. She couldn't hide the glee on her face. 'Something's gone wrong with Mr Parker's mailshot to our senior clients. I've had seven calls already and Mr Gee is not in a good mood.'

'Oh dear, what a pity, never mind!' I raised my eyebrows.

'And this,' Marilyn dropped a VHS cassette onto her desk, 'came into my possession from Antony this morning. It would seem that I was right about something!'

'What?' I was desperate to know what had been going on.

'Just you wait and see.' Marilyn tucked the video back in her desk drawer. 'Oh,' she frowned, ' or is this the tape?' She lifted another tape from her desk drawer. 'One's my special surprise and one is *One Hundred and One Dalmatians*.'

Before I could question her further, Arnold Gee flung open his door and glowered at me.

'Do you know what the fuck is going on here, Armstrong?

Because if you do I swear I'm going to fucking sue you for every penny you've got.'

'I have no idea what's happened, Arnold,' I smarmed. 'I just saw Karl and he's the only person who's touched that mailshot or his computer. Nothing to do with me. Sorry, you'll have to find another whipping boy.'

'A call from IBM, Mr Gee,' Marilyn interrupted. 'Do you want to take it now?'

'Jesus Christ!' Gee stormed, sprinting into his office to take the call. 'Fuck, fuck, fuck, fuck!'

Outside I saw Gee's head nodding as he apologised. His finger stabbed at his desk and he shook his head. Neil joined me on the sofa outside. He gave me a kiss.

'How's things?'

'Going like a charm!' I replied.

The lift pinged and Miles Stone stepped out. He strode across the office.

'Morning, guys. How are you?'

'Fine,' I replied

'A lot better than Allsop and Gee are today I should imagine.'

Neil shrugged his shoulders.

'Yes, and if you two had nothing to do with this I'm Olivia Newton John.'

'Hello, Olivia,' Neil retorted. 'You've changed.'

Miles grinned.

'Thought you were very good in *Xanadu*,' I added.

Marilyn stood and announced Miles Stones's arrival to Arnold Gee. Gee was still begging forgiveness on the phone and I heard him urge Marilyn to keep us all outside. We sat and waited. The peace was shattered by Karl sprinting to join us.

'Mr Stone, it's so good to see you again.'

'Parker, isn't it?' Miles said, his voice steely.

'That's correct.' Karl proffered a hand.

'I thought I made it quite clear at our last meeting that I never wanted to see your scum-sucking little arse again?'

Karl blanched. It really wasn't a good day. 'But I've done a great deal of work on the new design. It's very cutting edge, I'm sure you'll love it. I need to be there to explain it.'

'You drew up the design?' Miles asked with incredulity.

'Yes,' Karl jumped in before either Neil or I could speak. We sat back into the sofa and let Karl hang himself. 'I've worked on it solidly. It's a new design, new inspiration, very much the sort of organic whole you were looking for.'

'Organic whole . . .' Miles mused. 'Well, let's just hope that your "organic whole" is not just a synonym for another big wet turd you're going to drop in my lap. By the way,' Miles added, 'what has dropped into your lap?' Karl covered his stained groin with a sheaf of papers. 'You stink of fish.'

'Oh yes, ha ha,' Karl quaked. 'A little accident.'

Miles shook his head. Karl stood and clutched the designs under his arm. The nervous silence was broken by Gee flinging his door open again and welcoming in Miles Stone with more fake charm than I had ever seen from him before. His forehead was wet with perspiration.

Inside, Neil and I sat together, nervous and excited. Neil's leg twitched up and down next to mine. I loved the feel of his strong powerful quad brushing against me.

'Before we start, Arnold, I would just like to read you a letter I received from you today. I thought you might be interested.'

'I can explain,' Karl wailed.

'Don't interrupt!' Miles Stone ordered. Karl shrank back to his position behind the aspidistra. Miles Stone read his letter.

'From Allsop and Gee, Canary Wharf.
Dear Miles *fuck me till I fart* Stone,

We at Allsop *finger my love hole* and Gee are constantly striving to bring our clients the very best *fishy beef drapes* service, *pumping erections* and design. We are pleased to announce that we have recently *come in the face of a rabid baboon* and appointed Karl *breasts like melons* Parker to be Head of *fist-fucking* Development in our business design unit. Karl's experience *stuffing small furry animals into his rectum* at Allsop and Gee has included a number of award winning projects which concentrate on *come-shots, lesbians* original design for a reasonable cost *and a finger behind the bike sheds.*

Big Dogs Cock!

Should you or your partners have *haemorrhoids the size of a bunch of grapes* or any architectural needs in the near or distant future, please *whip me, strip me, call me Gwendoline* and do give us the opportunity to quote on your *tatty little scrotum* requirements. You can be assured of *eating my grandmother's shite and* the best of service at all times. After all, *you herpes-ridden cunt lesion*, the Allsop and Gee motto is "Tomorrow's *arse wipe* design at yesterday's *wet gusset* cost."

I am wearing skimpy ladies panties.

We look forward to speaking to you soon.

Melons, melons and more melons.

Yours sincerely,

Half a pound of breasts, please, vicar.

Arnold Gee

I'm a woman trapped in a man's body.

Partner'

Miles Stone read the letter with a straight face, emphasising every filthy phrase in it for effect. I was almost on the floor fighting to keep my laughter contained.

'Have you anything to say, Gwendoline or can I call you Gwen?' Miles asked.

Gee poured forth with a barrage of apologies, but Miles brushed them aside.

'Arnold, or is it Gwen? I can easily see that this is a mistake. What worries me is that it got out in the first place. Your security measures are appallingly lax. Don't you keep an eye on what your staff are up to? With modern technology you can even watch them pee these days. This letter doesn't fill me with inspiration that Allsop and Gee are a trustworthy organisation.'

'Miles, you know you can call me anything you like,' Gee simpered. 'I can assure you that something like this has never happened before and will never happen again. As for keeping an eye on my staff, I believe that you have to trust your employees to do the best work they can.'

I coughed loudly. Neil patted me on the back. Gee shot us a look. He began to realise he had been tricked, but now it was too late.

'We'll put that aside for the moment. Show me these designs.' Miles stood and Karl sprang, gazelle-like from behind the pot plant, to lay the plans for the proposed building on the coffee table in front of Miles. Neil and I both remained in our seats, hands clasped in our laps.

'It's new, it's organic,' Karl began as he unveiled the horror we had designed. 'It's based on the Cack house in Pennsylvania!'

'And what the fuck is the Cack house?' Miles asked, staring at the plans. 'A prison?'

'No, it's, it's,' Karl stumbled, 'it's a house!' He looked at me to help him, but my lips remained resolutely closed.

Miles studied the plans and then stood and turned his gaze on Karl. He was very domineering. Seeing his tight arse facing me, I nudged Neil. Delicately he licked his lips. I felt my cock begging to stir at the thought of probing Miles' tight butt again, of being able to suck his hole while Neil parted my own butt cheeks and slipped his hot wedge of man meat into my own cunt.

'Cack, this certainly is,' Miles announced. 'Prohibitively expensive, a waste of space, dark, dank, gloomy, dreary, a second-rate, thoughtless piece of mother-fucking shite!' The office was silent at Miles pronouncement. 'Is that clear enough for you, Parker?'

Karl was quaking.

'Is that an old stain in your trousers or have you just pissed yourself?' Miles continued.

'No, it's old. Its fish,' he added by way of explanation.

'I can smell it's bloody fish!' Miles screamed.

'I'm sure we can sort this out,' Gee began, trying to keep a hold of the situation.

'I can smell it from here!' Miles stormed. The aroma of rotting fish had filled Gee's office. 'What is going on here? Why am I wasting my time? I'm sorry, it's too late, Arnold, I'm going to give the commission to a new company.'

'Are you sure, Miles—' Gee began.

'I have never been more sure.' Miles turned and left, leaving Gee's office door wide open behind him.

Neil and I sat feeling smug. Neil squeezed my hand.

'I knew it, you bastards!' Gee exploded. Neil kept hold of my hand. 'You've been fucking each other all the time haven't you!'

'Yes,' Neil announced casually, standing up, 'and now we've fucked you too!'

'Don't bet on it. Wait till I talk to Karen,' Gee threatened.

'I wouldn't do that,' Neil threatened, his six foot three frame a powerhouse of muscle and violence. 'I've already talked to her about Wade and I, and explained your motives behind bringing her in. Oh, yes,' Neil grew in stature, 'I also told her about your snooping and your manipulation to get Wade and I separated. Not going to work this time, Arnold.'

'I'm only interested in what's done on company property during company time. I've broken no laws. I'm going to sue both your faggotty arses! Besides, I can make Karen feel a little worse about the situation, if I try.'

Neil was about to hit him. I sprang to my feet and held him back as Gee shrank behind Karl.

'Yes, a lot happens on company property in company time, doesn't it Arnold.' It was Marilyn standing in the doorway.

'Get out, woman!' Gee bawled.

Marilyn stood rooted to the spot. 'No, I won't, you ignorant little man. I've worked hard for you for a long time and what am I rewarded with? Rudeness, ignorance and spying.'

'I said get the fuck out, you old slapper!' Gee was screaming now. Neil was ready to hit him. With force I held Neil from jumping over the desk to flatten him. Karl was hopping on the spot, almost apoplectic with the turn of events.

'What do you think this is?' Marilyn said calmly, holding up the VHS cassette she had shown me earlier. Gee was silent. 'You see, Arnold,' Marilyn moved into the office, 'as a woman, I don't mind you reading my private mail, I don't mind you seeing what I write to my gynaecologist, but I will *not* stand for you reading the letters I write to my mother.' She dropped the cassette on Gee's desk. 'This is a tape of your office activities last night.'

Gee's face went white. Karl stopped twitching, paralysed with fear. Neil and I were awestruck with Marilyn's cool composure.

'Yes, the security cameras by the lift have been trained on this office for a few days now and I have here on tape your little aerobics exercise last night.' Gee grabbed the tape. 'Or should I call it *Baldie-locks fucks Parker Bear*?'

Simultaneously, both mine and Neil's jaw dropped. We turned to look at Gee and Parker. The veins on Gee's neck were pulsating. Parker looked as if he was about to faint.

'Yes, boys,' Marilyn continued, 'the special bond between these two happens every Friday night when Arnold becomes Sir and Parker becomes "the boy". I think you'll find his dog chain in the filing cabinet, as well as a medium butt plug and crates of lube. Their special bond occurs when Arnold's wizened spam javelin parts Parker's flabby butt cheeks. It's fun viewing, you should see it.'

Gee's hand whipped down and grabbed the tape. 'What do you want?'

'I think we're all leaving now. Speaking to Mrs Rogers is not a good idea as it'll mean I'll have to speak to every colleague, customer, newspaper, trade journal and fucking tourist in London that I can get hold of!' Marilyn clearly meant business. 'And we'll take six months' salary each, and if you keep your mouth shut, we'll keep ours closed too.'

'Take it and fuck off.' Gee slammed the tape in his desk drawer. 'There is a copy of that tape, just in case you have second thoughts . . .' she added.

I rushed and hugged her. 'Can I offer you a job, Mrs Allbright?'

'Certainly, Mr Armstrong. I've just become available.'

Neil waited behind. 'I always knew it,' he said calmly. 'You're a tosser, Karl, I can't bring myself to care about you. But you, Gee, you manipulated my wife's feelings in all this. That I won't forget.'

Outside Gee's office, Marilyn already had her things packed into a cardboard box. Hurriedly Neil and I emptied our desks. I was slowed only by Cheryl.

'You going then?' she asked.

'Yeah. Neil and I are setting up on our own.' I threw in some extra stationery.

'What's Marilyn doing then?' she asked, puzzled.

'She's coming with us.'

'Marilyn?' Cheryl sucked on a finger. 'Marilyn!' she exclaimed. 'Is she the other woman then?'

'Sort of,' I replied.

'You having a three-way with old Marilyn!' Cheryl gasped. 'We weren't in with a chance then were we?'

'No,' I nodded, grabbing my coat and heading for the lifts. Cheryl trotted after me. Marilyn, Neil and I converged at the lift. The doors were open and we loaded our things in as Neil held the doors. Cheryl stood outside.

'Why didn't you tell me you two didn't like young girls?'

'I tried,' I said as the lift doors shut and Cheryl disappeared from sight

'You told her we're gay?' Neil asked, putting his arms around both Marilyn and I.

'I tried, it wasn't easy,' I admitted.

Neil kissed me and then gave Marilyn a peck on the cheek. 'So Gee's been shoving his load up Karl's arse all this time!'

'Yes and that's been the root of the problem with you two. Gee thought he was going to be able to get Neil to join in his little Friday night fun and games. But then Mr Gorgeous Wade comes along, turns your head completely and utterly ruins his plans.'

'And that's why he hated me?' I cried. ''Cause of him?' I pointed at Neil.

'Yup,' Marilyn confirmed.

'But I'm worth it aren't I, Sport?'

I smiled at Neil, that effortless charm, his strong, rugged frame. 'Of course you are!'

The lift doors opened. There were crowds of people in the lobby, but no one moved to get into the lift. We pushed our way out, carrying our possessions.

'What's going on?' I asked.

'Oh dear!' Marilyn sighed. 'I must have given them the wrong tape. The tape Gee and Parker have must be *One Hundred and One Dalmatians.* The tape I sent to Antony in security is what is playing through every closed-circuit television in the building now.'

I peered at a nearby monitor. On it I saw Karl Parker, naked on all fours on Gee's desk, his neck held in a collar and chain, while a naked Arnold Gee threw dog biscuits at him and wanked on his stubby, greying little cock. Neil howled with laughter.

'Oh my God!' I gasped at the hideousness of the sight of Karl Parker's arse being fitted with a butt plug.

Miles Stone was watching a monitor near to the exit. 'What do you think?' I asked.

Miles smiled. 'I could never work with a guy who's cock is that small or with a guy who's butt is that tight!'

'Me neither.' I held Neil's hand, 'It's gotta be twelve inches or nothing.'

'Twelve inches!' Marilyn gasped, 'Then I think I've made the right choice working with you. You got any straight friends looking for an older woman?'

Neil laughed and took my hand down to his hefty packet. I could feel the heat from his man-rammer growing into life. 'If twelve inches is what you want, then twelve inches is what you'll always get.'

RUDE BOYS

Jay Russell

Malcom and Don, lithe young members of drum n' bass outfit *The Boot Sex Massive*, are out to kick-start their musical careers – if only they can keep their minds on the job. The trouble is, west London is just bursting with serious distractions – like Thom, the blond Aussie sound engineer, and Kam, the sexy Japanese student. Then there's Stevo, a skinhead who's making up for lost time, and big-hearted Bobbi, who just can't resist helping out a friend in need.

Not least, there's the capacious Prince Fela, African aristocrat, and his manservant Camara. Their legendary Notting Hill parties – with their promise that each guest will find a pleasure he's never found before – are sure to delight all comers. But, having searched for tenderness from Soho to the Gate, Malcom and Don both learn that real respect can be found closer to home . . .

0 7472 6065 6

MAN2MAN